KILLER WITHIN

KILLER WITHIN

JEFF GUNHUS

THOMAS & MERCER

Text copyright © 2015 Jeff Gunhus

Published by Thomas & Mercer, Seattle

www.apub.com

Amazon, the Amazon logo, and Thomas & Mercer are trademarks of Amazon.com, Inc., or its affiliates.

ISBN-13: 9781477822234

ISBN-10: 1477822232

Cover design by Salamander Hill Design Inc.

Library of Congress Control Number: 2014952438

Printed in the United States of America

For Nicole
I love you

GENESIS

Arnie Milhouse never considered himself much of a hero. Especially since no event in his first three decades on the planet gave him any reason to think otherwise. Even as his fingers flexed around the pen he was about to jab into the neck of the man in front of him, he still had his doubts.

Twenty minutes earlier, he passed the last of the boarded-up row houses that made up this Baltimore neighborhood and turned into Rocco's Convenience and Liquor, a place that seemed ready to live up to the promise of its name. There was plenty of liquor and not another soul to mess up the convenience of it all. It wasn't unusual for the store to be empty at ten thirty on a Tuesday night. Friday would have been a different story. Workers trading their paychecks for cheap whiskey and smokes. Old ladies down to run their Powerball numbers, high school kids scoping for someone to pimp them some beers. But Tuesday was as quiet as a church.

Arnie shuffled to the back of the store, curling his toes to keep his ill-fitting slippers from sliding off his feet. Vaguely, he wondered if he ought to have put on his shoes before leaving the house. He shrugged away the thought when he reached the wall of refrigerators in the back of the store. He opened a door and pulled out a milk jug. White flakes coated the plastic where past spills had dried, but the expiration date was still a respectable five days away. It would do.

He stood at the counter to pay for his milk, shooting for the minimum acceptable amount of interaction with the acne-tortured teenager brooding behind the cash register. The kid's face made him think too much about his own awkward adolescence for him to make eye contact for too long. He caught himself running his fingers over the pockmarks left from acne so bad it had made Arnie stay home from school some days in embarrassment. He remembered the jokes from other kids, the sympathetic looks from teachers, the tut-tut of the dermatologist who never found a way to help him. He felt a surge of anger at the kid for dredging up those painful memories. Arnie preferred to forget those days. Not that things were much better now.

"What's that?" the kid asked.

"What?"

"What's not better now?"

"Nothing," Arnie mumbled. He hadn't realized he'd said anything. "I wasn't talking to you."

The teenager rolled his eyes and held out his hand, nodding to the register's display that showed the amount owed.

Arnie handed over some cash and waited for his change, taking in the space around Rocco's cash register. It looked like a million other places with the yellow laminate surface stained and chipped away, rows of ninety-nine-cent packets of herbal supplements, a display of Harley-Davidson lighters, walls of breath mints, and racks of chewing gum.

Boring and expected. But then again, what in life wasn't?

Arnie hadn't always felt that way. Like any young man, he had once been full of expectation, ready for the road to rise before him in a never-ending adventure. Ready to make his mark. Slay dragons. Grab the world by its balls and squeeze until it screamed for mercy. But none of it was meant to be.

Things had started out in his favor. He was good-looking, filling out and growing into his own during college. He possessed a work ethic and was wicked smart. Even Mensa, the society of high IQs, had been impressed by his intellect and had sent him a document to print out, certifying that he, Arnie Milhouse, was a goddamn genius.

"You're so fucking smart that you're stupid" was his wife's favorite line, a battering ram that smashed into him the minute he had the poor taste to feel good about himself. Problem was, she wasn't wrong.

He overanalyzed every decision he faced, which made him indecisive and a chronic second-guesser. So he'd sought refuge in the certainty and infallibility of math and computers. Over time he turned meek and timid. He didn't stop to realize the mouse he had let himself become until it was the only thing he knew how to be. He was disgusted with the man he saw in the mirror, but it was the hand life had dealt him.

Then the door to Rocco's Convenience and Liquor opened and life took an unexpected turn.

It wasn't like in the movies. The bad guy wasn't dressed in gang colors, eyes darting around like a crack fiend, ski mask pulled down over his face. No, the guy who came through the door looked like a middle-American dad: blue jeans, a little faded but new enough; a clean white T-shirt worn under a rust-colored flannel button-down, hung open and untucked sleeves rolled up to midforearm, like he was going camping and just stopped by to pick up some night crawlers and ingredients to make s'mores. The man seemed so totally average and unthreatening that Arnie didn't give him a second thought. He was too tired to care. Too worried about what might be happening back at home.

Arnie pictured his wife pacing the small kitchen of their one-bedroom row house, checking and rechecking her watch as she chain-smoked her Kools and chewed down her yellowing nails. He figured she felt the same way he did: desperately hoping that little Jason, the product of their single, fumbling night together—a total mercy fuck, to hear her describe it—wouldn't wake up before she could get the hell out of there.

Arnie didn't know where she went or even care that much. Sometimes she came back smelling like another man. Some nights she didn't come back at all. Once, she disappeared for a week, one of the best of Arnie and Jason's life. Just when he allowed himself the giddy idea that she might be gone forever, she reappeared on their front porch, passed out, her face covered with bruises, a dirty, torn dress hiked up over her hips, ass on show for the entire neighborhood to see. He took her in and nursed her to health, fighting down the impulse each time he entered her room to cover her face with a pillow and put an end to his misery.

Leaving her at home was a risk. Jason wasn't likely to get up this late, but if he did, he'd want a bottle. Arnie knew if he didn't get home fast enough, his wife would get impatient and start slapping Jason on the backs of the legs to make him stop whining. A month ago, Arnie came home late from work and Jason's legs were bright red, welted up where his mom had used a flyswatter instead of her hand. For greater reach, Arnie suspected.

This act of violence against his little boy filled Arnie with a kind of rage he didn't know was in him. He did the unthinkable and confronted her, but she didn't back down. She screamed at Arnie. Punched him in the face. Told him to fuck off. That he was as much an annoying little prick as their son. That if he wasn't late, little fucking Jason wouldn't get fucking slapped, would he? She must not have liked the hurt look on Arnie's face because she grabbed Jason, yanking him up by the arm until only his toes touched the ground, and slapped at the backs of his legs until he was screaming. "Happy now, asshole?" She'd grabbed the car keys out of his hand and come back two days later, reeking of booze.

So no, Arnie didn't bother with the new arrival to the store. He just wanted to get the hell out of there, climb back into his Toyota Camry, and get back up the street before things got out of hand on the homestead.

He didn't want to be the reason Jason got hurt again.

But he was in a holding pattern. The teenager seemed to be stuck by the higher math required to make change out of the five-dollar bill Arnie had given him. He stood there, both hands in the drawer, mouth slack, eyes fixed over Arnie's right shoulder.

Arnie was about to wave his hand in front of the kid's face to snap him back from whatever mental vacation he was on when something hard and cold poked him in the back of his neck.

The instant he felt the pressure against his skin, he knew it was a gun.

"Easy. Don't move," a voice whispered inches from his right ear. "I won't hurt you if you don't move."

The voice was deep, smooth but with a gravelly rumble at the lowest register. Absurdly, Arnie thought the voice would be great on the radio announcing the weather. *Gray skies ahead, buckaroo.* "Stay calm or I'll blow your head right through."

Arnie nodded to let the man know he understood. No heroics here. Take the money and run. What did he care? He just needed to get home to Jason. That was all he cared about.

Arnie didn't say these things but he conveyed the message through slumped shoulders and a lowered head, the universal signs of subservience he'd practiced all his life. Practiced with his boss. With his father. His wife. Certainly a man with a gun deserved the same treatment.

"Good, stand to the side. Right there. You make a move and I shoot the kid. Got it?"

Arnie's eyes instinctively went to the teenager, who backed away from the cash register with his hands up until he ran into the wall of cigarette dispensers behind him. Instead of looking at his face, Arnie fixated on the name tag pinned to the poor SOB's shirt. "Hello. My Name Is EDGAR" it proclaimed to the patrons of Rocco's Convenience and Liquor, who, of course, never for one second gave a damn. Arnie hadn't either.

But now Arnie was glad he knew the teenager's name. Somehow it was important. And for some reason, Arnie wished the kid knew his.

He let his eyes move up to Edgar's terrified face. His cheeks were flushed with two thick splotches of crimson, but the rest of his face was the gray-white of dead skin. Even his zits looked drained of their color, only a faint pink instead of the painful, oozing bloodred visible just a few seconds before. His lower lip had caved and disappeared into his mouth, where the kid was chewing on it.

Arnie considered whether the lip biting was from nerves or if he was trying to stop trembling so he would look brave. The dark piss stain spreading out from the kid's crotch answered that question. Arnie didn't blame him. He watched a lot of cop shows, and he knew things usually went bad in a hurry for the fella who had what the guy with the gun wanted. Even though the robber looked like a soccer dad, he was holding up a liquor store at gunpoint, an act that reeked of desperation. And desperation and guns were a terrible combination when you were on the business end of a firearm.

An image came to Arnie's mind. It was an unkind thought, and he tried to squeeze it back into whatever dark place it had come from, but it refused to leave. So, when he looked back at the kid's name tag, he saw the new version that had come to his mind. It said: "Hello. My Name Is EDGAR and I Am Fucked."

"How you doin', Edgar?" the man with the gun asked. "You all right?"

Edgar didn't move. He stared down at the gun, his jaw working away at his lower lip.

The man moved the gun from side to side. Edgar's head swayed to the same rhythm, like a cobra dancing with a snake charmer.

"EDGAR!"

The boy flinched backward and finally looked up. A tiny rivulet of blood dribbled from his mouth. Arnie almost told him to calm down and stop chewing his lip, but he had been given his instructions. He intended to wait for the storm to pass. Do exactly as he was told. No muss, no fuss, as his old man used to say.

"Are you paying attention now?"

Edgar nodded, spilling a little more saliva-blood mixture from his mouth. It drained down his chin, and soon it was falling in long, wet strands to the floor. Edgar didn't wipe the blood away. Arnie understood. He and the kid were the same kind of animal. Just ride it out. No sudden moves.

They wanted to live. Shutting up was their ticket out.

"Put the cash in the bag. Hurry up."

The man was still calm, which Arnie took as a good sign. The crook was less likely to lash out that way. Of course, he was basing this analysis on nothing more than thousands of hours of watching cop shows on TV. This was the closest he'd been to real danger. It's not that he was a coward, at least he didn't think of himself as one; it was just that a thirty-year-old dad who spent fifty hours a week networking people's computers seldom stared death in the face.

Now, only four or five feet away from a loaded gun, Arnie thought he would be the one pissing his pants, biting his lip until blood gushed down his chin. But he wasn't. Instead, he felt a cool detachment from the situation as a growing sense of wonder and excitement worked its way up inside his chest.

It was the same way he'd felt last summer when he'd stood at the edge of the Grand Canyon. Right on the edge, toes touching the rim, so close that a gust of wind could have launched him into the abyss. With the outlandish scale of the canyon wrapped around him, he'd suddenly understood that the thousands of pictures he had seen hadn't conveyed a single thing about the place. But the experience—the experience told him everything.

That moment had revealed to Arnie a basic truth, something he felt sure he had once known but somehow had simply forgotten, beat out of him like a flyswatter taken to a baby's soft skin.

Life is revealed through experience, the canyon had whispered to him. *Not seen through a screen, or read about, or talked about. Experienced.*

And his entire life was a step away from experience; he was on the other side of the glass looking out, on the other side of the TV screen looking in.

Arnie had decided that day at the Grand Canyon to make changes in his life, big changes. But that was a year ago. And like every time he decided to completely change his life, not a single thing had happened.

But now, standing so close to danger, real danger, he felt the visceral power of raw experience, felt the pull of it even more than the canyon on that summer day, that pure day when the wind whispered his name, begging him to jump off the rim and float on the air currents for fifty glorious seconds before his brains bashed against the rocks below. This was different, not the explosive celebration of a fantastic ending but something better: the promise of a different beginning. Somewhere in the danger he sensed that there was a basic right he had denied himself his entire life.

He looked into himself, trying to understand.

And this internal view, for years a black wall of closed thinking, was suddenly a breathtaking vista. Arnie nearly staggered backward from the enormity of it.

"Now the drop box. The money in the drop box."

Edgar's eyes widened. The kid took half a step backward, the bag of money from the cash register still clutched in his hands.

"I . . . I can't open it."

"Bullshit."

"It's not bullshit, man," Edgar shouted, the stress forcing the words out in spastic bursts. "C'mon . . . like . . . like I care if you get the fuckin' money from this place."

Blood splattered down the front of Edgar's uniform. Arnie figured the kid must have chewed half his lip away for it to bleed that much.

"Open the safe."

"I can't."

"Do it now!"

"I told you, man, I can't . . ."

BAM.

Arnie fell back against a candy rack.

Skittles, M&M's, and Snickers bars flew everywhere.

Then screaming.

Edgar. *Jesus, this son of a bitch shot Edgar.*

Arnie looked up. The gun was pointed at his head.

"Up. Get up."

Arnie did as he was told. Any excitement he'd felt was gone. His stomach turned in on itself and he thought he might be sick.

"Shut up, Edgar," the man yelled. "You're not hurt. That was just a warning shot. Now open the fucking lockbox."

Arnie felt a surge of relief when he saw Edgar pressed against the back wall, still standing, but curled up like someone had punched him in the stomach.

Arnie realized that this man, this ordinary, average guy, meant to kill Edgar if he didn't open the safe. In his mind, he imagined the poor kid's head smashed open by the gunshot. But he realized that the image wasn't really of Edgar. It was Jason, or at least how he imagined Jason might look as a teenager one day. Suddenly, Arnie saw everything around him through a different lens. It had nothing to do with Edgar, or the man with the gun. It was all about protecting his own son in a violent world, a world in which Arnie always felt completely helpless.

He looked down at his shaking hands and realized for the first time in his life that his fear had somehow been transformed into rage. He hated everything about the man in front of him. He hated the way he pointed a gun at Edgar. Despised his tone of voice when he ordered them around. He resented that he kept him from going home to Jason. He was insulted that the man thought so little of Arnie that he robbed the store with him in it instead of just waiting a few minutes until he left. He hated everything about him. And he liked the feeling. He gripped his hands into fists and when he released them they were steady. He was done shaking.

On the counter next to Arnie was a pen. A thick plastic Bic. With the man's back turned, Arnie reached out, grabbed it, and clutched it in his right fist.

The man pointed the gun at Edgar again. He shouted something but Arnie couldn't hear it over the drumbeat of the blood that pounded in his head.

Arnie thought about his little boy at home, little Jason taking his hand and walking him to the couch so Arnie would hold him while he drank his bottle.

When that little boy grew up, what would he think of his father? The mouse of a man who watched life instead of living it? What kind of man would Jason be when he grew up if his model was the sniveling nobody Arnie had allowed himself to become? How could he stand by and do nothing while someone else's son died?

Arnie was back on the edge of the canyon, his toes dangling. The vista wrapped around him, calling to him, beckoning him to jump.

Then, from a dark, unknown place within his mind, came the gust of wind that pushed him over the edge and changed everything.

◆ ◆ ◆

Arnie lunged, right fist cocked back over his head, Bic pen sticking out from the fleshy circle formed by his little finger and the pad of his hand.

The man never saw him coming.

The skin gave little resistance as Arnie jammed the pen into his neck.

Before the man could jerk away, the palm of Arnie's hand slid up and forced the pen deeper, twisting as it went in.

The gun exploded.

BAM.

Sparks everywhere. The bullet hit one of the lights in the ceiling.

Arnie shoved his body weight against the man, twisting the pen from side to side, scrambling the man's veins, carving up his windpipe.

They fell together to the ground.

Arnie felt warm liquid splash over him. On his face, his neck, in his eyes. He tasted it on his tongue, salty and warm.

He crouched down, snarling, ready to attack again.

The man lay on his side, his back to Arnie, nothing but the top inch of the Bic pen standing up out of his neck, the rest buried in the flesh. Blood spurted out of the wound in arcs almost a foot high.

Wet gargles escaped his throat as he clutched at the wound.

Then the man twitched—horrible spasms, like there was electricity shooting through his body.

Suddenly, as if there were a power outage, the body slumped and ceased to move. The sounds stopped. Everything fell quiet.

Arnie looked up at Edgar, who somehow found the willpower to move around the counter to check out the body.

"I think . . . I think you killed him."

Arnie nodded. He didn't think he'd killed the man. He *knew* he had.

Somehow, Arnie was certain that just injuring someone wouldn't feel this good.

He started to cry, his shoulders jerking up and down, snot covering his upper lip. He had never cried like this before, never felt such a deep release, never felt so bare.

Never felt so fucking alive.

Even as the sobs racked his body, he knew the emotions were not only from killing the man; it was also the pain of so many years piled up on top of him. And then, in one action, he understood that none of that pain was necessary. He'd had it within himself the whole time to take control. To be the master of his world, not some sniveling servant. The elation of this truth had always been so close to him. The feeling of total power right there for the taking.

But with the realization came a rush of panic. The incredible high would fade. He knew it would. He had learned the hard way that nothing good in life lasted. And just like every other time, Arnie knew everything would go right back to the way it was before.

His body shook even harder as the feeling of raw power slipped away.

He couldn't go back. Not to his wife beating him down. Not to his bullshit job. Not to his insignificance. He refused. He wanted to feel that power again.

Needed to feel it again.

And again.

And again.

Arnie picked up the man's gun.

He would not let himself go back to the way things were.

He balanced the gun in the palm of his hand, savoring the weight of it.

How could he even consider going back, now that he knew what true power feels like?

He slid his finger over the trigger.

No more lies, Arnie promised himself. No more weakness. Never again.

He pivoted to his right, took aim at the spot between Edgar's eyes.

"What the—"

A cloud of blood sprayed out of the back of the kid's head, and his body dropped to the floor.

It didn't feel as good as killing the man, of course. But the rush was still there. The power. It was all there. And it was real. Accessible whenever he needed it.

But not if he got caught. Arnie's mind wasted no time on emotions but occupied itself by rifling through all the forensics shows on TV. Not the prime-time series with the good-looking actors, but the reality shows with the ugly people and the actual science. He knew all the tricks. He knew he had to be careful. He was smart, he'd always been smart, but the science was sophisticated now. He had to worry about the science.

Arnie wiped the gun off with napkins and put it back in the dead man's hand, feeling calmer than he'd imagined he would. He wrapped the limp fingers around the trigger and forced the gun to discharge once more. Probably unnecessary, but he couldn't be sure the gun powder residue on the man's hand from the first shot when Arnie stabbed him would demonstrate a controlled forward shot.

Adrenaline pumped through his system. The police would be there soon, and Arnie needed to get his story straight. There would be questions, newspaper interviews, probably television too.

He sat on the floor in the middle of the pool of blood, arms crossed against his chest, and giggled at the thought. He had jumped off the canyon wall and instead of falling to his death, he discovered how to fly.

THIRTEEN YEARS LATER

CHAPTER 1

Charlie Foxen clung to the possibility that sex might still happen. For a week now he spent all his free time, when he wasn't working at the bar, toting around bags of equipment and chauffeuring Allison Davenport to his favorite spots on the Chesapeake Bay. He'd sent all the signals, flashed his best smiles, applied an extra dousing of Axe cologne each day, even worked out at the gym before picking her up to make sure his flexed muscles were easily seen beneath his thin T-shirts. On most girls in Annapolis, the Charlie Foxen treatment worked like a trick. But this was different. This was a woman he was after. And maybe this woman needed a little more convincing to take him seriously.

He grabbed a roll of duct tape from the car and looked at the center of the beach. Down on the edge of the water, with a tripod balanced on pieces of wood to keep it from sinking into the sand, stood Allison, the most perfect woman Charlie had ever seen. That included the *Playboy* and *Hustler* women that kept him company during all those hours of bathroom intimacy in his teenage years. Those women were a different kind of look—too plastic, too made-up, and slutty. Besides, they were just pictures. Nothing compared to getting to know Allison. Nothing compared to seeing her now standing by the Bay with a storm blowing in ahead of her, the way she faced into it snapping pictures, her blonde hair thrown back by the wind, her tan skin standing out against a white sleeveless shirt, old jeans revealing just enough of a figure to make Charlie feel the blood thumping through his body.

He grasped the roll of duct tape a little tighter and headed down the beach, not quite believing what he was about to do.

Allison looked up from her camera's viewfinder long enough to see what was keeping Charlie. She wanted to attach a plastic shield to the camera body to block some of the glare coming from the sun's last rays of the day, but she'd left the tape in the car. It was an hour before sunset but the clouds were moving fast, and the best shots would be the seconds just as the clouds and sun met.

"Hurry, Charlie," she said. "We'll miss it."

Charlie waved and broke into a trot. Allison smiled. Charlie was a great find when she first arrived in Annapolis. She'd strolled into McGarvey's Saloon and Oyster Bar one afternoon and ate lunch during his shift behind the bar. She wasn't halfway through her beer before he offered to play host to her and show her the area and then another hour after that to convince her it was a good idea. The past week he'd never been far from her side and she'd grown used to having him around.

While she knew he considered himself quite a guide, her real motivation to have him along was to run interference on any other men trying to pick her up while she went about her work and keeping the curious at bay. People tended to leave alone a young couple out on a walk, and she enjoyed the space Charlie helped carve out for her. She suspected he was developing a little puppy-dog crush on her, even though she tried to send the signals that she wasn't interested. Judging by the way he looked at her, she guessed his interest in helping her wasn't just because he wanted to learn more about photography. Still, their developing friendship made her feel a little guilty that she had done nothing but lie to him since they met.

"Wow, it's really starting to blow," Charlie said with a whistle.

"Did you see that lightning over there to the south? I think I caught some of it."

"Long exposure?"

"Yup." Allison smiled. It was one of the few photographic principles Charlie understood, so he used it as often as possible in conversation. "Six seconds. Caught it right at the beginning."

"Cool."

"Did you get the tape?"

Charlie held it up. "How much do you want?"

Allison reached down into her bag to grab a black plastic lens hood she could use as a screen. "Just enough to attach this to the barrel. We only have a minute or two before we lose the sun."

When she stood up, Charlie was holding out a piece of tape toward her, just out of reach.

"Here you go," he said, nodding down at the tape.

"Stop fooling around, Charlie."

"Who's fooling around?"

Charlie's smile was all wrong. Blotches of red burned at his cheeks. Then Allison noticed his hand shaking.

Charlie couldn't keep his hands still. He'd never been this nervous before in his life. Nausea churned in his stomach and, in a flash of panic, he thought he might throw up.

Allison, shaking her head, took a step forward to take the tape.

Do it, Charlie, he said to himself. *What are you waiting for?*

He couldn't. He watched as she got closer, everything moving in slow motion, her eyes searching his for . . . what? Some kind of sign that he was interested in her?

Hell yes, you're interested. Do it, Charlie. She wants you, man. Don't be a loser.

Charlie waited until her hand was near his; then he reached out and grabbed her wrist.

He yanked her toward him, his other hand reaching out for the back of her head, his mouth open and seeking her out.

But then everything went wrong.

Allison's wrist twisted. There was sudden pressure on his groin. No. More than pressure. Pain. Baseball bat to the nuts kind of pain.

Then the world reversed itself and the Chesapeake switched places with the sky. It hung there for just a second before the natural order of things returned as he collapsed in a heap, the air knocked out of him by the hard landing.

He lay on the ground, his hands cupped around his throbbing testicles.

"Oh Jesus, Charlie," Allison said, dropping to her knees next to him. "Are you all right?"

Charlie's eyes squinted open. "Never better. Just give me a minute."

Allison patted him on the shoulder. "Is it bad?"

Charlie coughed and rolled to his side until he was up on one shoulder. He smiled weakly. "Where'd you learn to do that?"

Allison waved the question away. "You scared the hell out of me. I didn't mean to . . . I mean . . . are you all right?"

"Bruised ego and some sore nuts. Not really what I had planned." Despite the pain radiating from his groin, he managed to still feel embarrassed. "I just thought . . . I don't know . . . it's just . . ."

"You're a good guy, Charlie. You should know better than to pull shit like that."

Charlie looked down at the sand. "I know. I'm sorry. I just thought . . ."

She let him wallow for a bit, then pointed up to the car. "Why don't you wait in the car?"

"I can help—"

"I can manage. Go ahead and wait in the car."

Charlie nodded, rolled up to his knees, then hobbled up the beach, staggering like a vasectomy patient walking back to his car in the hospital parking lot.

◆　◆　◆

Allison watched him go and felt genuinely sorry for the poor kid. At twenty-one, Charlie was awkward and still trying to figure things out. She was sure he would have stopped if she had just pulled away from him and told him she wasn't interested. Incapacitating him may have been a little more that he deserved.

Then again, the kid didn't realize how lucky he was she hadn't hurt him worse than she did.

And although she felt bad, she wasn't sorry for the lesson she'd taught him. Come on too strong to a woman who doesn't want it and you just might get a swift kick in the balls.

"Damn," she said, looking out over the Bay. The sun was behind the clouds now. She'd missed the shot of the day. Still, she reminded herself as she glanced over to the large house perched on the cliff farther down the coastline, she got what she came for.

She smiled to herself as she packed up her gear and headed to the car. No matter the circumstances, it was flattering that a good-looking guy like Charlie would still go for her even though she had him by more than a decade. She decided to let him off easy and not make a big deal out of it on the way home.

CHAPTER 2

The storm was as bad as its reputation. The rain pelted them in thick sheets, and thunder rattled the windows of the rented Dodge Durango. Still, with the truck in four-wheel drive just to be on the safe side, Allison navigated the Eastern Shore back roads at full speed. Soon they were on Highway 143, heading north.

After a half hour of driving in silence, with the Bay Bridge finally in sight, Allison figured Charlie had suffered enough.

"You OK?"

"Yeah," Charlie said. "I screwed up, huh?"

Allison nodded. "Yes sir, you sure did."

"But I didn't . . . I mean, I just wanted . . ."

"Oh, I'm pretty sure I know what you wanted," Allison laughed. She felt bad when she noticed Charlie turn red and look away. "You're young. And when you're young you get a little impatient for things to happen. I know, I've been there."

Charlie nodded. "So you're saying I need to be more patient?"

"Exactly."

"And if I take it slow, then maybe . . . you and I . . . we could . . ."

"You're not listening to what—" She stopped when she saw the smile spread across his face.

"Got you," he said.

"Very funny."

"I've got it. I'm too young. Don't have enough going on to get a fine woman like yourself."

"You have plenty going on, trust me. You'll do just fine."

Allison rolled up to the tollbooth and paid her three dollars. The toll operator opened the sliding glass just enough to stick her hand through to take the money. The rain came in horizontally with the stiff wind coming off the Bay, and the roof of the booth didn't provide much protection. Allison drove off without getting a receipt for her expenses. A small thing, but another reminder that no one was reimbursing her for this trip.

"Where did you learn to kick ass like that anyway?" Charlie asked. "What do you weigh, about a buck thirty?"

"Watch yourself or I'll beat you up again."

"No, really. Are you some kind of karate-voodoo master or something?"

Allison laughed. "Karate-voodoo master? No, I don't think so."

"What then?"

"I just like to take care of myself, that's all."

"Took care of me," Charlie grumbled.

Allison poked him in the ribs. "And I'll do it again if I hear about you trying to kiss girls who don't want to be kissed."

"I got it," Charlie cried out. "Lord Jesus, get me back to my bar and out of this woman's car."

Allison smiled. "Speaking of your bar, I think you owe me a beer."

She never heard Charlie's response. Wasn't sure if he did respond, or if his mind froze along with hers at the sight of the red brake lights in front of them. All noise disappeared as the Durango crested the rise in the bridge. The storm faded away; the music on the radio dissolved. In fact, she didn't hear another thing until Charlie started to scream.

Her right foot pumped the brakes. Everything in slow motion.

She knew it wasn't going to be enough. Not with the wet road. Not going downhill.

Why were you going so fast? What the hell were you thinking?

The world moved to the rhythm of the windshield wipers.

Whirr-thunk

Red brake lights everywhere. Traffic stopped. People out of their cars.

Whirr-thunk

Some kind of open-bed truck with construction equipment on it. They would hit that first.

Whirr-thunk

Sideways. They were sliding sideways now. Looking across Charlie's body, through the passenger window. There's the truck.

Allison's own screams filled her ears, competing against the twisting metal from the impact. There were explosions everywhere around her. The air filled with smoke. Someone had a blanket over her face, trying to suffocate her.

Air bags. It's just the air bags. Relax, Allison. Relax.

Almost immediately, the pressure eased and she could breathe again. She pushed the air bag away and that's when she heard Charlie screaming. There was fear in the sound, enough fear to go around, but the pain was unmistakable. Something was very, very wrong with Charlie.

Allison clawed Charlie's air bag away.

"Charlie, what is it? What's wrong?"

"My leg! My fuckin' leg! Jesus Christ."

Allison felt the tension roll away. Charlie was hurt but he wasn't dead. Dying men didn't speak, they just kept screaming. Allison had heard those screams before and she knew the difference.

"Hold on. Let me see it."

She unclipped her seat belt and leaned over to Charlie's body. Quietly she said a prayer of thanks that the good people at Dodge decided the 2004 Durango should have both front and side air bags. Without the silk bag now deflating against the shattered passenger-side window, she was sure the rainstorm would be washing parts of Charlie's brain down Bay Bridge right now. Instead, the air bag had done its job, and they were just dealing with some minor issue with his leg.

But lifting up the front air bag, she immediately saw it was worse than she thought and something no air bag in the world could have prevented.

"Charlie, you have to promise me something, all right?"

"Aww, Jesus, it hurts! What's wrong? What's wrong with my leg?"

Allison got in his face. "Listen, you're going to be all right. I'm going to get help, but I want you to promise me something before I leave."

"What?"

"Promise me that you're not going to look at it. Promise me, Charlie."

"Shit, I promise! Just get help, all right?"

"OK. I'll be right back. Don't look down."

Allison crawled back into her seat and out the door. People were already crowding around the car, asking if she was all right. She glanced up the bridge. Other people were already running up the rise with flares to warn approaching cars.

A little late, guys.

A sudden scream from inside the Durango told her that Charlie had broken his promise and looked down. The side-impact air bags had protected Charlie's head but hadn't done anything about the metal spikes hanging off the back of the open-bed trailer. Several had penetrated the door and skewered the Durango like a sausage at a cookout. Two of these two-inch wide bars had pierced Charlie's leg, effectively stapling him to the car. It looked to Allison like the metal spikes were embedded in thick leg muscle, and blood loss was a big risk. He needed immediate attention. She shivered, thinking about what would have happened if the metal spikes were only a foot or two higher.

An ambulance siren cut through the storm raging around them. She made sure people around her knew Charlie needed help, then ran over to the passenger side, pulling her belt from her jeans to use as a temporary tourniquet.

"I looked down!" Charlie struggled to say when she appeared at the door.

"I figured. Looks nastier than it is. Ambulance is on the way but we need to stop the bleeding." She leaned into the car with the belt in hand. "This might hurt a little."

Charlie squinted against the pain as she slipped the belt under his upper leg and then cinched it tight. He jammed his head into the headrest, blinking back tears.

"Hang on, Charlie," Allison said, taking his hand. "Help's coming."

CHAPTER 3

It was after ten before she called for a cab to take her back to her room at Governor Calvert House, a historic bed-and-breakfast in town. Charlie had insisted she go home. In fact, he had insisted that he be able to go home as well, but the docs at Anne Arundel Medical wanted to keep an eye on him overnight. The gashes in his leg were sutured and it would be a while before he was playing in his Friday night basketball league, but considering how close he came to being skewered, he was in pretty good shape. She had refused to leave at first, the guilt from driving too fast in the rain wearing on her. But after Charlie all but begged her to leave, she gave in.

Reluctantly, she took a cab for the short ride back into the historic district of Annapolis. The bed-and-breakfast was located on the cobblestoned road that encircled the colonial statehouse, a beautiful building that was still home to Maryland's state legislature. With a red brick exterior, white-pillared front, and whitewashed portico, the capitol was the cornerstone of a town that seemed frozen in the eighteenth century.

Allison fell in love with Annapolis the first time she visited. Even as a teenager, she was attracted to the timeless quality of the place, the way the row houses stood vigil over the passage of years like ancient trees too important to change. She remembered her father driving carefully through the narrow streets, pointing out landmarks from travel guides he read on the flight out from California.

"There, Allison, there's the governor's mansion. They open that up at Christmas and anybody and everybody can walk in, shake the governor's hand and have a glass of punch. How about that? Over there, that's the state capitol. Actually, it was the capitol of the United States for six months when the Congress was moving from city to city. Not many people know that, you have to figure."

That was her dad, Mr. Trivia. And, in Annapolis, he was in historical footnote heaven. Where did Washington resign his commission as head of the Continental Army? Annapolis. Where was Kunta Kinte of *Roots* fame brought on land? Annapolis. Where was Navy hero John Paul Jones buried? Annapolis, of course. The United States Naval Academy, to be exact.

And that was why she had been in the car with her dad. To see the academy. To see what it was all about.

Two years later, they were in the car again but heading in the other direction. Not smiling like on that first day together, but her in tears and him barely holding it together. By then she had seen the academy. And she was leaving it behind her forever.

Only that wasn't really true, was it? She was sleeping a block away from the main gate. Closer to it than she'd ever thought she'd be able to stand. But she was really no closer to or farther away from the Naval Academy than she had been since she drove away that day with her father. The past was like a bill sent in the mail, chasing after her whether or not there was a forwarding address. Allison's memory of the academy had proven its staying power. Fourteen years and still going strong.

Goddamn place.

The cab pulled into the valet spot in front of the bed-and-breakfast, and Allison crawled out with some effort. Her entire body was stiff now that the adrenaline had released its hold on her. She felt like her bones had been shaken out of place by the force of the impact. All she could think of was a hot shower and a long night's sleep. But she wouldn't afford herself that small luxury. She still had work to do.

She turned to the valet. "Do you think I could load you up with these bags?" Allison dropped her shoulders and let her camera equipment slide to the ground. "I'm in room eight."

"Sure thing. I'll take care of it."

She reached in her pocket for a tip, but the valet shook his head. "That's all right, Ms. Davenport. I'm happy to do it for you."

She smiled, so tired that she almost forgot she was using Davenport as her name. "Right, thanks. I appreciate it."

Sucking in a deep breath, Allison leaned forward to get her momentum going in the right direction and headed down Glouchester Street for the short walk to McGarvey's. Charlie called in to let them know he was all right, but he asked her to stop by anyway. Little did he know that she had to go by there, whether she wanted to or not. She'd grown fond of the people at McGarvey's. After the night she'd had, she was actually looking forward to being around some friendly faces.

Besides, it was the least she could do for the kid. She had, after all, denied his advances, kicked him in the balls, and almost killed him, all in one day. At least he had a great story to tell next time his buddies talked about the worst dates they had been on.

Allison McNeil: bad date specialist. Wasn't that what Richard had said to her when she broke things off with him?

Oh well, she thought, *Lord knows it's the truth.*

McGarvey's had become a regular hangout since her arrival a week earlier. Lunch each day and a few drinks at night before turning in already made her something of a fixture around the place. Of course, some fixtures blend into their surroundings, like beige furniture or seldom-used ashtrays stuck in the corner. A young, friendly blonde woman with striking blue eyes and girl-next-door looks is hardly the kind of thing that blends in. And it wasn't Allison's goal either. Her goal was to stand out. Not too much. But enough to get noticed.

When she pushed open the first of the dark, wooden double doors, she could tell people inside saw her coming through the windows. Courtney, a young brunette with a shirt a few sizes too small, opened the second door for her before she could do it herself and ushered her to a chair at the bar as if she were pregnant and ridiculous for being on her feet.

"What are you doing here? Are you all right? Is Charlie OK?"

"Calm down, Courtney. Give her a chance, will ya?" It was Mick O'Donnell, the manager/father of the McGarvey's crew. He'd taken a paternal liking to Allison when she first arrived. For some reason, he assumed that "freelance photographer" was the same thing as being broke, so her bill usually ended up half the amount it ought to be. A few of the other waitstaff huddled around her, waiting for her to speak.

"Charlie's doing great," she announced.

Everyone nodded and grunted their approval. It was the same news Courtney had heard Charlie give over the phone, but somehow hearing it from someone in person made it real.

"Tell us the truth, Ali." Mick smirked. "He cried like a baby, didn't he?"

Allison shook her head. "No, no. He took it like a man. Not a word."

Mick clapped his hands together. "Attaboy, Charlie."

A girl pushed her way from behind the first row of people. Allison recognized her but didn't know her name.

"What happened? Weren't you paying attention?" she demanded.

Silence from the group. The words came out as an accusation and lingered in the air for a few seconds before the chorus could react to her.

"It was an accident."

"Yeah, just an accident. Lay off, all right?"

But Sarah was staring Allison down, unmoved by the protest around her. Intuition kicked in, and Allison understood what was going on.

She's Charlie's girlfriend, or wants to be. Look at how she hates me.

"Yes, Sarah, I feel awful. I should have been going slower." She wanted to say more, maybe explain what had happened, tell her how she had done her a favor by teaching Charlie a few manners, but there was no way to say it. Sarah turned and marched off.

Mick wrapped an arm around her and whispered in her ear, "Don't worry about that one; she's a little sweet on Charlie is all. We were all a little worried."

"Me too, Mick. I was too."

Mick smiled, and Allison had a flash memory of being around her grandfather, such comfort, such easy familiarity. How was it that she had known these people for only one short week and could feel like she belonged with them? And how would they react when they found out the truth about her?

"Hey, Stan!" Mick shouted. "Get this girl a beer on me, right?"

Allison was about to protest and head to her rendezvous with a tub of hot water and freshly pressed cotton sheets, when she caught sight of the man at the other end of the bar. Her stomach turned over and an adrenaline rush surged through her.

"Thanks, Mick," she said, her voice shaking. "That sounds great."

"You got it, Ali. All right, everyone back to work. I don't want to see anyone bothering this poor girl. Let her drink her beer in peace."

With a chorus of groans, the little crowd melted back into the restaurant to bus tables, deliver hot plates, and collect tips from wealthy tourists. Allison took two long drinks from her beer and tried to figure out how she was going to introduce herself to the attractive man who she had just noticed noticing her.

CHAPTER 4

The issue took care of itself within a few minutes. The man stood up and walked toward her. Allison watched him in the clouded mirror behind the bar to make sure he wasn't just getting up to leave.

Even though Allison had spent hours studying the photographs she had of the man, she took in his appearance. Unlike the first day she saw him at the bar when he was in jeans and a loose collared shirt, tonight he was dressed in full corporate conservative: dark tailored suit, white shirt with French cuffs, shoes buff-polished so that they even picked up the dim lights in the bar. The allowance to casualness was an undone top button and a muted blue tie nudged down a few inches from his neck. Where this made some guys look like a cheap knockoff of a Dean Martin lounge act, the man carried it off.

The man's face was more rugged than handsome, a face that said the owner had done hard time in life but had survived with stories to tell and self-confidence intact. His hair was neatly trimmed and combed back, no effort made to disguise a receding hairline. If Allison didn't know better, she'd have guessed he was in his late thirties. He was actually forty-four, the same age as Richard, but her ex certainly didn't possess the same animal power of the man almost standing next to her.

She just wished she didn't look like shit warmed over for this chance meeting she'd been angling for all week.

"Hi there," the man said. "I couldn't help but overhear about your bad day."

Allison pushed back her hair over her ear and smiled softly. "Yeah, it's been a tough one."

"Mind if I sit with you?"

Direct and to the point. She liked that. But the voice in her head warned her, *Don't seem too eager. Play it cool, Allison. Play it cool.*

Allison shrugged and took another sip of her beer. The man tipped his beer toward Stan, indicating two more.

"I'm fine with this one, thank you. I'm about to head home," she said to the man when the beers arrived.

"These are both for me," he said, smiling. "I'm sure it won't go to waste in this place."

"Do you come here a lot?" Allison cringed as the words came out of her mouth. What was she, twenty years old and falling back on cheesy pickup lines she'd learned in teen movies? She had to be a little cleverer.

"Whenever I'm in town. I live over on the Eastern Shore but I come over for business occasionally. Sometimes for pleasure. How about yourself?"

"Short version?"

"Short or long. I'm not going anywhere."

Allison looked away and pretended to be embarrassed by the attention. "All right, short version. Ready?"

"Fire away."

"Freelance photographer. In town for a week now, probably here for another week or two, shooting pictures of the Chesapeake."

"For what publication?"

Allison laughed. "Yet to be determined."

"Ah, working on spec. Now, that takes some guts. I like that."

"I'm not sure about guts, but it's the way to do the work you like as opposed to the work you have to do, you know what I mean?"

"Amen, sister."

It's a natural flow to ask what he does for a living. Don't ask, though. Give him room.

Allison let the silence drag out between them. Finally the man filled the gap.

"What was it like tonight?"

"What do you mean?"

"I heard you ran into a little trouble," he said.

"The accident?"

"Yes," the man said softly, "it sounds like it was pretty horrific."

Allison cocked her head to the side. Her new companion's voice had changed—a bit lower, but it wasn't an attempt at sympathy or consolation. There was an edge to it now, an eagerness that hadn't been there just seconds before.

"It was bad. Charlie, the kid who works here as a bartender—"

"I know Charlie."

"Yeah, he's OK, though. There was some farm equipment on the truck we hit. Some metal poles bored through the door and went through his leg."

"That's awful," the man said in a voice that said it wasn't awful at all, but exactly the kind of thing he wanted to hear.

Allison tried not to read too much into it. People flock to accident scenes, don't they? It is human nature. They don't slow down at the roadside accident to help, too much blood, worries about AIDS and lawsuits for doing the wrong thing. No, they slow down to see the damage. To look at the poor son of a bitch on a stretcher and think, *Better that poor schmuck than me.* It was the man's next question that unnerved her.

"Tell me," he said, his voice lowered to a whisper, "what did it feel like right before the accident? What did it feel like in those few seconds before the impact? When you knew what was coming but couldn't stop it. How did it feel to be so close to death?"

Easy, Allison, don't blow it.

Allison slowly turned away from the man's intense stare. She took a drink from her beer as if considering her answer carefully. Finally, she turned back and said, "Shitty. It felt shitty."

The man's face went blank with disappointment, but then the skin at the corners of his eyes creased as he smiled and then started to laugh. "That's perfect," he said. "I couldn't agree with you more." He raised his beer toward her. "To the shittiness of the near-death experience."

Allison finished off her first beer and eyed the second one waiting for her. Decision time. She'd worked on this meeting for a week, but it would be for nothing if she pushed him too far. She made her move and stood up.

"Where are you going?" the man asked.

"It's late and it's been a rough one. I'm heading back to my place for a long bath and an even longer sleep."

"Fair enough. It's been a pleasure. Perhaps I'll see you down here again."

"Maybe," Allison said, trying to sound offhanded. She called out to Mick and Stan that she was leaving and they waved good-bye. She put her hand lightly on the man's shoulder. "Have a good night. Enjoy those beers."

"I never caught your name," the man said.

"Allison Davenport."

"Nice to meet you, Allison. My name's Arnold Milhouse. People call me Arnie."

She shook his outstretched hand and hoped he couldn't feel it trembling. "Good to meet you too, Arnie. See you around, OK?"

"You bet."

Allison left the bar, second-guessing herself for leaving so quickly. She wondered if she should have spent more time talking to him. But getting the attention of a millionaire required not giving him what he wanted, making him want more, making him start the chase. She felt confident that she now had Arnie Milhouse's attention. It was just a question whether he would take the bait. As she walked down the street, she tried to dredge up the confidence she needed to see her plan through.

She reached into her purse and felt her Glock 44 on the bottom right where it was supposed to be. The feel of a loaded gun always made her feel better.

Still, she fought down a surge of panic that she was blowing her first real chance to make a connection with Arnie. She just hoped she read him right and hadn't ruined her chance to find out if he really was who she needed him to be.

Back at the bed-and-breakfast, she ran hot water in the sink. Taking the bar of soap, she manically scrubbed the hand that had touched Arnie. She always knew that before it was all over she would have to get her hands dirty. After years of waiting and planning, she was prepared to do whatever it took to succeed. Still, part of her clung to the idea that after it was over, no matter what she had to do, no matter how she compromised herself, she could somehow remain clean in the end. As she scoured her hands raw trying to erase the sensation of Arnie's touch still crawling across her skin, she doubted whether that was possible.

She threw the soap in the sink and turned off the water. It didn't matter. Success was the only thing she cared about. The only thing that mattered. She had to keep telling herself that. Eventually, she hoped she would start to believe it.

CHAPTER 5

Arnie Milhouse watched Allison leave the bar, appreciating the view as long as he could before the door swung closed behind her. He knew talking to her was a mistake; there was too much going on right now to get distracted. Still, the heat from her brush with death had emanated from her and made meeting her irresistible.

He chugged down the last half of his beer and chuckled to himself.

"Either it was all that, or maybe you talked to her because she was so hot," he said under his breath to the reflection staring back at him, the guy in the suit and the loosened tie looking pissed off that his partner had gone chasing skirt when there were important issues to be dealt with. Arnie paid his tab and headed out.

The storm left as fast as it had come, blown out in a few hard hours of rain and thunder. The humidity, bad enough without the rain, coated the world with a thin sheen of moisture. Arnie had been farther south on business many times and knew that humidity could be worse, but that was no consolation as sweat started to build on the nape of his neck as he walked to his car.

He decided the threat of more rain was low, so he pressed the button on the dash of his BMW M6, lowered the top, and then drove out of the Main Street parking garage. The low murmur of the powerful engine filled the garage. Arnie rubbed the stick shift around the palm of his right hand, relishing the subtle vibrations from the transmission. He had never been a car nut until he purchased his first high-performance toy to celebrate his first win in the stock market. Back then it had been a Mustang, only because it was the first dealership he had come across. The Mustang had less finesse than many of the cars he'd owned since then, but it was full of piss and vinegar. He still had the Mustang in the garage, but now he was into whatever was new. Whatever was fast.

The tires of the M6 chirped as he rounded the corner out of the parking garage and headed up Main Street to Church Circle. He took the circle fast enough to lose traction in the rear wheels. He corrected the fishtail into the turn onto College Avenue, roared past the back side of the governor's mansion, and yanked a hard left onto Bladen. From there he opened up the powerful German engine and headed for the on-ramp to Route 50 and the Bay Bridge. He was sure the accident on the bridge would be cleaned up by now, so he figured he had a thirty-minute trip back to the house.

Arnie pushed Pink Floyd into the CD player and cranked the volume. Top down, saying fuck-all to any posted speed limit, wind hitting him from all directions, he sang along with Roger Waters.

Tomorrow was going to be hell. July 17 was always the worst day of his year. And for that day only, he wished he could have exactly what Pink Floyd was singing about. For one day he didn't want anything to do with the vivid intensity that had once saved his life and now ruled it. Tomorrow, he wanted just what the song and the bottle in his hand promised. "Comfortably numb" sounded just fine to him.

◆ ◆ ◆

Half an hour later he made the turn down the quarter-mile stretch of driveway leading to his home. He slowed down a little, partly to keep from running into one of the deer on his property, but mostly to extend the time he had left on his trip.

The road was lined with trees on either side, so that when it finally opened to the circular drive that curved in front of his home, the effect was like a curtain being whisked back from a prize on a game show. And that was exactly how Arnie thought of the house: a ten-thousand-square-foot waterfront prize awarded to him for having the balls to play it big in the stock market of the roaring nineties. The fact that there wasn't a "For Sale" sign at the front of the drive was his prize for being smart enough to pull his money out before the tech crash.

While the dumbasses around him had taken margin calls with trembling hands (and occasionally concluded that the only way to answer the call was with a firearm to the head), Arnie sat on the sidelines like Scrooge McDuck, swimming in his stack of cash, tut-tutting at the people around him pissing away their fortunes. Then, once the dust settled, after the real damage had been done and the panic of weak minds had run its course, he swooped in on the carrion and snapped up positions to make another fortune in the recovery.

And now they wanted to take it all away from him.

Arnie pulled into the four-car garage that stood detached from the home but joined by a covered breezeway. He turned the engine off and remained in the car, listening to the click and pop of the engine cooling down. He closed his eyes and leaned back against the headrest and replayed for the hundredth time his meeting earlier that day.

CHAPTER 6

The call from the FBI was unexpected. Arnie had been questioned by police before and always found it exhilarating. But the FBI? The fucking FBI? That was a different potato altogether, wasn't it?

The agent was polite, almost embarrassed that he had been sent on his task. He called Arnie's home first, which Arnie knew was a good sign. If they had something solid, something real, the Bureau didn't extend a courtesy call. No, they banged down the front door wearing flak jackets, guns blazing. On the phone, the agent said there were some questions he needed to ask, that somehow Arnie's name came up in a case he was investigating. Arnie lied and said he was going to DC on business anyway the next day, and he'd be happy to meet the agent in town.

Old Ebbit Grill was a favorite of the Washington in-crowd, the power elite, as they preferred to be known. Located across from the Treasury Building, one building away from the White House, Old Ebbit Grill fed presidents, cabinet secretaries, and every manner of rising and falling star for the last five decades. Dark wood interior, lots of brass, deep booths where information could be whispered in false confidence to reporters, where dirty liaisons could begin and end, where state secrets could be sold over a nice pinot noir. It was the perfect fixture in a city of deals and people on the make.

The agent had been sitting at the bar, a half-full bottle of Pellegrino in front of him. Arnie picked him out immediately. A JCPenney suit in an Armani world. The agent glanced to the front door every few seconds, obviously nervous, probably uncomfortable, Arnie suspected, to even be in the same building with the booze lined up behind him while he was on duty. He was young, fresh off the farm. That was a good sign. They were sending the kid out on a busywork assignment. Just running down sketchy leads no one else thought were worthwhile.

But that was what made Arnie nervous. Something had brought the kid to him. Something had brought the FBI into his life. That was unfuckingacceptable.

"You must be Special Agent Dewitt."

The agent grinned and looked around. "I'm that obvious, huh?"

Arnie returned the smile. "Not at all. Frank, the manager, is a friend of mine. He pointed you out to me. That's all. I'm Arnold Milhouse. You can call me Arnie."

"Yes . . . great . . . I have a booth ready for us. Or would you rather walk?"

"Are you going to tell me some bad news? Something we shouldn't discuss in polite company?"

Agent Dewitt blushed; he actually blushed right there in front of everyone.

Arnie slapped him on the back. "Well, whatever it is, I'm sure it's nothing these walls haven't heard before, right? Let's grab that booth."

Arnie ordered a glass of wine and made small talk with the agent until the waiter returned.

"Mind if I order something to eat?"

"No, go right ahead."

Arnie ordered the chicken Caesar. "And anything my friend wants."

"I'm fine, thank you," Agent Dewitt said.

Once the waiter left, Arnie sat back in the booth and took a sip of his wine. "All right, Agent Dewitt. How can I help the FBI today?"

"Sir, first let me assure you that the questions I ask you today will be held in confidence and are part of an ongoing investigation. You are in no way currently a suspect in the case I'm about to discuss."

"Well, that's good to know," Arnie said and laughed, even as his stomach fell away at the word *currently*. Did it mean something? Was it just standard procedure?

"I tell you this because, although you are not a suspect, you obviously still have the right to have an attorney present."

"Look, I appreciate all the foreplay, but let's just get down to it, shall we?"

Agent Dewitt nodded and pulled out a pad of paper from the inside pocket of his jacket. "Do you now or did you ever have a relationship with a Suzanne Greenville?"

Suzanne Greenville. How the hell did they bring that to his door so quickly? Lunch suddenly got a lot more interesting.

CHAPTER 7

Arnie was aware of interrogation techniques employed by the police. He made it his business to know. For the last thirteen years, he used every available research tool to educate himself about police procedures and forensic evidence. When he thought about that first night in the convenience store, he shuddered to think how naïve he was to believe that watching a few TV shows prepared him to evade the police. It was only dumb luck and a couple of overworked detectives assigned to his case that let him get away with it.

The Internet made things easy with details about blood splatter patterns and crime scene analysis as simple to find as travel tips for a beach vacation. The most informative were the tell-all books from some of the FBI's most accomplished profilers, who provided step-by-step descriptions of their greatest cases along with commentary on what mistakes the criminal made. To Arnie, it was like having a blueprint to follow. The key wasn't just having the information; it was knowing how best to use it.

Even a greenie like Agent Dewitt here would know the basics. Words didn't mean much; it was the body that mattered most. Liars looked up and to the left, accessing the creative sides of their brains.

They looked down in shame. They fiddled with things in their hands when they were nervous.

Arnie picked up his fork and twirled it in his hand. He looked down at the table, then up as if clicking through his mental Rolodex of names.

He tried for embarrassed and nervous, but on the inside alarm bells were screaming for him to jump up from the table and get the hell out of there. Better yet, stab his fork through the little FBI fuck's right eye, scramble his brain a little, then get the hell out of there.

He shook his head. "Suzanne Greenville? Doesn't ring any bells."

Agent Dewitt nodded in . . . what? Sympathy?

"Mr. Milhouse, I understand that this can be"—he leaned forward and whispered—"can be a little embarrassing. I have reason to believe you know very well that Ms. Greenville was a call girl who worked here in DC and Northern Virginia. A very highly paid call girl." He let that sink in for a few moments, obviously hoping Arnie would fill in the dead space. "See, Ms. Greenville had a long-term plan, call it her retirement plan. She was working on a tell-all book and she had plenty to tell."

"I still don't see how . . ." Arnie pretended to be flustered.

"Ms. Greenville knew her story would be better with pictures, so she had a camera behind the bedroom mirror." Agent Dewitt slid a small photograph from his notebook, keeping it facedown on the table. "Would you care to see yours?"

Arnie felt the heat rise to his face. He shook his head "no" and watched the agent push the photo back into his notebook.

"All right, obviously I did know Suzanne. I'm sorry. I just . . . you know . . ."

Agent Dewitt held up his hands. "It's all right. Trust me, this same conversation is happening all over DC this week. A few being conducted by people far above my pay grade, if you know what I mean.

Some people deny it even after we show them the pictures. Afraid of wives, I suspect."

"I don't have to worry about that."

"You're one of the lucky ones, then."

"My wife died in an accident twelve years ago. In fact, tomorrow is the anniversary of her death." Arnie put on a distant look, then stared down at his hands.

The agent cleared his throat. "I apologize, Mr. Milhouse. I didn't know."

Arnie let the tense silence drag out, gathering the agent's guilt and sympathy as chips to be used later in the game. He suppressed a smirk at the thought that his no-good, waste-of-a-human-being wife had been useful for something at last.

Finally, the agent continued. "So, you did know her, then?"

"I used her on two different occasions." Three occasions actually, but he didn't plan to talk about the last one.

"Do you have the approximate dates?"

"This was over a year ago."

"Ballpark it for me."

"I'd say the first time was the end of July last year. The next was a month after. But you already knew that, didn't you?"

Agent Dewitt suppressed a smile, but he didn't answer the question. He wrote something in his notebook. "Any other times?"

Arnie shook his head. "No, like I said, just twice."

"Did she talk about any of her other clients with you?"

Arnie shook his head. "That sort of thing doesn't exactly instill confidence, you know? When you do something like that, you're betting on discretion."

"That discretion makes this investigation more difficult."

"So, what's going on? What did she do? Blackmail someone with these photos?"

"Suzanne Greenville was murdered three weeks ago. Rather gruesomely, I'm afraid. We have reason to believe it's linked to other murders."

"You mean like a serial killer." Arnie's stomach muscles tightened. He felt a rush saying the words out loud.

"Something like that."

"I haven't read about it in the papers."

"It's public information. Just buried on page fifteen or something. Most people don't realize that on any given day there are dozens of serial cases being worked by the FBI."

"That many?" Arnie asked.

"They really only flare up with the public if there's an angle."

"You mean like the Boston Strangler."

"A good nickname helps too."

"Or something juicy like a call girl with a hidden camera?"

The agent took a sip of water and gathered his papers together. "Yeah, well, I think it's best for everyone involved if that little detail never got out. Wouldn't you agree?"

Arnie wanted to smile at the agent's weak attempt to appear menacing, but instead he nodded seriously. "Of course. I just can't believe there are so many serial killers walking around."

"The world is a violent place. But you already knew that."

Agent Dewitt looked up as he said the words. An alarm went off inside Arnie's mind. For one second, he thought he caught something new in the agent's eyes. An intensity and intelligence that hadn't been there before. In a flash, Arnie considered whether Dewitt had been playing him for a fool all along. The "gee-whiz, I'm-just-a-junior-agent-on-shit-duty" routine all a masterful ploy to get Arnie to lower his guard for this one question.

"What are you referring to?" Arnie asked. He felt his heart pound, and he cursed himself for the weakness. He slid one hand off the table and pinched his own leg painfully, trying to calm himself. Agent

Dewitt glanced down and appeared to note the movement. Arnie stopped immediately.

"I read about the kid at the convenience store," Agent Dewitt said. "That double homicide up in Baltimore. Nasty stuff."

Arnie tried to look rattled. It didn't take much effort. "I—I don't really . . ." He took a drink. "I don't like to think about that night."

Agent Dewitt watched him for what Arnie thought was a beat too long. Then the agent's vacant look returned. "I understand. Sorry I brought it up. There are some real sick puppies out there." It was his turn to look down at his hands. "You wouldn't believe some of the things I've seen since I joined the Bureau."

Arnie could hear the pain in the young man's voice. He'd already decided not to underestimate Agent Dewitt, but he wished he could question him.

"Did you see Suzanne Greenville, Agent Dewitt?"

Did you see her severed hands and feet? The way the wound across her throat hung open?

Did you notice that her mouth was stuffed with her own feces to make your profilers think it was about revenge?

Right now, are you looking for someone who was abused by their mother, an orphan maybe? Did the murderer cut her feet off so she couldn't run away the way Mommy did? Her hands so she couldn't hit anymore? Is that what your profilers are telling you, Agent Dewitt?

"Yes, I'm sure you have seen some terrible things," Arnie said, trying to sound consoling. "I couldn't do your job. I'd have nightmares for sure."

The agent looked away and Arnie allowed himself a quick smile. Yes, the young agent had nightmares. Severed limbs. Blood pouring from open wounds. Flies crawling across the dead girl's eyes, sucking away the oozing moisture. Nightmares for sure. Somehow that made Arnie feel better.

"Anyway," the agent said, "here's my card if you think of anything that might help. Anything she might have said, you know, anything at all."

"You'll be the first person I call," Arnie said. "Should I . . . I mean, I understand that what I was doing was technically illegal."

The agent waved him off. "This is purely a murder investigation. I don't believe there is any interest in pursuing the . . . clients in this case. For now anyway."

"Then I don't suppose you'd like to leave that photograph with me? It's all a little embarrassing."

"Sorry. Goes back in the evidence locker. But don't worry, they're all under seal."

"I understand. Just thought I'd ask."

The agent nodded good-bye and left Arnie to pick at his Caesar salad. Unfortunately, as Arnie replayed the conversation in his head, he found that his appetite had disappeared. He called for the check and decided to visit his banker to start making arrangements.

Now, ten hours later, Arnie was sitting in his car, stewing over the memory of the meeting. He was thinking through all the possible ways to dispose of Agent Dewitt and his smug, grinning face, when . . .

CHAPTER 8

. . . the side door leading to the breezeway out of the garage opened, and Arnie jerked upright in his seat. Fear clenched at his stomach. He couldn't see who had opened the door, but it didn't matter. His raw instinct told him it was Agent Dewitt at the door. The FBI knew all about him. It was a trap. Right there in his own home.

Arnie reached under his seat, his fingers scratching the metal guides and bits of leather as he groped for the Beretta M9 taped there. His heart thumped in his chest, adrenaline pumping through his system. The *clank-clank* of the locomotive in his brain bleated out for him to hurry. His hand wrapped around the butt of the gun and he tugged at it.

In spite of the fear of being caught, he trembled at the glorious thought of shooting Agent Dewitt through the head, of seeing that little puff of red cloud appear out the back of the man's head as the hollow-point round liquefied the agent's brain, and then blew a six-inch hole through the skull.

He had the gun loose from the tape just as the overhead lights turned on.

"STOP. FEDERAL AGENTS. FREEZE."

Arnie could have sworn he heard these words. That they were not just a figment of his hopped-up brain.

He raised his gun and took aim at Agent Dewitt's head.

Agent Dewitt's eyes widened in astonishment. Then he let out a short, high-pitched yelp and raised his hands over his head like he was in an old western TV show.

The Beretta's trigger was set at thirteen pounds of pressure. Arnie would later wonder how close he had come. Ten pounds? Maybe even twelve? No more than a twitch away from pulling the trigger and blowing away the head of his little boy, not Agent Dewitt at all, but Jason. Poor, thirteen-year-old Jason, standing there, paralyzed more with shock than fear.

Arnie pointed the gun at the ceiling and released the trigger slowly and put the safety on. He choked back a sob, the realization of nearly destroying the only thing he loved in the world crashing in on him with such intensity that it was almost painful.

"Hey, Jason. It's OK. Nothing to worry about. See, I'm putting the gun away."

Jason lowered his hands but didn't say anything, as if he were still unsure if his dad meant to shoot him or talk to him.

Arnie fought to control the tremble in his voice. He quickly decided blame and anger were the best substitutes for the guilt he felt. "What are you doing up, sport? Where's Anita?" Arnie said, upset that Jason's nanny had him up past midnight.

Jason stood up on his tiptoes to follow his dad's hands as they disappeared under the car seat to redeposit the gun. "We were watchin' a movie. She fell asleep like always, so I stayed up." Then, with more enthusiasm, he asked the real question of the hour. "Was that a real gun? Can I see it?"

Arnie got out of the car and walked over to his son and kneeled in front of him. He loved the frankness of youth. No bullshit about this boy, no sir. "No, you can't see it. And I never want you poking around looking for it either."

"Why do you have a gun?"

"Some people have bodyguards who watch out for people who want to hurt them or kidnap them. Some people have guard dogs watch over their homes for them. Understand?"

"Yeah."

"Well, we don't have bodyguards, right? And we don't have guard dogs. So why do I have the gun?"

Jason mulled it over, then finally said with a smile, "Because you're our guard dog?"

Arnie grinned, pleased as always with his son. "That's right, Jason. I'm the guard dog. And I'm one mean SOB. I'll never let anyone harm you. Understand?" Jason nodded. "All right, give me a hug."

Jason gave him a half hug with one arm. Arnie found himself missing the overboard showing of affection from when Jason was younger. He cringed at the thought that one day he might ask for a hug and get offered a handshake instead. Until that day, he was happy to get at least the half hug.

"I almost peed my pants," Jason said, stepping back. "You really scared the shit out of me."

"Language," Arnie growled. Jason looked properly chastised, but Arnie knew he was enjoying testing his limits. "But I bet you'll remember this night. If you'd fallen asleep watching TV, it'd be like tonight never happened. If you're not going to do something you're going to remember, what's the point of living that day?"

"I'd rather remember a night for some other reason than being scared," Jason said. "You're the one always saying fear is weakness."

"You're right. There are better ways to make sure you remember nights like this. Ways that make you feel so alive you can't believe it. Ways that make it so you don't have to be scared."

"How?"

Arnie laughed. "I'll teach you some day. You're a little young still."

"But I'm fourteen now. That's old enough."

"You're almost fourteen. And that's not even old enough to be up past midnight on a school night."

"It's Friday."

"All right, then it's past my bedtime. Let's hit the sack. We're up early tomorrow."

Before Jason could lodge his protest, Arnie spun him around and walked him out the garage side door and through the breezeway to the main house. He was still a little shaken from how close he had come to destroying the only thing in the world he loved.

He was too on edge, and it was getting dangerous. At least he felt more confident after meeting with his banker that the proper arrangements were in place in case the impossible happened. If the FBI ever put the pieces together, they would have a tough time finding him. With little or no notice, Arnie felt confident that he and Jason could disappear forever without a trace. And for the first time, Arnie wondered if that scenario wasn't more of a likelihood than a distant contingency.

"Are we still taking the boat out tomorrow?" Jason asked, snapping Arnie out of the cyclical thoughts of his paranoia.

Arnie suppressed a groan. He had conveniently blocked out tomorrow. "You bet. Bright and early, we're Annapolis bound. Weather permitting," he added.

"I just checked online. We're fine."

"Good, now get upstairs and get changed. I'm going to wake up Anita, then I'll be up to tuck you in."

"Are you going to use the gun? Make sure she remembers this night?" Jason said eagerly.

"Upstairs, mister. Don't be causing problems."

Arnie watched his boy bound up the stairs, wishing for all the world that tomorrow was already behind him. As he walked through the foyer on his way to the media room where he imagined he would find old, snoring Anita sprawled out on the couch, he was surprised to find himself latching on to the one detail of the day that seemed minor compared to everything else that had happened.

Maybe it was because it made the trip the next day more bearable. Maybe it was walking through a quiet house that seemed to beg for a woman's presence. Whatever it was, he found himself hoping he would run into the woman at the bar tomorrow. Allison. That was her name.

Perhaps they would have a love affair. But more likely, the interesting and beautiful freelance photographer would end up being the next adrenaline rush he needed. He'd discovered that the more beautiful the woman, the greater the rush of the conquest. Anyone with money could get a woman into bed. That wasn't a conquest; that was a hobby. But to stamp out the life from another human being, that was another matter altogether.

Tomorrow might not be that bad, Arnie thought. *It might not be that bad at all.*

CHAPTER 9

Allison woke at six in the morning, and no matter how much she willed her body to keep sleeping, it wouldn't comply. Finally, she pushed off the covers and draped her feet over the side of the bed and rolled herself over, groaning with each small move of muscles that had tightened overnight. Her neck especially felt like a thick collar of bruised flesh, and she sat on the edge of the mattress, stretching carefully from side to side until she loosened up.

Allison had gotten used to a routine since arriving in town a few days earlier. Up early and out the door while the other guests at the Calvert House were still nestled in their down comforters and high-thread-count sheets. Down the street to City Dock Café, a coffeehouse where the baristas remembered your drink and the scones were baked fresh every day. A jumbo skim mocha for the road and she was off with her gear to shoot a few hundred photos in the morning light. Then back to town to drop off her stuff and go for her daily run. Five miles on off days. Ten when she was on. "On" and "off" were based on her stress level that day or the beauty of the place where she was running. Annapolis had given her many "on" days for both reasons.

She could treadmill run or pound a track if she needed to, but a place like Annapolis made things easy. Running through the colonial streets under a canopy of leafy trees, across the bridges over the Severn River, through the academic serenity of St. John's College's manicured campus, she felt like she could run forever, soaking up the endorphins rushing through her bloodstream. Each day she picked a new route, often just making blind turns to see where her legs would carry her. There was only one rule. While civilians were given free access to the Naval Academy campus, she had no desire to go there.

The stress from the last week pushed her as well. Running had always been her outlet, and she needed that outlet not only to get through the emotions of being back in this place, but to help her focus on her goals. She had never done anything like this before, and she knew she needed to keep her edge in order to pull it off.

She decided to change her routine today, though. She put on a sports bra, sweats, and a T-shirt and headed downstairs with a baseball cap on, pulling her hair through the hole in the back. There were already a few guests down in the common area, reading newspapers and drinking coffee. One man, the one she knew would be there waiting, the one dressed as always in beige Dockers and a tucked-in polo shirt, glanced up at her as if he might say something. She turned away from him and heard the paper rustle as he flipped the newspaper over on his lap. Allison grabbed a banana from the morning table and chugged down a full glass of orange juice before heading out the front door.

Normally she only did a few cursory stretches before starting her run, but this morning she timed herself and stretched out for a full ten minutes while she consumed her banana. She knew she shouldn't even run at all, but she needed it. The accident had left her more rattled than she would admit to anyone. That and the first real contact with Arnie Milhouse had combined to make this a true on day if there ever had been one. She thought she might even push it a little and hit twelve miles today.

Jeff Gunhus

Stretches over, she bounded down the flight of wooden stairs
that led to State Circle and headed right, circling around the capitol
grounds. It was still early so the gaggles of tourists and schoolkids
were sitting en route to the nation's little known, six-month capitol. A
few gardeners roamed the shrubs that outlined the crisscrossing walk-
ways meandering through the grounds. Her main spectators were the
dozens of squirrels that chittered eagerly at her, fat little rodents that
thrived off an unhealthy diet of potato chips and Cheetos and whatever else tourists used to coax the animals into the rangefinder of their
cameras.

She followed the spin-off from State Circle, passed by the governor's mansion—See sweetie, that's where you can shake the hand
of the governor and get a free cup of cider at Christmas. How about
that?—did the small loop around Church Circle and headed down
Main Street to City Dock.

Here too it was early enough so that she avoided the usual throngs
of people that crowded the streets. Like the locals at most tourist attrac-
tions she'd visited in her life, Annapolitans had a healthy respect for the
dollars tourists brought in but an even healthier desire not to be around
them very often. Early morning still belonged to the locals, though:
the shopkeepers, the guys cleaning the streets, the local cops grabbing
some coffee at City Dock Café. Allison had always been a morning person for this reason. There was a vibe in the morning that disappeared
later in the day, something that changed after the day settled into a
rhythm and the early promise that this particular day might be different gave way to the plodding certainty that today would actually turn
out to be the same as all the others. But the morning always held so
much promise, and Allison liked being part of the people who shared
the same hope, no matter how briefly.

She'd settled into a rhythm by the time she got to the end of Main
Street and ran down parallel to Ego Alley, the short canal that led from
the Bay into City Dock. Ego Alley was called that for the type of person

who paid extra money to tie up his or her boat along the canal wall, and really was an impressive display of yachts, both sail and power. Tagged with the moniker "The Sailing Capital of the United States," Annapolis didn't disappoint in its display of vessels.

As she made the turn to head back to City Dock and headed left over the bridge to Eastport, Allison glanced up at the smooth curves of the Naval Academy Visitor's Center. Her dad had loved the museum there. In pictures and artifacts, it described the role of academy graduates in the nation's wars, in the space program, in the embodiment of honor and service to a greater cause. It looked all well and good to her seventeen-year-old eyes, but it was nothing compared to what she saw watching her dad. The way he stood in awe of the place, squeezing her hand tightly when his own excitement welled up in him, the way he almost choked up when reading the quotations aloud to her from the walls of one of the displays, the quotes about honor and dedication to sacrifice. The words had stirred her, but the tears that welled in his eyes did her in. He never asked her to go or even pressured her to apply, but there wasn't a recruiting pamphlet in the world that could have done to her what seeing her father like that had done. She knew right then that she had to do whatever it took to get accepted and become an officer in the US Navy.

Allison put her head down and lengthened her stride. She focused on her breathing, pushing the memories back where they belonged. She'd force them away permanently if she could, but years had taught her that was impossible. The best she could hope for was some good old-fashioned repression. There was too much at stake with her pursuit of Arnie Milhouse to get distracted now. She beat the sidewalk with her Nikes and headed over the Eastport Bridge.

As her pace quickened, she left behind the dark cloud of thoughts that had hovered around her all morning. Dark and bitter, these memories brooded about the confident woman running away from them. But the darkest memory, the worst of them all, did not worry like the others. Allison knew she could never run far enough or fast enough to get away from it completely. That memory refused to be relegated to the shadows for too long. Little did she know that it was about to be thrust back into the harsh light of day.

CHAPTER 10

The Maritime Republic of Eastport was a small batch of homes and restaurants just over a short drawbridge from Annapolis. Visitors seldom realized there was a different name for the area, but the residents sure did. In colonial times, Eastport was the center of some of the Bay's most important boat building and also home to a large contingent of the area's oyster and crabbing fleet. Allison ran the outer road of the peninsula, passing by the last holdouts of wooden boat manufacturers who were fighting the good fight against the fiberglass hull with high-end wood kayaks for weekend warriors. On reaching the end of the point of land, she turned south and started to run the grid, following the road to the water on the other side, moving down one street and crossing the small peninsula again.

The sun was well up over the horizon now, and the seasonal humidity mixed with the steady evaporation of last night's showers made the air thick enough that she imagined she was less running than swimming through the streets. She wished she had worn shorts instead of the heavy sweats. She had long since soaked through her T-shirt and it now hung from her side, tucked into the belt line of the sweatpants. Her jog top still gave her plenty of support. Even though she had to put up with a few more looks from passersby, she felt it was worth the trade-off to be able to survive a little longer in the rising heat.

She stopped in at a gas station right before the bridge to Annapolis and bought a bottle of water. She felt good, much better than she thought she would. With the accident, it was probably smarter for her to take it easy. She hadn't bothered to ask the doctor. No doubt he would have suggested a couple of days of rest, maybe a trip to a masseuse or even a chiropractor, but that wasn't for her. No, the surety of a good run was exactly what she needed, and if the payment was being miserably sore later on, she would happily pay the price.

She allowed herself a few minutes of rest, sipping the cold water and stretching out her back. She tried to work back through her meeting with Arnie but surprisingly found herself thinking about Richard instead. Maybe it was the sheen of sweat covering her body, or the blood pounding through her system, but it was the sex she remembered. Not the desperate, passionate clawing at each other that marked their long reunions after being apart but the marathon sessions on long, lazy weekend mornings, when they could take their time exploring each other's bodies and work their way to a shared crescendo that left them both exhausted.

She smiled at the memory, savoring it. Usually thinking about Richard turned bitter, reliving the fights, second-guessing her decision to end things between them. But not today. She wondered why.

Allison poured a little water on the back of her neck and straightened as the small stream trickled down the length of her spine. She finished the bottle and restarted her run, crossing over the bridge down by the Marriott and back through City Dock and took Prince George's Street out.

This led her by the South Gate of the Naval Academy, but a left hook took her alongside the fifteen-foot wall that protected the grounds from unwanted visitors. Soon, St. John's College was on her left. Even during her time at the academy, she felt it was an odd juxtaposition.

A small liberal arts school, St. John's was known for attracting esoteric thinkers. Usually brilliant and always quirky, St. John's students liked to grow their hair long, wear sandals even in snowstorms, and sit in coffeehouses arguing about the origins of leftist philosophy. On the other side of the street, Navy midshipmen signed up for a world of structure and self-discipline. Despite the differences, there was a tradition of mutual respect between the two institutions, solidified each year by the unlikeliest of sporting events, an annual croquet tournament.

The road became narrower, and she crossed a bridge that spanned Navy Creek, home of the academy's boathouse for the crew and skull teams. Farther on, she came to a T intersection. To the left was the road back toward Annapolis that would take her by the Navy Stadium, where she had gone as a teenager with all her classmates to cheer on the often losing but always hard fighting Midshipmen. Turning right at the intersection would take her along the road that paralleled the outer wall of the academy grounds, over to Navy Bridge, across the Severn River and then up into the million-dollar homes that lined the river.

She jogged in place, trying to gauge how far she had already run and how much longer each direction would take her. Finally, she chose to go right and head toward the bridge. A simple decision, no more than a flip of the coin really, but one she later wished she could take back.

CHAPTER 11

The midshipmen from the Naval Academy were out in force. Dozens of them, both men and women, decked out in dark blue shorts and white T-shirts with "USNA" printed across the front. On most mornings, Allison ran into at least a few runners wearing that outfit. Physical training, or PT, was part of the drill at the academy just like in any military program, and it wasn't uncommon to see a few midshipmen out running the bridge or through town, but this morning was different. This had the look of a timed run, a regularly scheduled check to make sure there were no physical stragglers in the midst of the nation's finest. The runners each had a number taped to their clothing, the same as a marathon or 10K race. Instructors lined the path, not barking instructions like in some bad training-camp movie, but simply eying each midshipman as he or she came by, letting them know they were being appraised, letting them know, honor code or not, there would be no shortcuts taken on this course.

Allison had been one of them once. She had run the timed course with her classmates. She had been competitive too, finishing in the top ten, not only of the women but of all finishers. She'd taken some flack for it from some of the guys, especially since the instructors used being beaten by a girl as an insult to hurl at the ones who finished after her. At the time it felt good, but the price later had been too steep, too unfair.

Even though the bridge was open to the public, something made her stop in place and prepare to turn around. She felt a rush of shame. *You're not a little girl anymore, Allison. Run where you want to run.*

She was surprised by the voice in her head. The voice that encouraged her and pushed her when she felt uncertain usually sounded like one of her parents, her father mostly. Research showed that it was the same for most people, although the word *encouragement* was often substituted with *belittled* or something similar. This internal dialogue was the subject of Allison's senior thesis at UCLA. "No matter how well my life goes, my father is always there to shit on my parade" was the opening line of the paper, a quote from her own mother who hadn't seen her father for more than two decades. This negativism wasn't Allison's experience, though. Her parents were always supportive.

But the voice in her head this time wasn't either of her parents. It was Richard.

She hadn't spoken to him for months now, but there he was again, in her head, pushing her along. And worst of all, she knew he was right. Which was the most awful thing about Richard to begin with: that indeterminable rightness about everything.

At least without him here, she could take his advice without feeling self-conscious about her own identity or without the power struggle that plagued their relationship. *Had* plagued their relationship, Allison corrected herself. That was no longer an issue because the relationship was no longer there to be plagued. She'd seen to that.

Guilt throbbed inside of her, heating up like a low-grade fever. For all of his issues and all of his faults, Richard had done everything right. She was the one who had gotten scared and pulled back. Allison had dated plenty of guys but never allowed things to get serious. Always pulling the plug long before anyone got too close. Being with Richard was the only real, adult relationship of her life, but eventually it went too far, too fast, and became too scary. One day everything was great between them; the next he started a discussion about kids. Soon after, they were on the long slide downhill toward the abyss, Allison self-sabotaging all the way down.

Richard was patient through it all, knowing exactly what she was doing, even understanding the reasons why. But it didn't stop her from ending things in one cataclysmic fight. At first ending it had been hard, and self-doubt had led her to pick up the phone on more than one occasion, reconciliation on her mind. But he was a good-looking, upwardly mobile guy, and he hadn't stayed single for long. She told herself it was for the best and tried to shrug it off, but she let it eat at her. The fact that she hadn't been in a relationship since was testament to that. But what else was she supposed to do? Besides, she had Arnie Milhouse to keep her occupied right now.

Allison started up her jog again, deciding to let her mind wander back through the minefield of her and Richard's relationship for the next mile or so. She was reliving a trip to Napa Valley when she hit the downward slope of Navy Bridge and saw the police car in the intersection below holding traffic back for the runners to cross the street.

She slowed a little on the downhill. There was a bottleneck of people at the base of the bridge. Orange cones made some space in the road, but most of the runners stayed on the sidewalk as if the slow-down were a welcome relief from the pace. She glanced across the bridge to see about crossing, but there were cars coming in both directions. And she guessed that the cop at the intersection wouldn't appreciate her jay-walking on the downhill side of a blind rise. So she allowed herself to filter into the group until she was shoulder to shoulder with the other runners, all of them carefully jogging forward at the same pace.

She heard the instructor's voice before she saw him. It was a heavy, thick sound, with nasal tones that belied the owner's southern origins. There was undeniable strength in the voice, as if a megaphone had been implanted in the man's larynx. It rang out over the panting and heavy breathing of the group, calling them names, yelling for them to dig deeper.

Allison's mouth went dry. Her throat constricted painfully. She tried to slow down, but the runners around her pushed her forward.

The voice called out as if moving cattle through a shallow river crossing.

No.

No, that's not possible.

Allison felt the ground buckle beneath her feet. She reached out to the person next to her for balance.

It can't be.

The kid beside her had her by the elbow now. She thought she heard him ask if she was all right, but the words came through as if spoken underwater. The concrete beneath her feet turned into sand. She couldn't quite get her feet to work right.

Then she was in the air. It wasn't a far drop, just the height of a curb, but her stomach rose up with the disturbing realization that the ground was no longer where it belonged. A quick jolt of panic accompanied the step down, as if her brain were suddenly seized with the possibility that the ground had indeed disappeared entirely and there would be nothing to break the fall.

But the ground was there and it slammed up into her foot, throwing her momentum forward into the back of the person ahead of her. She clawed at the shirt to regain her balance, but she was too far gone. She fell, making first contact on the asphalt road with the heels of her hands. Instinctively she rolled onto her shoulder, tucking her head away.

The runner behind her tried to leap over to keep from stepping on her, but the boy's shoe caught the side of her head and he tumbled over, taking a few other people down with him. Most of the runners, well aware that the clock stopped for no one, kept flowing around them, doing their best to step around the jumble of sweaty limbs sprawled out in the road.

Allison clutched the side of her head where the boy had kicked her while the world throbbed in and out of focus. She was disoriented so that when she lowered her hand and saw the blood there, it took her a few long seconds to understand that the blood was from the scrapes on her hand and not from a head wound. It only felt like the kid had put a hole in her head.

The few runners who had stopped had melted away back into the rush of white T-shirts. Allison knew she needed to get to her feet, she needed to get away, but she couldn't make her body do it. Chills ran through her torso. Her arms shook. Tears streamed down her face. She could only manage to push herself backward along the ground, away from the voice, away from the man. *Run, Allison, run away before it's too late.*

The man with the voice pushed past the last of the onlookers. Allison was looking toward him, but the last person to move out of his way had left her looking directly into the sun. She put her hand up to shield her eyes. She needed to see the man, to verify what she already knew, holding out in the far corner of her mind that she was wrong; it was just nerves, just bad memories catching up.

The shadow in front of her moved in closer, reaching out for her. Part of her brain knew the man was reaching down to help up a civilian jogger who had fallen down in the middle of some serious young people doing a serious run. But the second the face was out of shadow and she could see the man reaching for her, that part of her brain ceased to exist. A small part of her persona, locked away in heavy solitary confinement for so many years, burst out from its cell and took over. Allison was eighteen again. Defenseless. On the ground. Out of breath from running. And the face was coming toward her. Reaching out to grab her. Leering at her, mouth slightly open, moist, pink tongue visible through the cracked lips and tobacco-stained teeth.

That face, reaching out to steal something from her that could never be given back.

Allison did exactly what she had done when she was eighteen.

She screamed.

And she screamed.

Until the face was gone and someone told her it was all right to stop.

CHAPTER 12

The day started just as every July 17 had started for the last thirteen years. Arnie woke up, crossed the bedroom floor unsteadily, and threw up in the toilet. Now a different man from the loser throwing up in his two-bedroom shithole thirteen years ago, he couldn't help but think about that poor SOB as he heaved out the booze in his system into the porcelain bowl.

In his mind, the Arnie Milhouse living in the row house in Balti-more wasn't really him; it was someone else entirely. The Arnie Milhouse he knew today was a self-confident millionaire, the man who took a very healthy life insurance payment from his wife's untimely death and parlayed that into a small fortune. He was self-made, beholden to no one. This intruder, this person from a parallel universe that looked like him in the mirror wasn't a reflection of who he really was. It was just a false echo from the past, one that meant nothing to him now.

Only he knew that was a lie.

That poor bastard meant everything to him.

If it wasn't for that skeleton of a man finally standing up to the world, Arnie Milhouse wouldn't be where he was today.

So, no matter how much he hated the man for his weakness and his timidity, for the dozens of times he had just looked the other way when his wife had mistreated their son (mistreated, hell, it was criminal abuse, pure and simple), no matter how little a man he had been, Arnie-today took his hat off to Arnie of thirteen years ago for finally getting the cojones to stand up and take charge.

Arnie gargled some Listerine to get the puke taste out of his mouth, spit in the sink, and looked up at his reflection, staring into his eyes as if he might find something unexpected hiding there.

"You OK, Dad?" a tired voice said behind him.

Arnie turned to see Jason in his boxers and a T-shirt, rubbing his eyes, hair sticking out in all directions. "What are you doing up?" Arnie asked.

The boy shrugged. That was fast becoming Jason's answer to any question his dad asked. That and "I don't care." Arnie supposed it was natural for a boy entering his teenage years, but not his boy. Arnie knew he would soon have to teach Jason that *I dunno* and *I don't care* just weren't going to cut it around him. Not today, though. This wasn't the time.

"I heard you throwing up. Are you sick?"

Arnie put his arm around the boy and walked him back to the bedroom. "Probably just something I ate last night. I'll be fine."

"So we're still going out on the boat?"

"Hell yes. I mean, heck yes."

Jason giggled at what a prude his dad was, and Arnie soaked up the boy's presence. The twinge came again as he realized the days were numbered that it would be just the two of them. First would be high school and girlfriends. Then college, hopefully in-state and close by, but Jason had been talking about Harvard. Then marriage, his own kids. Soon it would just be a periodic phone call and a couple of trips a year. Life was going to take his boy away from him.

But today Jason was all his. Well, mostly his. On many days, but always on this day in particular, Arnie had to share Jason with a ghost.

"Do we have the flowers for Mom?" Jason asked.

"No, not yet. There's a place in Annapolis. We'll pick them up there so they'll be nice and fresh."

Jason sat on the edge of the bed, looking out the wall of windows that framed a view of the Chesapeake Bay. "Do you miss her still?"

Arnie sat next to him, wrapped an arm around his shoulders and lied. "Yeah, I do. She was a good woman, your mother. She loved you so much."

Jason smiled. Arnie knew his son didn't remember anything about his mom. What memories he did have were from carefully selected photos that Arnie had put together in an album. He had burned most of the pictures of his wife. All the ones where she had a cigarette in one hand, a can of cheap beer in the other, eyes glazed over from whatever drug she was on that night. Gone were the pictures of her partying with random men she'd picked up at the bars. No, the pictures told a different story and it had nothing to do with the truth. And that was the point. The truth hurt, and he wouldn't let anything hurt his boy.

"I miss her," Jason said. "I wish she hadn't died."

"I miss her too," Arnie lied. *I wish I'd killed her earlier than I did*, he added to himself. Not too early—she had, after all, given him Jason, but a day or two after childbirth would have been fine.

"All right then, First Mate Milhouse. Are we ready to embark on our adventure on the high seas?"

"Yes sir, Captain," Jason said, bouncing off the bed. "Ready to go."

"That's a funny uniform there, sailor," he said with a nod to Jason's pajamas. "How about we go with something a little more conventional? Breakfast in five minutes and then we'll get going."

Arnie smiled as Jason turned and raced off to get changed.

A day on the water with Jason would be great. There was peace on the water that he didn't get anywhere else and, after yesterday, peace was exactly what he needed. The threat he'd felt so strongly yesterday after the interview with the young FBI agent had been weakened by a night's sleep. He started to suspect that yesterday's stress had been an overreaction. He knew that a connection between Suzanne Greenville and him had always been a possibility, but he hadn't anticipated involvement from the FBI.

But now it was here.

She took pictures of me when I was with her. They have a direct connection between the two of us.

He sat on the edge of his bed and drew in several deep breaths to slow down his thinking. Certainly the contact with the FBI was disturbing, but they thought of him only as one of many wealthy johns caught on film by a dead prostitute. Certainly that connection wasn't strong enough to make him pick up everything and move.

Still, Arnie couldn't shrug off the cold pit in his stomach. The FBI had his name in the file of a homicide victim. That happened once and he was just another unlucky guy caught on film by a whore writing a tell-all book. The next time his name turned up, even circumstantially, the computer would spit out his name and raise a red flag. The legitimacy that his money afforded him would give him some camouflage but not forever.

He was upset at his own complacency. The preparations he put in motion yesterday for Jason and him to disappear if they needed to were long overdue. Being connected to the Greenville woman wasn't completely unexpected. In retrospect, he knew better than to hunt so close to home. Especially with someone he saw on more than one occasion.

He spent some time reflecting on why he had done it. Not the killing. The reason for that was obvious. But the risk profile was out of sync with his other conquests. He'd realized that the increased risk was exactly what had made it so much more exciting. Like a drug addict, he'd recently found himself needing a stronger fix. That was where all the serial killer copycat bullshit came from. It was why Suzanne Green-ville had happened. And it worked. He'd never felt so alive.

But now the thought of running was taking that feeling away, replacing it with something totally unacceptable: a sense of weakness. Logically, it made complete sense to be ready to disappear, but he loathed how it made him feel. The slow-burning anxiety in his stom-ach. The paranoia that made him look over his shoulder every few minutes. It was a constant reminder that the old Arnie Milhouse, the cuckolded asshole who didn't know how to stand up for himself, was still inside of him. Ready to slink back from his long exile. Sniveling. Whining. Ready to turn him back into the sorry excuse for a man he had once been.

The new Arnie Milhouse refused to let that happen, on this day of all days. He wouldn't give in to the fear. Or to the voices shouting in his head to be cautious. To hell with that. Instead, he would double down and push harder. The photographer he'd met the night before suddenly came to mind. Amanda, no, Allison was her name. Smart, beautiful, and hard to get. Just the challenge he needed right now to shake off the weakness threatening to seep into his bones. She could have a role to play in his game with the FBI. A very fun role. And if not, he could easily think of other uses for her. It was exactly what he needed. A dis-traction to take his mind off things. Especially today.

Arnie dreaded the visit to the cemetery in Annapolis, the lies he would have to tell, the emotion he had to fake. As a rule, such things didn't bother him, but with his son it was different. He was honest with him about everything else. Well, almost everything. He still hadn't shared the one thing about his life that freed him from the miserable curse before the transformation. Before that night at the convenience store when the entire world suddenly made sense to him.

That was another lesson that would have to wait. But not forever. Someday Arnie would teach his son how to be a man. He would teach Jason the proprietary blend of domination and power that came with killing. Teach him how his existence before killing was like being an empty balloon, formless, pliable to anyone who chose to stretch and bend you.

But he would teach his son that he didn't have to accept the emptiness. That there was a way to change the world and to change yourself in it. A way to be filled with confidence and passion until you felt ready to burst from your own skin. Yes, Arnie would teach his son to kill, but not yet. Not today. Today was a time for honoring the dishonest memory of Jason's drugged-out, child-abusing slut of a mother. The truth of life would wait for another day.

◆ ◆ ◆

The Chesapeake lived up to her reputation as one of the finest boating waters in the world. The morning clouds broke halfway through the trip, and the water transformed into an endless blanket of gold sequins, each small wave reflecting its own personal fire from the sun. The double hull of the forty-five-foot catamaran sliced through the calm waters with only a slight aft-to-stern swell belying the incoming tide. Arnie stood behind the wheel in the center of the craft, a stainless steel thermos of coffee in his hand. They had started the journey under power from the twin Mercury engines, but a soft breeze out of the south had made for an easy sail across the Bay.

"How are we doing, bubba?" Arnie called out.

Jason was on his favorite lookout point, the taut elastic net stretched between the two hulls in the bow of the boat. He liked to hang suspended directly off the water, wind in his face, pretending that there was no boat at all and that he was by himself, flying just feet above the surface like the gulls that followed them on either side of the boat. He looked over his shoulder.

"What's that?"

"I said, how are you doing?" Arnie shouted over the wind.

Jason gave him a thumbs-up and a wide grin.

Arnie slugged back the last of his coffee and checked his bearings. Navigating the Bay in clear weather was simple. At night or in rain it was a little trickier. When he first started to boat, Arnie had been caught unexpectedly out in a storm. That time in a smaller vessel, by himself and with a lot less experience. By the time the Coast Guard rescue patrol pulled him aboard and towed his waterlogged craft into harbor, he had a new appreciation for good old Mother Nature. And an impatience for the next storm. Since then, he'd gone out based on the promise of bad weather, in love with the fury and the danger that a storm could bring. As a result, Arnie had become a decent sailor in a short amount of time. This too would be instrumental in his disappearance, if it came to that. He pushed the idea back angrily and tried to clear his mind of thoughts of running and hiding. Instead, he focused on the girl from the night before and plotted how things might go between them.

They lowered the sail and came into Annapolis under motor. He steered south of City Dock and came up Spa Creek. After waiting fifteen minutes for the next raising of the Eastport drawbridge, they motored through and docked at their slip at Olde Towne Marina.

After some quick hellos to some of the live-aboards whom they had gotten to know over the years, Arnie and Jason secured the boat and headed into town. First to the florist, where Jason was allowed to choose whatever flower arrangement he wanted. And then a fifteen-minute walk to the cemetery, where Jason was allowed to remember his mother in any way he wanted.

Arnie kept quiet as they laid the flowers on the grave, hating the woman even as his son softly told the person he'd never known that he loved her. Arnie was glad to see Jason didn't cry. For a few years, Jason had cried pitifully when they came with flowers. Now it seemed the boy was maturing and, while still missing a mother, was probably starting to realize that he really didn't know this particular woman buried in the ground at his feet. Arnie wondered if there wouldn't be a year that July 17 came and went without either of them mentioning it. If they had to run, that year might come sooner than he thought.

CHAPTER 13

Allison rubbed the side of her head and once again assured the police officer that she was all right. The cop, the only person who had been able to finally calm her down, wasn't buying her story, but she really didn't give a shit. At least her hands had stopped bleeding. Her head still ached like the kid who had kicked her had been jogging in steel-toed boots instead of sneakers. Right in the temple, right where it hurt.

Craig Gerty.

Still an instructor at the academy.

What were the chances?

"So you sure you're all right, ma'am?" the police officer asked her for the fifth time.

"Yes, I'm sorry about that," she said. Her stomach still churned from the overload of adrenaline and bile. She felt queasy but didn't think she was going to lose it. A small victory given the situation. "Really, I should be more careful."

The cop raised an eyebrow as if to ask, *And the screaming? You really haven't explained that horrific screaming display you put on, you know?*

"I'd feel better if you got yourself checked out. Make sure everything is all right."

"Everything's five-by-five," Allison said, throwing a little law enforcement lingo in there to lighten the mood. "I told you, I was in that bad accident on the bridge last night. Seeing blood kind of freaks me out to begin with, so you can imagine . . ." She let the words drift away, as if that explained the freak-out display she had put on earlier. And now. Even now, twenty minutes after the cop had calmed her down and walked her away from the gawking runners, her hands still trembled.

Craig fucking Gerty.

And I lay there on the ground. Screaming my head off.

"OK, then. If you're all right."

"I'm fine. But I could use a ride home."

"I have to stay here for the next half hour, but you're welcome to wait."

"That'd be great," Allison said. "I'll even promise not to bleed on anything. Mind if I wait in the car?"

The cop mumbled that it would be fine and, red-faced, scraped the empty fast-food wrappers off the passenger seat.

Allison sank into the seat, her body suddenly stiff from the accident the night before, the eight-mile jog, and, now, the spill on the asphalt. Not to mention the psychological drain of the last few days.

She put on a brave face for the cop, but now with the doors closed and the world outside shut out, the emotions flowed freely over her.

It wasn't the fearful panic that came back to her; it was the anger. A decade of anger. A decade of countless scenarios she had played out in her head of what she would do if she ever ran into Craig Gerty again. But the anger was directed at herself. Anger mixed equal parts with shame and disappointment.

She beat her fist into her leg, closed her eyes, and leaned back against the headrest.

Craig Gerty's face loomed in front of her. She jerked up in the seat, looking through each of the windows to make sure she was alone, to convince herself that he had left for good. No one around except her new cop friend and the straggling end of the timed runners.

She had to get a hold of herself. She refused to let the piece of shit get inside her head again.

Allison didn't know if Gerty had recognized her or not. The whole encounter was blurred to her, a TV show watched in fast forward, all the central elements clear but the details flying by too fast to see with any kind of precision. He hadn't stuck around; that was for sure. But that didn't mean anything. It wasn't like Gerty had a record of giving a damn about people. Still, it might mean that he knew who she was. And that could make things complicated. What she was doing in Annapolis was too important to let that shitbird screw things up.

She leaned over to the driver's side and depressed the door lock. The doors thunked comfortingly. She leaned back in the seat and closed her eyes again.

This time a face appeared, but it wasn't Gerty.

It was Richard's face. Full of concern for her. Full of compassion.

She was tempted to linger on the image, but she forced it away and replaced it with Arnie Milhouse. Serious. Handsome. Wealthy.

Arnie was why she had come all this way. He was the reason she was here after all these years of hard work, after so many setbacks and doubts. She wasn't about to let anything get in her way.

◆ ◆ ◆

"Go ahead and grab a table for us," Arnie said, nodding toward McGarvey's.

"Where are you going?"

"I'll be right back."

Jason rolled his eyes and trudged off to the restaurant. Arnie watched him and resisted the urge to chase him down, mess up his hair, and race him to the restaurant door. It would have been the easy thing to do, but Jason was old enough that he needed a little reality check. He needed to let go of this day a little. Besides, chances were that Allison wouldn't even be at the inn, in which case there was no harm except a little emotional bruising, nothing a couple of crab cakes couldn't fix.

He walked up the narrow, cobblestoned Duke of Gloucester Street toward State Circle, flanked on either side by wooden row houses. Except for the overhead power lines strung up in messy loops from the rooftops, Arnie imagined the view on the road hadn't changed much in a hundred, maybe even two hundred years.

He turned right on the Circle and headed over to the Calvert House. He stopped and laughed out loud to himself. He was nervous. Not by much, but he couldn't think of a time in years when meeting a woman had made him even the slightest bit nervous. But now, standing half a block from where a woman he had barely spoken to the night before might or might not be waiting for him, he felt the faint flutter of butterflies swirling around his stomach. It was such an unusual feeling that he stood on the sidewalk, trying to decide what it meant.

Why did this woman intrigue him? She was beautiful, but he had been with beautiful women before, the sort that always seemed to find themselves on the arms of wealthy men. Arnie decided it was because the contact had been so short. All the blank spots about her could still be filled in by his imagination, and in his mind he made her into something she very likely wasn't. It was always the way. The women started off with all the promise of real beauty, but they all turned out to be whores after his money, after his attention, after something. He was smart enough not to use them for his killing rush, but there hadn't been one where he hadn't had to fight down the urge. Recently, he wondered why he had bothered resisting the temptation.

This one was likely no different. The delight he felt at the forgotten sensation of being nervous withered away as he remembered a dark time when he used to live every minute of his day with this kind of nervous fear.

He didn't like being reminded of his weakness.

In fact, he hated it.

That Arnie Milhouse was dead, dead as his wife, dead as that kid in the convenience store, dead as the dozens of people he'd used to feed his confidence and his power over the years. He would not allow that Arnie to return, no matter what he had to do to prevent it. The butterflies in his stomach dropped dead in midflight, suffocated by the hot rage suddenly burning inside of him.

A police cruiser pulled up alongside him and stopped in front of the Calvert House. The door popped open, and the object of his anger stepped from the car. Allison leaned back into the cruiser and Arnie overheard her say, "Thanks again, officer."

The Annapolis PD officer leaned toward the passenger-side window. "You sure you're all right?"

Allison pulled at her sweats. "Nothing a washing machine won't fix. Again, thanks for the ride. I appreciate your help." She shut the door before he could say anything else and waved good-bye through the closed window.

When she turned to walk up the stairs of the Calvert House, Arnie was there to greet her.

"Trouble with the cops, huh? What'd you do, jump the wrong fence or something?"

Allison flinched and did a double take. She caught herself, smiled, and brushed back her hair, even though it was an impossible mess. "Hi. You're the guy from last night, right?"

"I'm that guy," he said. "Arnie."

"Right, sorry." She put her hand to her face. "As you can see, I'm having a hell of a day."

Arnie put on his best sympathetic look. "What happened?"

"Just me being clumsy. Took a tumble off a curb while I was running."

"Are you OK?" He nodded toward her legs. "Looks like you spilled a little of the red stuff."

"I'm fine, really. No big deal." She paused, but when Arnie didn't say anything, she gave a little wave and said, "Well, it was good to see you again. I'm heading in for a shower. Take care."

She had already taken a few steps toward the Calvert House before Arnie could jump in. "I . . . I was actually up here to see if you were around."

Allison turned toward him with a shy smile. "Really?"

Arnie took stock of the smile. It registered interest but not too much. He had been right about this one. She was going to be a challenge. "I sailed over this morning from St. Michaels with my son. We were about to have lunch at McGarvey's and then take a cruise on the Bay. I thought you might like to come along."

Allison made an obvious glance down at Arnie's ring finger. He saw the look and held up his left hand to show a bare finger. Allison smiled. "Sorry, caught me. I've just been down that road before."

"My wife passed away over ten years ago."

"I'm sorry, I—"

Arnie waved her apology away. "No worries. A strange man you met in a bar tracks you down to ask you out for a boat ride, it's natural to wonder."

Allison shook her head. "Still, thanks but I don't think that's a good idea. I really need to clean myself up and get a change of clothes. Maybe some other time?"

The door to the Calvert House slammed shut on the porch just above them. It was loud enough to startle them both and make them look up at the red-faced man standing on top of the stairs. He looked at Allison expectedly, as if he had finally gotten up the courage to talk to her, but his face went blank on seeing Arnie. The man rushed down the stairs, hands stuffed into his pockets, mumbling a mangled combination of an apology and telling them both to have a nice day. Arnie watched him go, amused.

"Looks like you have more than one admirer here."

"Oh, him? Yeah, I see him every morning in the lobby. I talked to him over a cup of coffee the first day I was here. Software sales. Almost put me back to sleep. Ever since then I've tried to avoid conversation with him."

"I think he's a little sweet on you."

Allison blew by the comment. "Anyway, thanks for the offer. It was nice of you to think of me."

Arnie felt the opportunity slipping away. "Listen, like I said, my son and I will be down at McGarvey's for the next hour or so having lunch. We'd love to have you come out with us for a little afternoon cruise. If you decide you'd like to come, either meet us there or at Olde Towne Marina. Do you know where that is?"

"Behind St. Mary's, right?"

"We're the yellow catamaran. *Sweet Ride.*"

"*Sweet Ride?*"

"All my son's doing. If it was up to me, I would have named it *Endurance* or *Intrepid.*"

"*Sweet Ride*'s better."

"That's what my son tells me. So, can we expect you?"

Allison smiled. "No promises, but if I get myself together, I'll try to meet you at McGarvey's. Don't wait for me, though, all right? I might have to get some work done."

"I have a thirteen-year-old son who loves to sail. No waiting will be allowed."

"Come on, Dad. You said five more minutes ten minutes ago."

Arnie sipped his third Diet Coke and glanced at his watch. He'd stretched out the lunch as long as possible, but it had been more than an hour since he'd spoken to Allison. He'd already paid the bill, so when Jason complained a second time, he nodded. "You're right; let's get going."

They cleared out of the restaurant with a few good-byes and headed through town to St. Mary's. Less than ten minutes later they were at the catamaran, getting ready to throw off the lines and get under way. Arnie was thinking of the next way he would arrange an encounter with Allison, when a woman's voice called out from the shore.

"Have room for one more?"

Arnie waved at Allison, now wearing shorts and a white sleeveless blouse and toting a backpack of what he assumed was photographic equipment.

"You made it."

"Sorry I cut it so close; I had a long call from the editor who's interested in doing a coffee-table book with my pictures. I thought I missed you."

"Glad you made it. Come aboard."

Jason came up from below deck and locked eyes with Allison. "Oh man," he blew out with sagging shoulders, then turned and went back down the stairs.

Allison looked at Arnie. "Are you sure this is a good idea? I think someone wants his dad all to himself today."

Arnie reached out a hand to help her on board. "He's fine. Trust me, once we get under way, he won't even notice you're here."

Allison hesitated but finally took the outstretched hand and climbed onto the deck. "This is an impressive boat."

"Thanks. She sails great. We'll get some awesome pictures for you today."

Allison took a seat, lowered the sunglasses that were perched on her head, and soaked up the sun beaming down the teak deck. Jason appeared when his dad called and, with a cold look in Allison's direction, went about the work of casting off lines and stowing the buoys.

"Look, your not-so-secret admirer," Arnie said, pointing to the bridge ahead of them.

Allison raised her sunglasses and squinted in the direction he indicated. On the end of the bridge, leaning over the edge and staring at the catamaran, was the man from the bed-and-breakfast. "It is. That's Dockers-man."

"What's that?"

"I forgot his name so that's what I call him. He wears Dockers pants every day."

"It's a little creepy that he followed you down here. Do you want me to talk to him when we get back?"

"Oh, he's harmless. I can handle Dockers-man all by myself." She stood up and waved at him. "Hi there. Yeah, you."

The man stood up and marched away off the bridge.

"That wasn't very friendly," Allison said, pretending to be offended.

Arnie chuckled at the man's expense and angled the catamaran for the bridge that was just starting to rise. He stole glances at Allison when he thought she wasn't looking, marveling at her tan skin, smooth complexion, and a figure that he had even seen his son take notice of. He found himself hoping it wouldn't be necessary for her to die, even though part of him knew such thinking was useless. She would have to be killed because of the nervous fear she had caused in him, that bitterly cold reminder of the man he once was. The complication of people having seen them together simply made the game more exciting. The rush more intoxicating.

He returned her smile and rifled through his mental catalog of the different ways he might do it. Years of studying killers had given him a vast library of options from which to choose. Everything from the sublime to the grotesque. But he wanted something special for her. Something original.

They motored out of the harbor, Arnie lost in a daydream of hot blood and carved-up flesh, all sound-tracked with imagined screams for mercy from the beautiful woman in front of him.

Just another gorgeous day on the Chesapeake Bay.

CHAPTER 14

FBI Special Agent Scott Hansford watched the catamaran slide through the harbor until it made the turn south into the Bay and out of view. He was just about done playing nanny to Allison. What started as a favor to a friend and an excuse to spend a few days in Annapolis away from the Washington DC cesspool had turned into a major pain in his ass. First Allison refused to talk to him; now she was openly calling attention to him as if he were some kind of stalker. That and she made him look like a fool by constantly sneaking off and losing him.

Scott pulled his phone out of his pocket to call Richard and tell him he had better things to do with his time.

But as he scrolled through the contacts on his phone for Richard's number, he lost his momentum. Scott realized that calling now would inevitably lead to the question of the last time he saw Allison. He didn't feel like having to explain how she blew past him and ended on a boat sailing out to the middle of the Bay with Arnie Milhouse. *At least the kid was with them,* Scott thought. *How much trouble could Allison really get into with a fourteen-year-old on board?*

Still, he knew Richard would never let him hear the end of it. Scott slid his phone back into his pocket and decided to wait it out a little longer. He wondered if Richard's interest in Allison's comings and goings was professional or personal. Likely a little of both, he concluded. Scott didn't mind. He just didn't understand what everyone saw in Allison. Sure, she was good-looking and smart. But as far as Scott was concerned, she was just a walking liability that left a trail of damage wherever she went.

Scott hoped she would wrap up her little foray into Annapolis sooner than later and that he would escape unscathed by the experience. After that, if he had his way, he would never cross paths with her again.

CHAPTER 15

Allison snapped some pictures of the aft of the catamaran with her handheld Nikon 100 and tried deep, controlled breathing to calm her nerves. She still couldn't believe she was on the boat with Arnie. Couldn't believe that she had taken up his offer after the meltdown she had just had. But, she had argued with herself in the mirror after a hurried shower at the Calvert House, it was the whole reason she was in Annapolis to begin with.

Yet so much was on the line that she hadn't been able to shake the feeling that she was rushing things. Her mental state after the run-in with Craig Gerty was fragile at best. Even she knew that if it weren't for the adrenaline rush from having things progress so fast with Arnie, she might very well be back in her room at the Calvert House right now, under the covers in bed, crying herself to sleep.

That was probably why she was on the boat, she thought, multitasking her self-analysis and snapping off a series of photos of two racing yachts slanted at nearly forty-five-degree angles as they bent over against the wind. She knew she should have waited until she had her emotions in check, but the other option was to deal with Gerty.

"How's Charlie doing?" Arnie asked.

"Good. He's out of the hospital and back home. On crutches instead of a wheelchair. In good spirits, though."

"Good spirits? When isn't Charlie in good spirits?"

He's not very happy when you kick him in the nuts, she thought. "Yeah, he's a good kid." She looked up to the bow of the boat, where Jason sat cross-legged on the net stretched between the two hulls. "Is Jason all right? He seems upset."

"He's a little mad at me. Pouting like any thirteen-year-old does from time to time."

"It must be hard," Allison said. "Raising him by yourself."

"Not so bad. I'm lucky to have control of my schedule. I have help too, but I try to be there as much as I can for him."

Allison nodded. "What is it that you do?"

"Investments."

"You must be pretty good at it. Following in the family footsteps?"

Arnie cracked a smile. "Is that a nice way of asking if I was a spoiled rich kid or if I earned this stuff myself?"

"No—I—I mean . . ."

"I'm just giving you a hard time. My folks split up when I was a teenager. Dad took off. Mom took to the bottle. So I left when I was sixteen. You know, the all-American childhood. Not sure what happened to either of them."

They were quiet for a few moments, the unsettled silence between strangers when an unexpectedly private thought is shared for the first time.

"My folks divorced when I was in college," Allison said. "Just called me up one day to say they'd only stayed together for my sake and now that I wasn't home, it didn't seem necessary to keep up the charade."

"They told you over the phone?" Arnie said, as if this slight were so much worse than his own story.

"Mom remarried a week after the divorce was final, so I think it'd been going on awhile. Dad still lives alone."

"Usually it's men who remarry. Looking for someone to take care of them."

"No, once was enough for him, I think. My dad's really big on people being able to take care of themselves."

"And you? Ever been married?" Arnie asked, pulling a line to tighten the foresail as the wind shifted a bit. "Or are you really big on being able to take care of yourself?"

Allison laughed. "God, no. Freelance photography means constant travel. I've never met a man who was willing to put up with that and me at the same time."

"So nothing against marriage, just selfish men."

"Yeah, I guess you could say that. Or that I'm too selfish myself to compromise."

"Compromise is overrated."

"Says the bachelor," Allison said with a laugh.

Arnie turned serious. "You know what you want from life and you're living it. I respect that. Most people spend their lives wishing they were doing something else. They buy into the drudgery of daily life, the consumerism, the fifty-hour workweek, buying weekends by wasting weekdays. People waste their lives away, not even complaining, just accepting the shittiness, the smallness of their existence. How can they not feel like there's something bigger out there for them? Why don't they chase after it?"

Allison watched as Arnie's body language told the story beneath the words. The veins in his neck became more pronounced. The knuckles on the wheel turned white as he grasped the wood. He wasn't talking to her but rather straight into the wind, not shouting but with the strict sternness of a father talking to a child, chastising, teaching a lesson.

"Because they're afraid," Allison said softly, surprised to find that she actually agreed with him. "They're afraid there's nothing better."

Before Arnie could say anything, his body language changed again. He stood up straighter and looked out over the deck. "Jason, get down from there. You know better than that."

Allison looked up to the bow and saw Jason balanced on the net near the tip of the aft hull. He had a life vest on, but it hung loose off his shoulders, obviously not snapped in the front. The water was rougher on the open Bay, and the catamaran was making fast work of the waves that crested before them. Jason had to have heard his father, but he didn't acknowledge him.

"Teenagers," Arnie mumbled to Allison, but she could see the fear in his face. He clambered forward. "Jason. Jason! Get back from the edge and put your life vest on correctly. Right now, son, or we're—"

Arnie froze halfway to the front of the boat. The bow dipped down into the trough of a swell, and the catamaran's speed pushed them through the wave. The bow dug under the water briefly, and Jason was lost in a wall of churning foam. The catamaran rose out of the wave, and the boy slammed back into the hull, hitting his head with a sickening *thunk*. He had one arm flung over the hold line, legs dragging in the water, the life jacket half off his body.

"Jason!" Arnie cried out.

The catamaran dipped into the trough of the next wave, and water tugged at Jason's legs. He was holding on weakly with one arm. His other hand held his head.

"Hold on, Jason. I'm coming."

A wave washed over Jason's midsection, and the catamaran hit the bottom of the next wave trough hard enough to loosen his grip. The water swirled around him and, in a rush of foam and spray, Jason was gone.

Arnie shouted and pushed his way through the rigging to the edge of the boat.

Allison was standing in the rear of the craft and saw the bright orange of the life jacket racing past them as the catamaran sped through the water. On pure instinct, she ran toward the back of the boat and dove into the water.

Even in July, hitting the water took her breath away. She treaded water until she saw a flash of orange bobbing on the crest of a small wave not more than fifteen feet to her right.

She swam over to it but it was just the life jacket. No Jason.

Sucking down a deep breath, she dove in, her eyes open and stinging from the salty water. Visibility was nonexistent anyway.

She flailed her arms around wildly, grasping through the murky water. Nothing.

She heard the whirr of a motor underwater. The catamaran was coming back.

C'mon, kid. Where are you?

There! She brushed up against something with her right hand.

Her lungs burning from lack of oxygen, she reached out and took hold of the boy's body.

Jason was deadweight as she pulled him to the surface, breaking the water just as she thought her breath would give out and she'd suck water into her own lungs.

The catamaran was closing in fast, so she floated Jason's body in front of her, one arm slung across his chest to keep his head up and the other stretched out, treading water.

Seconds later, Arnie had the catamaran maneuvered next to her and strong hands lifted Jason onto the deck.

By the time Allison pulled herself up the ladder, Jason was already spitting up water and sputtering from the CPR being performed by his father.

She collapsed on the deck, relief washing over her as the boy took full breaths and started crying.

Crying was good. Crying meant alive.

Allison caught her breath and steadied herself. She looked up at Arnie to make sure he was all right. She wasn't sure what she expected:

gratitude, relief, joy, something. But what she got was as unmistakable as it was brief, quickly and artfully replaced by a mask of concern for her own well-being. But before the false expression could find its proper place, Allison saw the rage burning just under the surface. While most parents would have loved Allison for what she had just done, for some reason Arnie Milhouse seemed to hate her for it.

And for the first time, Allison felt afraid of the man she was chasing.

Allison rocked in time with the swell, feeling the power of the water through the wheel of the catamaran. She fixed a bearing on the three radio towers in the distance that stood sentry outside Annapolis.

Arnie came out of the main cabin and slid the glass door behind him. He carried two bottles of beer and handed one to Allison. "Here, you deserve this."

Allison took a long pull on it. The cold liquid cut through the briny taste left in her mouth from the Bay water. She tipped the bottle toward him in thanks. "You know, I really don't mind if you want to sail home. I can take a taxi back to Annapolis."

Arnie shook his head. "After your heroics you deserve the red carpet treatment. That was something else. You didn't even hesitate. I hardly realized what had happened, and you were already in action."

Allison smiled and tried to look embarrassed by the compliment, but the alarms were going off. His tone was only slightly masked incredulousness. She knew the question that was coming next.

"So, where'd you learn those reflexes? Does freelance photography lend itself to life-saving skills?" It came out like casual conversation, but Allison sensed the underlying suspicion. *Who are you really?*

Allison laughed. "You'd be surprised. When you take the wrong pictures, it's usually your own butt you're trying to save." Arnie chuckled and took a drink from his beer. It didn't make her feel any better, though. She could feel his eyes scrutinizing her, testing her. "Three summers lifeguarding spoiled rich kids at Camp Fellowship when I was in college," Allison lied. "It's been a few years, but some things don't leave you, I guess."

"Well, on behalf of my spoiled rich kid, I'm glad you were around."

"I didn't mean—"

"I know," Arnie said smiling, seeming a little more relaxed. "Since I lost his mother, Jason's been everything to me. I can't think of what I'd do if I lost him. Thank God you were here. You saved his life. I won't forget that."

"Well, let's call it a team effort and just thank God he's all right."

Arnie nodded and looked away.

Despite the kind words, she couldn't shake the feeling that he was somehow angry at her intervention. Was it a blow to his ego? A woman saved his son instead of him doing it himself? Did that minimize his role as caregiver? No, it wasn't that. It was about power over her. The position of power had reversed. That must be it. She wondered if—

"What are you thinking about?" Arnie asked.

Allison realized that he was staring at her again, and she wondered how much of her concern had registered on her face. She craned her neck from side to side. "Thinking I'm going to need a massage before all this is over."

Arnie held up his hands. "These hands give a great massage. For the right price, they're all yours."

"The right price, huh? Do you charge by the hour?"

"I was thinking more along the lines of dinner. Have you tried Harry Browne's yet?"

"Walked by it. A little pricy for a freelance photographer's budget. I'm not sure your hands are worth that much."

"I'm buying. All you have to do is agree to come."

Allison pretended to weigh the options carefully. "Well, if that's the only way I can get the back rub, I guess I'll pay the price."

"Perfect." He slid around behind her and put his hands on the base of her neck. She felt him lean forward and then his mouth was next to her ear. "Just relax," he said. "I'll take care of you."

Allison tried to suppress it, but a shudder passed through her body, and her skin turned to gooseflesh where he touched. "Sorry, I'm just a little cold," she said, trying to hide her repulsion.

Arnie pulled back his hands. "I'll get you a dry towel."

She leaned into him before he could stand. "No, it's all right. I'm fine." He put his hands back on her and she steadied her breathing, reminding herself that there was a chance Arnie might not be the man she suspected he was. The evidence was circumstantial. Not enough to build a case on. But she had to know the truth, regardless what it cost her. If that meant letting him feel in control of the seduction, then so be it. One way or the other, she had to find out the truth about Arnie Milhouse.

CHAPTER 16

The day spent waiting for the date with Arnie tortured her with too much time to think. After a restless night of half dreams and fitful sleep, she rose before dawn and set out early to take photos. But the camera never left the bag. Instead she found herself walking the path that twisted along the Chesapeake shoreline, sorting through the emotional baggage that had been heaped on her the day before.

She knew on her arrival in Annapolis that there were ghosts waiting for her on every corner, that being in the town could be the grindstone on which the dulled edges of old memories were rechiseled so they could pierce her again. But Arnie Milhouse was a perfect opportunity for her. Passing up the chance meant admitting the ghosts' power over her. And that was a failure she would no longer permit herself to tolerate.

But that was before Craig Gerty showed up.

Walking the solitary beach, arms hugged across her chest, tear-filled eyes focused on the step immediately in front of her even while the world lit up in the sun's gorgeous hues of oranges and yellows, she wondered if she knew what the hell she was doing.

Before coming back to Annapolis, she had been so certain, willing to do anything to achieve her goal. As hard as it was to admit, she had doubts about Arnie. There was something dark there to be sure, something she'd seen in his eyes on the boat. But she found herself second-guessing what it all meant. She supposed the conversation tonight would tell her what she needed to know. She found herself hoping she had been wrong about Arnie the entire time. And if she was, she wondered what she intended to do about it.

Arnie drove up to the valet at the Calvert House at seven forty-five, fifteen minutes early for his date. Harry Browne's was only half a block away from the inn, a convenience measured to make the night as pleasurable as possible.

"Good evening, sir. How long will you be parking with us?"

Arnie gave the kid a wink and a ten-dollar bill. "Might be a few hours, might be overnight. Just depends."

The valet grinned, both at the insinuation and because Arnie had spotted him checking out which president was on the bill now in his hand. Arnie could tell the kid was considering his own snappy comeback, probably weighing the appropriateness versus the possibility that he might step over the line with the juicier comments he could make. Arnie threw him the keys. "You got it covered?"

"Yes sir. Enjoy your night. Good luck to you."

Arnie nodded and walked up the steps of the Calvert House.

From her second-floor room, Allison watched Arnie park his car and talk to the valet out front. She had been ready for the last half hour but knew she wouldn't appear downstairs a minute before eight, ideally five minutes after. She had Arnie pegged for a punctuality freak and being a bit late would set just the right tone. She walked around her four-poster bed over to the bathroom and dumped three Tylenols into her hand. She washed them down with tap water, praying that was enough firepower to beat back the stress headache using the back side of her right eye as a punching bag.

She checked the mirror, turning to the side to make sure her dress hung properly. She'd gone with a simple black dress, a staple of women on first dates. Slenderizing, sexy, and easy to accessorize. She tugged at her bra to bring her cleavage into balance and pulled the neckline up slightly. Conservative, sexy, and slutty all came down to a matter of inches, and Allison made sure she came down between the first two looks instead of the third.

At eight o'clock, the phone rang.

"I've come to collect payment for services. One dinner date for one massage, if I remember correctly," Arnie said.

"Are you downstairs already?"

"We said eight, right?"

Allison paused as if checking the time. "Yeah, I'm sorry. I'm running a little late. I'll be down in a few minutes."

"I'll be here."

Allison hung up the phone and sat in the overstuffed Queen Anne chair in the corner of the room. She sat quietly, running through possible lines of dinner conversation. Five minutes passed and seemed an eternity, but she forced herself to wait another five before going to the bathroom for one last check of her hair, and then headed out the door for what could be the most important date of her life.

"Jason can't stop talking about you," Arnie said, taking a sip of his wine.

"I'm just glad he's feeling better," Allison replied, raising her glass. She knew she had to limit her alcohol intake tonight so she could keep her edge, but she had to admit that the glass of wine she had already consumed with their appetizers and the second with their meal had done wonders for her headache. "It must have been a scary experience for him."

"They bounce back from anything at this age. One day disaster, the next it's back to video games and texting for hours."

"I thought that was just teenage girls who did the texting thing."

Arnie laughed and leaned back as the waiter cleared his plates. "You wouldn't believe it. I walk in there and he's got five or six conversations going simultaneously. He tried to show me how to follow along on the different threads, but I was lost immediately."

Allison watched Arnie's body language change when he talked about his son. He sat up a little straighter and leaned forward, almost squirming in his seat from his enthusiasm. She wondered if her father ever spoke about her like that anymore. She knew at one time he did. There wasn't a person in town that didn't know she was accepted to the Naval Academy. The news of her leaving the academy was disseminated at a slower and more hushed rate. She wondered if now—

"Hey, where'd you go?" Arnie said, waving a hand in front of her as if trying to induce her out of a trance.

She smiled but inside she chastised herself for losing concentration. "It just seems like you and Jason have such a great relationship. I admire that. It can't be easy as a single father."

"I travel a lot for business. That part is hard. But he's at an age where we can hang out and do fun things together. I only worry about when he stops wanting to do stuff with his aging old man. Now, that will be hard."

"I thought you were in investments? I pictured you sitting in a little room surrounded by computer screens, watching the numbers roll by. But you travel a lot, huh?"

"Yes, I have some real estate interests, and I sometimes will visit a small company before buying their stock."

"So, you are a cautious investor," Allison baited.

"I don't think I'd use the word *cautious*," Arnie said, shifting in his seat almost imperceptibly. "I'm pretty aggressive in what I do."

"You don't believe in caution?"

"I think cautious people sit on the sidelines too much. What they explain as prudence usually is nothing more than fear."

"But can't fear be a good thing? You know, like the way fear of getting hurt keeps kids from touching a hot stove?"

"Ah, but that's different. That's experience. You touch the stove once and you get a burn; you cry but then it heals. The experience has taught you an appreciation for the power of the stove to hurt you. But from that experience it's up to you to decide how much fear you let into your life."

"But you're not talking about a stove, right? You're talking about people."

Arnie took a sip of wine as the waiter delivered their crème brûlée desserts. When the waiter left, Arnie leaned across the table. "Other people are the source of most fear. Not always that they can hurt you directly, but indirectly. You know, through their scorn, their pity—"

"Their judgment."

"That's right. How people, even strangers we'll never see again, judge our actions, or even how they *might* judge our actions, keeps most of us watching life instead of living it. Our nature calls for action, but being bound in society means that we're strapped down by the judging nature of society. Think about it: some people fear public speaking more than death; that's how much we allow ourselves to be sucked in and limited by the need to conform."

"Yeah, but put a gun to their head and say, 'Get out there and talk or I'm pulling the trigger,' and they wouldn't think twice. The will to live is stronger than fear."

Arnie smiled, appearing to enjoy the argument. "No doubt. But no one is there to hold that gun to their head to make them overcome the fear, so instead they become a slave to it. Soon their life is nothing but weakness, a numb life not really lived."

Allison raised her glass. "To a life lived and not merely survived."

"I'll drink to that," Arnie said.

They touched glasses and sipped their drinks. Neither spoke. Allison wondered if Arnie would try to turn them back to small talk now that things were just starting to get interesting. She decided not to give him the chance. If she was right about him, she knew exactly the direction to take. "If you have this philosophy that fear diminishes the life experience, you must do things to fight your own fears."

"What fears?" Arnie asked with a smile.

"You have to fear something."

Arnie shook his head. "I used to fear a lot of things. I was paralyzed by it. I walked through life flinching at shadows."

"What changed?"

Arnie lowered his voice and Allison noticed that while his right hand casually swirled his wine glass, his left hand grasped his dessert fork in a white-knuckled grip. "I took control. I reached a limit of abuse and simply decided to no longer accept my fear."

"You make it sound so simple," Allison said, surprised at her sudden longing to understand this man's secrets, to somehow make her own fear disappear. She forced herself to concentrate.

"Like most things, it's simple. What people lack is the desire to see the answer and then the courage to implement the solution. But it is simple, Allison. That much I can promise you."

Allison met his piercing eyes and felt exposed before them. In some inexplicable way, she understood there was an offer on the table for her to have a way out of her pain. She suddenly felt that she had gone too far.

"Well, this is awfully heavy discussion to have over crème brûlée," she said.

"I'm sorry, I shouldn't have . . ."

"No, I enjoyed hearing your ideas. I think it's fascinating. I think we should discuss it further the next time we go out on your boat."

"Are you asking me out on a date?" Arnie asked.

"Yes, and I'm using your boat to do it. How do you like that?"

"Actually, I like it quite a bit," Arnie said, finishing his wine.

Allison raised her own glass to her lips and took a deep drink. She thought of the road that had brought her to this moment, everything she had endured during the past ten years. This scene had played out a hundred times in her mind and never once, so close to her goal, did she expect to feel uncertainty. Doubts clouded around her and she had the uncomfortable sense that she was on the verge of making a horrible mistake.

Could it be that she was wrong about Arnie? Her evidence was all circumstantial, otherwise she wouldn't be at dinner trying to pry secrets out of him. Her facts were compelling, but only because she didn't believe in coincidences. And because her gut told her she was right about him. Only it was that same instinct that was wavering now.

It seemed almost a cruel trick to have second thoughts so late in the game. After months of being absolutely sure Arnie was the right man, she found herself suddenly nervous that she'd gotten it all wrong. Or maybe, after getting to know him, she wanted to be wrong.

With another deep sip of her wine, she resolved to do whatever it took to find out for sure, even if that meant continuing the date late into the night. Right or wrong, she had to see this through no matter the consequences. She just hoped those consequences turned out to be less severe than what she had come up with in her imagination. She finished her drink, put on her best smile, and did her best to hide the sense of terror building inside her.

CHAPTER 17

Arnie left his conquest naked in the other room, sprawled out on the cheap motel bedspread, used up for now, sore, spent, bloodied. He went into the tiny bathroom, chipped plastic veneer on the counter, mold blackening the grout, and he stood naked in front of the mirror. The bulb that stuck out from the wall was at least twice the wattage needed and the harsh light turned his skin pasty gray. *Like the belly of a dead fish*, Arnie thought.

The rest of the image was no more flattering. A regular exerciser, there was not excessive fat on his body, no spare tire that most men seemed to acquire when they entered their middle years. Instead, lean muscle quivered under his skin. Besides a dusting of hair on his chest and nipples, the only other body hair was a thick patch of pubic hair that framed an unsatisfactorily average-size crank.

He scrutinized his penis more closely. It hung limp, more shriveled than usual, as if exhausted and afraid of what it might be asked to do next. He had already removed the condom, tied it closed, and stored it safely away in his bag to dispose of off-site. Now he dug carefully through his pubic area to make sure there were no abrasions. *Leave no fluid behind*. If Arnie Milhouse had a motto, that would be it.

He looked back into the mirror, leaning in close to get a good look at his face. Not ugly but, truth be told, not a pretty one either. The ears were a little large, nose a bit small, mouth too thin for the size of his face, everything just a little out of proportion. But he knew that the woman in the room next to him wasn't attracted to the face or the body. She was attracted to the money. The aura of it. The power of it. Sure, he made the overtures, but it didn't take much convincing to get her to come with him to this motel room, cheap and dirty because that was his thing. He was eccentric, and she said it turned her on. And once here, she knew what to do and all the nastiest ways to do it. It was like after a lifetime of practice, she finally had the audition for the guy rich enough to warrant her entire bag of tricks.

Arnie took the tricks in stride and taught her a few new ones along the way. He tried to stay in control, but he'd been so pent up that he couldn't help but get a little carried away.

He swabbed the ends of his fingers carefully with alcohol to get the woman's blood from under his nails. These cotton balls, now smudged with blood, also went into his bag.

It had been three days since Jason had gone over the side, and he almost lost his boy. Three days to think about what life would be like without him. Three days to get more pissed off about being shown up on his own boat. To have someone else be his son's rescuer. His son's hero.

He heard the woman groan in the room next to him. *Serves her right,* he thought, feeling the rage from that day surge through him again. A quiet voice buried deep inside whispered that he was being unreasonable, that he ought to be happy she was there. Then there was another, more persistent voice. One that stayed with him no matter what he did to separate himself from it. Always beating on him. Always finding fault.

You better be glad she was there to cover your worthless ass.

He winced and rubbed his temple. If he concentrated hard enough, sometimes he could make the voice go away. Sometimes he could kill it all over again.

Piece of shit. You were just gonna let him drown. Let him sink to the bottom.

The voice took a stronger hold. Somehow, it was wrapped around his brain; it was barbed wire tied into a cinch around his brain, yanked tight.

"Leave me alone," he whimpered.

Leave me alone, the voice whined back. The cinch tightened. He yowled in pain and collapsed to his knees.

If it was up to you, Jason would be on the bottom of the Bay, fuckin' crabs swarming all over him like ants on a pile of puke.

"You're not real. I don't have to listen to you."

Bullshit, you don't have to listen to me, Arnie. I carried that little som'bitch for nine months until he crawled his way out of my innards, I will get some goddamn respect. Even if it is from a useless little piece of shitcake like you.

"Shut the fuck up!" Arnie cried, bent over and crouched on the floor, rapping his head against the wall. Tears streamed down his face. He couldn't help it; the pain was unbearable.

Piece of shit.

"SHUT UP!"

Head into the wall.

Useless.

"SHUT UP!"

Harder, into the wall.

Moron. Idiot. Loser.

"I'll knock us out if I have to," he snarled.

Stupid fuck, the voice whispered, but softer now, letting go. *Stupid mother fuck.*

Arnie braced himself, ready to ram his head into the wall if the voice rose up again. But slowly, the barbed wire dissolved, like temporary stitches, and just melted into the gray flesh.

Carefully, he got to his feet, wiping tears and snot from his face. He took deep cleansing breaths, ran some cold water, and splashed it over his naked body.

In the next room, the woman groaned.

Arnie thought he hit her harder than that. The fact that she would be regaining consciousness so quickly was just another insult. It didn't make him angry, he was already back in control of that, but it served to clear his head of distractions and refocus him on the business at hand. The voice was gone, thank God, but the beating hung over him, casting doubts and making him remember too much of his former self.

Fortunately he knew just how to get over it.

He flipped his penis idly with his index finger and wondered if he had any more sex left in him. Two times was actually pretty good, he thought. But he had been pent up, and the first time in his pants outside the motel door hardly counted. He wished he could make it through one more session to really make the woman pay.

Arnie checked his watch. After two in the morning. He put aside thoughts of sex. He was ready for something a lot more interesting.

Tools. What tools did he have?

He looked around the bathroom and considered the options. It reminded him of choosing clothes. Everything seemed either too pedestrian or too exotic. There was no "right" style, nothing he could put his finger on and describe to someone what his taste was. But like the federal judge said about pornography, he knew it when he saw it.

The problem was having too many options. Arnie figured the average young American never stopped to consider just how many items they are surrounded with on a daily basis that can be used to kill someone in a creative and satisfying way.

A toothbrush through the eye socket. A hot iron to the face. A shower curtain wrapped around a head and tied off with a power cord. Old-fashioned pillow to the face. More creative, miscellaneous objects in the orifice of choice. A shower rod, a plunger, a coat hanger bent out the wrong way.

Arnie's head rolled over the possibilities and he felt the rush building up, more powerful than the sex, violence the ejaculate ready to force its way out of him.

Sex made him feel empty. Killing filled him. It engorged him.

When he looked down, he saw that he had an erection.

He was ready.

Arnie blew himself a kiss in the mirror. "Enjoy yourself," he whispered. "Take your time." He walked back into the room to the blonde just now stirring on the bed. "Hello there. Bet you're thinking, 'Thank God I'm still alive,'" he said smiling. "Bet you're thinking, 'How could this happen to me?'" He pulled up her hair until her face was even with his. "Don't worry. Soon enough, you won't be thinking anything at all."

CHAPTER 18

Pete Dawson figured he was just about the only one at the Taj Mahal Motel not getting any nooky, and it kind of pissed him off. He thought through the list of girls he knew, thinking of who might go for a little booty call. But the list lacked both length and any real chance that any of the girls would even talk dirty to him on the phone, let alone come over and service his needs.

"If you want something done, better do it yourself," he said out loud to the empty cubicle that served as the Taj Mahal's front office, lobby, breakfast area, and, on most nights, P. Dawson's Grand Palace of Jacking-Off.

Pete giggled at his own cleverness. His other favorite was "When in doubt, rub one out." His buddy Ahram told him that one. Ahram the A-rab was always saying the most hilarious shit. Pete would laugh until his side hurt at some of the guy's sayings, promising himself that he would remember it and trot the comment out later as his own original thought. Ahram didn't mind. Hell, he'd even work on some of the funnier ones with Pete until he had them down. But damn if he wouldn't forget just the same. Pete knew he wasn't the sharpest knife in the block; not stupid mind you, he wasn't some kind of retard, but not prone to remember things he even meant to remember.

But "when in doubt, rub one out" had stuck with him sure enough.

He opened the lower left drawer and found his stash of hand lotion. "Damn if this dry weather don't chap my hands," he'd complained when his boss had asked about the bottle.

He had all the right tools. He had the motivation.

Now all he needed was some inspiration.

That fine blonde that checked in earlier would do the trick. Perfect tan skin, those shiny blue eyes, way classy by the Taj standards. He'd actually fantasized she was checking in by herself, but the way she was paying with crisp twenties and a quick look over her shoulder gave him the score. There was a dude waiting in the car for her, probably married and sneaking around on some overweight soccer mom somewhere. Didn't get a good look at him, but why would he? He wasn't going to waste time looking at some dickhead when the finest-looking pussy of his two years at the Taj checked in. He imagined that lucky son of a bitch was wailing away on her right then and there, hitting the real thing while he was stroking at the idea of it.

"Fuck that," he said, knowing he needed to at least try for a little more.

Months of practice and planning taught him which rooms worked best for a little sneaky-peeky. When the best-looking girls came in, he made sure they were located in just the right room. His dream was to set up cameras in some of the rooms, maybe even a webcam. He knew it could be done; he'd seen enough porn sites online that advertised them, but like most of his big moneymaking ideas (he had lots), the fact that it sounded really complicated made him happy to talk about it and just leave it at that.

He grabbed a small handful of hand cream and set out on his mission.

The hottie and her shadowy boy toy were in room 16, a dilapidated bungalow-style building in the back. It was dark out there, set away from the glare of the parking-lot lights and the main building of the motel. As far as the Taj went, this forty-nine-dollar-a-night room was the freaking Presidential Suite. And, courtesy of Pete Dawson, room 16 had several night-lights plugged into the electrical outlets to provide a little mood lighting for whenever lovers happened to be beating up the bedsprings that night. Sometimes the lights got turned off, but usually people coming to a place like the Taj were eager enough to get humping that they didn't even notice them, leaving Pete with enough of a light source for a damn decent show.

Pete strolled casually through the parking lot, cupping his lotioned hand to his side, as if he were doing a regular security check. He doubted anyone gave a shit what he did at two in the morning, but it was part of his game. He was undercover. Covert ops. Operation Handjob.

He chuckled at that one, hoping he would remember to tell Ahram the A-rab about it. That was rich. Operation Handjob.

When he turned the corner around the main building and saw the little bungalows out back, he started to get excited. The blonde was totally hot and the idea of seeing her buck naked, getting rammed if he was lucky enough, was starting to get him a little hot.

He broke into a little jog, sticking to the shadows as much as possible, humming the *Mission: Impossible* theme to himself.

There was a row of bushes on either side of the front door under the two windows. The blinds were pulled, but Pete had planned for that. The corner of the last five or six slats on either side were cut off so there was a nice peephole that was almost impossible to notice from the inside. Even from twenty feet away he could see the glow of the nightlights in the room.

It was going to work.

He started to get an erection at the thought of it.

With a quick glance around to make sure no one was watching, he crossed the distance to the bungalow and crept in between the wall and the bushes.

He peered inside to make sure getting set up was worthwhile. His eyes adjusted quickly to the dim interior. Tits. He saw tits. He couldn't believe it. She was naked, sure enough, and the dude was on top of her. Another quick detail. Her hands were tied to the bedposts.

Fuckin' A.

Pete pulled away from the window and wiggled out of his jeans, pushing them down to his knees. The bush scratched at his ass, but he ignored it. This was too good. He fiddled with his member until he had it all lubed up, then put his face back to the window.

The man had her straddled, a knee on each side of her hips. The woman was beautiful in the orange light of the room: smooth skin, huge breasts that seemed to stare at him, jiggling just enough to make him groan softly as the man shifted his weight over her. Pete couldn't see the woman's face, it was turned the other way, but that was all right. He had just the view he needed.

The man was talking to her, but Pete couldn't hear anything more than a murmur through the window. From the gestures it looked that they were into some rough play, a little S-M maybe. In fact, the man had something in his hands that looked like some kind of wicked sex toy. A fake knife—shit, maybe a real one. And he was dragging the point lightly over her skin, up from her navel, over her breasts, slowly, slowly, across her throat, talking to her the entire time.

Then he slapped her. A little harder than Pete imagined he would, but he figured the girl must like it that way. Hey, different strokes for different folks.

Usually Pete would have laughed at that one, considering that he was half-naked beating off in a bush, but he was getting an uneasy feeling. He'd never understood the bondage thing. Why get into all that when there's just good old-fashioned fucking right there for the taking, you know?

Then the girl turned her face.

There was a gag across her mouth. One of her eyes was swollen shut. Even in the bad light, Pete could see blood smeared from her nose down across her cheeks and chin and matted up in her hair. The one eye that was still able to function lolled around in the socket until it came to rest on the exact spot where Pete was staring at her through the window.

Just then the man reared back with the knife and plunged it deep into the woman's chest. Her back arched. Feet twitched as if the knife were filled with bolts of electricity.

A woman's scream filled Pete's head.

It was a few seconds before his brain told him the scream was impossible. The woman was gagged. He was the one screaming.

Pete shut his mouth, but it was too late.

He heard the man's feet hit the wood floor inside and thump toward him.

Shit, shit.

Pete turned to run but fell into the bush, his jeans still wrapped around his knees.

He fuckin' killed her.

Clawing his way through the bush.

It can't be real. Can't be.

The door flew open behind him. He was through the bush but his jeans were still a problem. He shuffled forward, a pathetic sight, lotioned prick getting in his way, testicles trying to crawl up into his stomach because he was so scared.

He didn't look backward. Didn't want to because he knew what was there.

The son of a bitch with the knife. And, in some insanely quiet place inside his mind, he knew what was about to come next.

In the last split seconds still available to him on God's good earth, all he could do was feel ashamed that his mother would find out what he had been up to. She gave him life, and he'd spent it spanking his meat outside of motel rooms watching strangers have sex.

He sucked in his last breath and decided to go out screaming, but the man behind him had a different plan. A powerful hand pulled him back by the hair, yanking his neck backward. A shadow passed his peripheral vision; then he heard a gurgling sound and felt a hot gush down his chest. He fought to hold on, to get a second chance, but the hot rush faded along with everything else. And then, at the end, an unnecessary cruelty. The sudden awareness about his wasted life.

I'm sorry, Momma. I'm sorry I made such a mess of things.

So, more ashamed than afraid as the darkness washed down over him, Pete Dawson died. Inside the Taj Mahal Motel, the people he had checked in that very night screwed, slept, and drugged themselves into submission, not giving a damn about his shame, his waste, and certainly not his death.

◆ ◆ ◆

Arnie dragged the kid back toward the bungalow. A double kill, it'd been a while since he'd done that. Later he would worry about how close he'd come to blowing it. What if the kid hadn't screamed? What if he had called the cops? But right then, covered in the blood of two victims in one night, he felt like a goddamn warrior king. And why not? He owned these two bodies. He had killed and he would get away with it like he always did. The voice in his head was gone. Not forever, he'd been down this road too many times before to be fool enough to think that. But it was silent, pouting in the corner because he was too strong for it. No, more than just strong. He was a fucking god.

Arnie positioned the bodies on the bed next to each other and pulled out his knives from a small suitcase. Every muscle in his body tensed up with expectation and excitement. The night was still young. And it was time to play.

CHAPTER 19

The itch was unbearable. In his mind, he took a fork and gouged it into his leg, ripping an inch into the flesh and grating it back and forth, feverishly sloughing off all his irritated, itching skin, even if it meant peeling back his leg until only the bone remained. At least the maddening burn and tingle under his cast would be gone.

Charlie Foxen opened his eyes and knocked his knuckles against the top of the hard cast covering the top half of his leg and extending down past his knee. The percussion he played helped a little. It hurt too, but the pain was far better than the constant itching.

He knew it meant the wound was healing and that it was a good thing, but if one more person told him that, he was going to hit them in the face. Knowing the facts didn't change the reality. And the reality was that he was about to go out of his freaking mind.

Charlie knew he couldn't complain too much. Four days since the accident and he was already getting around pretty good. He'd been on crutches before, back in high school when a cornerback from Derry High blew out his knee and any chance he had for a football scholarship, so he knew the drill.

And he was already back to work. Mick, an old curmudgeon of mythic Irish proportions, had taken it easy on him. Hell, even seemed happy to see him.

"Leave the boy alone," he told everyone, personally propping Charlie up as he walked into McGarvey's. "Let him sit and get off the leg. Stan, hurry now and get the lad a drink on me."

Of course the special treatment had the half-life of an open beer at a frat party. An hour later, Mick was barking orders at him and telling him to get his gimpy ass in gear. Now, a day later, it seemed Mick had forgotten Charlie had even had an accident, ever been to the hospital, and he certainly didn't give two shits to the dollar about the massive cast on his leg.

Charlie wished he could forget it all just as easily. If it wasn't for the infernal itching. If he could only . . .

"Hey there, Charlie. Leave that alone, now. You're concerning the customers with all that scratching."

Charlie looked around at the empty bar, then back at Mick reading the newspaper at the booth in the corner. "Mick, it's ten in the morning. There's no one here."

"Aye, but I'm here, aren't I?"

"How about some sympathy? This thing's itching like crazy."

"What do I look like to you, Florence fuckin' Nightingale?"

Charlie squinted in his direction. "Not really sure who that is. But if she's a really fat chick with extra skin around her neck then maybe—"

"Watch it now," Mick growled. "Besides, the itching means—"

"It's healing. Yeah, I've heard." Charlie picked up a glass and did what all bartenders around the world did to fight the boredom: started to wipe spots off with a towel. "Mick, you heard from Allison at all? She said she'd come in yesterday, but I haven't seen her."

"No, I haven't," Mick said, putting down the paper. "Heard she's been going around with that rich guy, Arnie Milhouse."

"Yeah, small town, huh? I heard the same thing."

"Shit, Charlie. I'm the one who told you. What'd they do, operate on your brain while you were in there?"

"If you knew you told me, why'd you tell me again like it was something new?"

Mick shrugged. "Makin' conversation, my potato-headed friend. Just makin' conversation."

Charlie chuckled and picked up another glass. "What do you think of him? Milhouse, I mean?"

"Nice enough, I guess. Quiet. Something a little odd about him, though."

"I think the same thing, but I can't figure out what it is. It's like he's a little off, you know?"

"Like milk just on the wrong side of spoiled. Not bad enough to make you wrinkle your nose but enough to make you open the new jug."

Charlie laughed again. "Are they all like you back in the old country?"

"No, the Irish are a mean lot. Not nice like me." Mick sipped his drink, a worried look on his face. "You say she was going to come in yesterday?"

"Allison? That's what she said. But you know how she is; could have heard about a neat-looking tree to photograph on the Eastern Shore and off she'd go."

"You're a little sweet on her, aren't you, buck?"

Charlie felt his face get hot. He flashed back to the beach when he'd tried to kiss her. He had gotten a swift kick in the balls and delivered Airborne Express on his back for the trouble. He checked out Mick's expression, suddenly terrified that Allison had told people about his clumsy attempt. There was amusement lining the corners of the man's mouth, but not the out-and-out hilarity that the real story would have provoked. No, Allison was good to her word. She hadn't told.

"Damn, Mick, what's not to like, you know? She's smart, funny, drop-dead gorgeous."

"And going around with a millionaire."

"Yeah, I guess."

Mick stood up from the table and walked up to the bar. "You really think there's something off about our pal Arnie?"

Charlie shrugged. "I don't know. More so than any other rich guy that takes away the girl of my dreams? Probably not. Why, you worried about her?"

"A little. Call it a feeling. Why don't you give her a call and see how she's doing?"

"If you say so," Charlie said, secretly pleased to have a reason, no matter how thin, to give her a call. "Should I finish up here first?"

Mick hesitated and Charlie thought the old man might ask him to stop what he was doing and call her right away. But whatever the impulse, it was pushed back into place. "Nice try. Why don't you give her a call on your break?"

Charlie nodded and went back to work, thinking about how Allison looked on the beach that day, how it felt holding her hand while they waited for the ambulance to arrive, and how much his damn itching was about to drive him out of his mind.

CHAPTER 20

When Charlie did call later, he wasn't able to reach Allison. Little could he know it was because Allison was dead to the world as she lay sprawled out on the bed, covers pulled up tight around her, blinds drawn to block out the late morning sun. Her cell phone rang loud enough to break through her sleep but not enough to motivate her to get up from bed.

She lay in place, eyes open slightly to the dark room but not really taking in her surroundings. With Arnie out of town on business for two days, she gave herself time off for good behavior and slept in with the help of a couple of Ambien and Percocet. It wasn't like her but she knew she was exhausting herself, driving out the demons by cranking up the exercise over the last three days, and if she didn't recharge the batteries she would start making mistakes. Deep, dreamless sleep was what she decided she needed. If it took a little prescription help to make that happen, so be it.

Now, lying in bed with the blurry numbness ebbing away, she reviewed her progress. She had seen Arnie each day since the boating accident with Jason, until he left yesterday morning for Miami, Florida, for a quick business trip. It was progressing well. She was still the hard-to-get woman, the challenge that the self-made man couldn't resist. Flirtatious enough in style and manner to keep him interested. Stand-offish enough to keep him guessing. Like any seduction, it was a game, a game she felt confident she was winning.

But she took no joy in it. The sense of cold dread that had filled her since the morning on Navy Bridge (fucking Craig Gerty, what were the chances?) had seeped its chill into her blood and bones. There wasn't a second when the thought of Gerty wasn't with her, ready to jump to her forebrain without warning. Even when she managed to push it back, it never strayed far, constantly angling for another grand entrance into her consciousness.

She felt a rush of shame as she lay in bed and remembered last night. Late afternoon, really, the sun was still up when she had decided to retreat. She saw herself throw the pills down her throat, biting her lip to control the sobs that had started unexpectedly and refused to quit. Goddamn tears over old bullshit that was long since behind her. Bullshit that had happened to a weaker person who used to cry like this all the time, curled up in her bed like a little kid and waiting for the world to go away. Trying desperately to block out the memory of that night, the night that changed her forever. Blocking out her father's shame of his daughter who couldn't hack it at the academy. She thought she had already battled and beat back these demons but not even close. They had been just crouching in the shadows, biding their time, waiting to pounce and rip into her all over again.

And now she was back in bed, hiding the way a kid hides from a thunderstorm or the boogeyman under her bed. Only this monster was real. And Allison had some grown-up pharmaceuticals at her disposal.

Even though she as making progress, Allison knew she should pack her bags and get the hell out of there. It wasn't a question, just a fact. The whole thing was uncharted territory. She would be dangerously out of her depth even if she had nothing else clouding her judgment. Part of her knew Gerty was the real reason for the Percocet, and that part of her was scared what else the urge for numbness might lead to.

Arnie wasn't back for another day, so she didn't have to decide right then.

What she did have to do was get her sorry butt out of bed and into the shower before the entire day got away from her.

She grabbed for the cell phone and scrolled down the menu to see who the missed call was from. It was a local number, area code 410. She decided to call it back later. She pulled herself out of bed. Her limbs felt so heavy and stiff that she imagined she knew what it felt like to be covered in concrete. She made it to the shower, not daring a look into the mirror, and tried to wash off the soreness and sense of shame.

A change of clothes later and she did feel better. Before noon she was down the stairs and into the Calvert House lobby. She half expected to see Dockers-man in his morning spot, reading the paper for the fifth time as he waited for her to come down the stairs, but the lobby was empty. She was famished, so she bounced out the door and headed for Main Street. She was hungry for a soft-shell crab sandwich at McGarvey's, but she stood Charlie up last night and he usually worked the lunch crowd. She felt bad about it, but she just wasn't in the mood to talk right then. Instead, she headed to Mangia's, a pizza place at the end of Main down by City Dock. Comfort food.

She promised herself that she would go down to McGarvey's that night to make things up with Charlie, but right then she still needed some time to herself to put her head on straight. A couple of quiet hours and a large pizza to herself sounded like just the ticket.

CHAPTER 21

A little past eight o'clock, Charlie was still hanging in there. He had been off the clock for a few hours but he didn't have much to go home to. Paid or not, he preferred to be at the bar. In the same way most Vegas dealers weren't big gamblers, Charlie, like most bartenders, wasn't much of a drinker, but he liked the people and he liked the vibe. Especially on a night like this, well into the summer, when they were packed to the rack with tourists and locals alike. When his personal Ms. America, Allison, finally showed herself, he was doubly happy he'd hung around.

"Well, there you are, young lady," he said. "What's a guy have to do to get some attention around here? Bleed to death?"

Allison squeezed through the crowd to the end of the bar and gave him a hug. "I'm sorry. Something came up. How are you? How's the leg?"

"Itches like a son of a . . . you know," Charlie said.

"Like a son of a bitch?"

Charlie laughed. "I was trying to be polite, but what the hell, right?"

"Right, what the hell? How about I buy you a beer for standing you up last night?" She waved at Stan behind the counter and he deposited two beers in front of them. She raised a bottle toward Charlie. "To air bags."

"To air bags," Charlie agreed. "May we never have a need for them again."

"Amen, brother."

They sipped their beers and watched the throbbing crowd for a while. People were standing shoulder to shoulder, a scene more likely in New York or San Francisco than Annapolis. But there they were, a weird amalgamation of sandal-wearing boaters, suited businessmen, and funky youngsters from St. John's, all crowded into McGarvey's dark interior to scoff down local brew and suck down some of the best oysters on the Eastern seaboard.

"I hear you're hanging out with that dweeb Arnie Milhouse," Charlie blurted out.

Allison slapped him softly on the shoulder. "Arnie's not a dweeb. He's a nice guy."

"He's nice and rich, if that's what you mean."

"And you think that's why I'm interested in him?"

Charlie shrugged. "All I'm saying is the guy's, like, super-rich and kind of a dweeb. Maybe you just like dweebs," he said, smiling. He craned forward to see Allison's expression, just to make sure she knew he was only poking fun at her.

"Maybe I do."

"Which explains—"

"Why I didn't go for you? OK. I walked into that one. Cheers."

Charlie sucked down his beer, bobbing his head to the thin bass line warbling out of the cheap speakers above the bar. "I'm serious, though. I get a strange vibe from that guy."

Allison looked surprised at Charlie's assessment. "I don't have an agenda. Just hanging out, seeing where things go."

"Has he tried anything?"

"Charlie!"

"I'm just saying . . . 'cause . . . you know . . ."

"Not that it's any of your business, but no, he hasn't tried anything. He's been a perfect gentleman."

Charlie felt both ecstatic and let down. That bastard Arnie hadn't gotten anything either, but he was playing it cool. Cooler than he had, that was for damn sure. Besides, a guy like that, with that kind of money, it was only a matter of time. He chugged down the rest of his beer just thinking about it.

"Whoa there, cowboy," Allison said. "What kind of pace are you on?"

"I'm fast-tracking the evening. C'mon, bottoms up. Next round's on me."

"I don't think—"

"C'mon, you stand me up, you put me in this cast, it's the least you can do." Charlie was happy to see her laugh and then down her beer.

"All right. I'm having one more, but then I'm heading home. Don't be getting any ideas."

"No, ma'am. I learned my lesson, thank you very much. Just a couple of friends having drinks. No kicking or karate-guru stuff will be necessary."

Stan lined up two more beers, and Charlie handed one to Allison. "To new friends." He pulled back his beer just before they toasted. "Correction: to new friends who are not dweebs."

"Charlie, you're terrible."

Charlie grinned. He may have lost the girl to the rich guy, but at least right now she was with him. And he wanted to enjoy it as long as possible. It was to be a much shorter time than he thought.

CHAPTER 22

An hour later, Allison knew she had to stop drinking and head back to her room. The warning sirens in her mind weren't blaring, but they were whining at a low-level frequency, just enough to point out that she was tipsy and on her way to drunk if she didn't get out of the bar. Her cheeks felt a little numb and the conversation around her was no longer words, just a pulsating tempo that gave the room around her its texture. But she was having a great time, and the stress release was just what she needed. Charlie was on a roll and had her laughing until she was wiping away tears. Still, she had to keep in control, and she knew a few more beers might just push her over the edge.

"All right, big guy. I've got to head out of here," Allison said.

"Aw, c'mon. Stay a while longer. There's a blues band coming in at ten."

"Negative. I've got an early day tomorrow. Can't have shaky hang-over hands when taking pics at six in the morning."

Charlie, who had already fought this battle twice in the last half hour, looked resigned. "All right, do me a favor, though."

"What's that?"

"Stay for one more drink."

"Charlie!"

"I'm kidding. Hold on to my seat for me. I've got to take a monster leak. Been holding it forever."

"All right, but don't be chatting up girls on the way back. I need to get."

"I'll be as fast as I can, but the leg here isn't exactly crowd-friendly," Charlie said as he pushed himself out of the bar stool and grabbed his crutches. "Back in two shakes."

"Any more than that and you're playing with it," Allison called out, and it was Charlie's turn to laugh.

She watched as he pushed his way through the crowd; then she slumped onto the bar stool, suddenly lonely in the crowded bar. And tired. So tired.

If she had been looking to her left, she might have seen the man approaching. Instead, it wasn't until a body pressed into the space next to her that she knew someone was angling for the spot. She planned on leaving once Charlie got back, so she didn't say anything.

"Thought I recognized you. You're all grown up now, though."

Every muscle in her body clenched at the sound of the voice.

"Wasn't sure at first. Thought you were just some whack-job that day on the bridge. But I've been watching you tonight. You're looking fine, Allison. Just fine."

Allison forced herself to look up, her face set. Civilian clothes, jeans and a too-tight yellow golf shirt stretched over bulging musculature. The liquid courage coursing through her bloodstream pushed away the shock from seeing him right next to her. "You still look like a piece of chewed-up dog shit, Gerty."

Craig Gerty didn't laugh, not even a smile. God saw fit to bestow him with a hawk nose and shallow cheeks that threw off any chance he had of ever being called handsome. Acne scars had created rough skin and craters on his neck and chin line, and a military cut couldn't disguise the fact that the man was rapidly losing a battle with his hairline. Craig Gerty did not do well with comments about his looks.

"I still think about you from time to time," Gerty said with a sniff. "Think about our time we had together. Do you ever think about it, plebe? Ever think about me?"

Allison stiffened at the word *plebe*. It was what upperclassmen and instructors called first years at the academy.

She turned toward him, willing her voice to come out strong. "Why don't you get the hell out of here?"

The surprise on his face made Allison feel a small triumph. *No, I'm not some eighteen-year-old you can fuck with, Craig. Now get the hell away from me.*

"You've turned into an uppity little bitch, haven't you?"

Allison looked straight ahead, willing Stan at the other end of the bar to turn around and make eye contact with her. There were so many things burning inside of her to throw at Gerty, but this wasn't the place, wasn't the time. A blowup in here would have people talking, and it would get back to Arnie.

Even with the booze, she knew she couldn't jeopardize that. She reached down her leg to her shin and felt the bulge there beneath the loose pant leg. Just a quick pat, just to feel better, just to know it was still there.

"Like I said, Craig. Fuck off, will you?"

She said it loud enough that a few people around her cocked their heads, eavesdropping but trying to be discreet. The words came out trembling, but Gerty read them the wrong way. He mistook the rage in her voice for fear. Sensing what he thought was weakness, he pushed in even closer.

"You know, plebe, you were one hot little number back in the day."

Allison clenched her hands together.

"Do you still have a tight little ass on you?"

She looked away. "Stop it," she hissed, barely in control.

"What say I give you another chance, plebe?"

He was leaning into her now, she could smell cheap, musky cologne mixed with boozy breath. She turned away from it. Her throat constricted and she had to gasp for air, as if Gerty that close to her had somehow blocked her airstream.

"I'll give it to you real good this time, plebe."

Allison dragged the back of her hand across her forehead and wiped away a layer of cold sweat. The walls around her throbbed, bending in and out like giant bellows at a furnace. And the heat. The air was suddenly impossibly thick. The images around her began to quiver as if she was looking through heat distortion off a steaming highway. She was suddenly very conscious of the weight of the gun holster wrapped around her ankle.

"Tell me something, plebe . . ."

He was so close now that his tongue, his disgusting, slimy, down-her-throat tongue was almost flicking into her ear. Her brain screamed for her to jerk away, but she was frozen, no longer in control right when it counted most.

She hardly noticed her right hand creeping down the outside of her thigh. Working down toward the ankle.

"I want you to tell me the truth . . ."

There was a wet sound, him licking his lips.

". . . are you still a screamer? Cuz I still love that shit."

He slid a hand across her lower back.

The break in her thoughts came with its own soundtrack. There was an actual *crumph*, like the distant sound heard on a clear mountain day, a dam giving way a quarter mile upstream, the kind of noise where you knew that there was no use running because what was coming next was big and impossible to escape. There was a second of silence before the voices in her head poured out like a flood of hate.

Kill the mother fucker. Kill him.

Allison pivoted on the bar stool, knocking Gerty's arm off her body. Gerty, both surprised and drunk, fell backward. If not for the wall of people behind him, he would have gone to the ground.

In the few seconds he took to stagger to his feet, Allison was off the stool, down on one knee and going for her gun.

Son of a bitch. Let's end this right now.

Then there was pressure on her forearm, a claw that dug into her flesh and yanked her up off the ground. She vainly made a last grasp for her gun but only got a fistful of her pant leg.

She pulled back, but the claw wasn't letting go.

Allison looked up.

The energy immediately drained out of her body, and she stopped struggling. She didn't say anything either. There was no need.

Special Agent Scott Hansford pulled her gently toward the door.

"Move," he said under his breath.

"Scott, you don't need to—"

"Now, McNeil," he said.

Allison did as she was told. Behind her she heard Gerty's voice, but she didn't bother to turn around. Scott said, "Go get another beer, buddy; fun's over." The tone of voice, strict and disciplined, must have found purchase on Gerty's military mind, because she didn't hear a response to it.

She burst through the doors into the humid night air, finally shaking off the hand clutching her elbow. She didn't turn to look at him, but she didn't walk away either. She knew the time for walking away had passed.

"My car's parked right over here," Scott said. "Get in; I'm driving."

Allison couldn't even bring herself to nod. She just went toward the car the man had pointed to, her muscles burning from the small effort it took just to keep herself upright. The fresh air felt good at first, and the quiet of City Dock compared to the constant roar in the bar, but now her stomach started to tumble over itself.

She leaned over and threw up into the gutter. Her abdomen retched until the muscles cramped into tight little clusters and only thin lines of stomach acid came from her mouth.

I was going to kill him.

The thought came through clearly as she stood in the street, hacking and gagging.

Scott waited beside her, neither patient nor impatient, just there. When she was finished, he held out a cloth handkerchief. Allison took it and wiped her mouth.

"Thanks, Scott. Thanks for being there."

Scott looked unimpressed by the gesture. He held out his hand. "Let me have it," he said.

Allison hesitated but offered him back his handkerchief. Scott swatted it away, his face reddening with anger.

"Goddammit, McNeil. You know what I'm talking about."

She actually didn't know what he was talking about, her mind still playing catch-up, the alcohol and adrenaline mix adding to her disorientation.

Scott, taking this as just one more insult, nodded to her ankle.

She immediately understood. She hesitated but quickly gave in. Reaching down unsteadily to her ankle holster, she removed her gun and handed it to him. He checked the safety and slid it into his pocket.

"You want this too?" she asked. She pulled out a bifold leather wallet from her purse and flipped it open. It was an ID. The picture on it showed her with hair pulled back, a serious expression on her face. But it wasn't a driver's license. It was her most prized possession and invested her with the title that meant more to her than anything.

Special Agent Allison McNeil.

The letters "FBI" were emblazoned in bold, dark blue letters above her name, dominating the credentials the same way the Bureau dominated her life.

Scott shook his head. "Put that away. What do you think this is, the old West? That turning in your gun and badge will make it all go away?"

"C'mon, Scott."

"C'mon, Scott?" He leaned in close to her. "You've been performing unsanctioned surveillance on a person of interest in an ongoing investigation. That's an obstruction charge right there. Let alone the dozens of ethical issues with the whole thing. Then I just witnessed you about to pull a gun in a bar on a civilian."

"He would have deserved it," Allison said, trying to sound surer of herself than she felt.

"Jesus, McNeil," Scott shook his head and pointed to her credentials. "Keep them. I'm pretty certain someone will be taking them from you soon enough."

He took her by the arm again and directed her to the passenger side door of a black sedan. She let him open the door and guide her inside, covering her head with his hand as she got in, like she was a perp. Before he closed the door, Allison reached out and got his attention.

"What I said before, I meant it," she said. "Thank you for stopping me."

Scott was about to say something but apparently decided against it. He closed the door and hustled around to the other side of the car.

Allison had seen the look on his face, though, and intuited what he had wanted to say.

You fucked up, Allison, old girl. Better you than me, though, if you know what I mean.

Yes, she had screwed up, and her little chaperone wasn't about to cut her a break. And he shouldn't either. She had just about shot a civilian in the middle of a crowded bar.

A shudder passed through her, and a more than normal amount of saliva filled her mouth again. She swallowed hard.

She had a long drive ahead of her, at the end of which there would be hell to pay. She closed her eyes and found herself wishing she had a few pills with her to make the world go away.

CHAPTER 23

Charlie came through the doors from McGarvey's just as the sedan pulled away. Chatting up one of the new waitresses Mick had hired, he'd missed all the action with the guy who messed with Allison. Stan filled him in, though, making it clear that he hadn't seen any of it himself or he would have come across the bar and throttled the bastard. Stan didn't know the man Allison had left with, but she had seemed to know him well enough.

Charlie peered through the darkness, trying to get a look at the man, but got nothing. The car had to stop for an elderly couple taking their own sweet time to cross the street, and that gave Charlie the chance he needed to check out the license plate. He said the tag numbers and letters out loud to himself until he fished a pen out of his pocket and scribbled them down on his cast.

He pulled a cell phone from his pocket and scrolled down to find the new number he had stored there only a couple of days earlier.

The person on the other end of the line picked up immediately. Charlie explained what had happened in the bar.

"I told you to watch her. Where were you when this man came and got her? How could this happen without you seeing who it was?"

"Hey, I had to take a leak, man. What do you expect?"

The cold silence on the phone told Charlie that the man expected more. Much more.

"But I did get the license number," Charlie offered nervously.

"Good. Good boy. What is it?"

Charlie read the license number off his cast, wondering why his voice was trembling. He used a pen to scratch over the number. If he saw Allison again, he didn't want her seeing it. The man asked if there was anything else, then told Charlie to find out more about the man Allison was talking to before she left. The one that upset her. Without saying good-bye, the man hung up the phone.

Charlie hung up and felt a little queasy about what he had just done. His little undercover snooping had sounded like fun at first, but now he felt kind of ashamed. But, he figured, Allison would move on soon and forget about him all together. She made her feelings very plain on the beach that day, right?

Besides, he needed the money big time and the man at the end of the line was willing to pay plenty of it just to know what Allison was up to while he was out of town.

It made Charlie feel a little better to know that even rich bastards like Arnie Milhouse were as insecure as the next guy.

Like Arnie, though, Charlie couldn't help but wonder who had been driving the sedan. Charlie wondered if Arnie would let him know after he tracked the tags down. He doubted it. The guy had sounded downright creepy tonight. A little psycho, you know?

Charlie turned and saw the guy who'd screwed with Allison stumble out of McGarvey's, Mick standing in the door behind him, his thick arms crossed over his chest. The man grumbled a few cuss words back toward Mick but then stumbled over to Middleton Tavern right next door and disappeared inside.

Charlie headed in that direction, not really sure what he intended to accomplish following the guy. He wanted to beat his face in, but the guy was huge, and Charlie, hobbling around on his crutches, wasn't exactly in fighting form. One benefit of going to Middleton Tavern was that he could drink without Mick hovering over him. And getting a serious drink on was exactly what he felt like doing.

He was more than a little ashamed that he'd sold out his new friend for a few bucks. He thought about coming clean with Allison the next time he saw her. He decided to call that Plan B. Plan A was to wash away his guilt with as many beers as his low-limit credit card would allow and see if he felt better in the morning.

CHAPTER 24

By the time Charlie Foxen was bellied back up to the bar, doing his damnedest to score with the new waitress, the black sedan hit the freeway, west on Highway 50, and picked up speed through the night.

Neither of the vehicle's occupants spoke, or gave any inclination they intended to for the rest of the entire trip. Scott stared straight ahead, radio off, needle hovering just the slightest amount over the speed limit.

It would be another hour at least. Then, Scott hoped, his part in this mess would be over, and he would never have to see Allison McNeil again.

CHAPTER 25

The room was larger than it needed to be. A long table of highly polished wood sat in the center facing a single wooden chair. The officer who escorted Allison into the room told her to sit in the chair and wait. Then he turned on his heel and left her alone. That had been more than ten minutes ago.

It was cold in the room, but she wiped sweaty palms against her uniform. She wasn't sure if she would have to shake any hands, but she wanted to be ready to make a good impression if she did. The ceiling soared more than twenty feet above her, plenty of room for the banners that covered the walls. She spent time inspecting them, working through the Latin phrases on each. She felt nervous but in control. After all, she hadn't done anything wrong.

A door behind her opened. The footsteps sounded distant and hollow on the wooden floor and they bounced around the massive room. Even though the people were walking together, she could still pick out one set of footsteps different from the others. Heel-toe. Heel-toe. Slightly higher pitched than the others.

Good, she thought, *at least there is one woman.*

There were five people, all uniformed naval officers. They would be both judge and jury for this case. Allison suppressed a groan when she saw the woman. They had met before.

Suddenly Allison couldn't decide what to do with her hands. Everything seemed to send a signal. At her sides, too nervous. On the handrails of the chair, too casual. Crossed on her lap, too prissy.

She had the ridiculous idea to sit on them, and that calmed her down. Even though she was nineteen years old, the absurd still had that effect on her.

The panel took its place at the massive table. She tried to read faces but got nothing back from any of them.

She fidgeted in her chair as the judges took theirs, none of them making eye contact with her.

"We have read your report, Ms. McNeil," the man in the center said—too suddenly, it appeared, by the surprised reaction of the other members of the board. She noticed this and wondered if the others thought there would be introductions, some small talk, but the man in the center was obviously in charge, because no one spoke up to correct his abrupt beginning. "And first let me say that we were shocked by what is contained here."

She ran her eyes down the line of faces. They were all staring at her, fixing in her direction severe expressions reserved for military statues. Only at the end of the table was there any reprieve. The woman gave her a small smile that may or may not have been meant as reassurance. Regardless of the uniformed woman's intention, Allison felt comforted.

"The purpose of this closed-door session is to determine whether to move forward with an Article 32 hearing," the man in the center continued. "That will be a *public* questioning that will result in a recommendation on how the charges should be addressed. The superintendent will make the final determination whether there will be a court martial, or if the case will be dropped. As a board it is our duty to examine the details in an objective manner and render a decision based on the facts at hand. Before we go on, does any . . ."

"I have a question," the woman said.

The man in the center looked impatient over the interruption, but he yielded to the woman who was no longer smiling.

"Thank you." She turned to Allison. "I read your report, and I personally find the contents deeply troubling."

Allison swallowed hard and felt the sting in her eyes. She promised herself that she would not cry, no matter what happened, but there was something about the way this woman said the words *deeply troubling.* As if she was saying that as a woman she understood the costs and the pain more than the men sitting next to her and because of that she was reaching out to help.

"Yes, ma'am," Allison replied, not knowing if there was a question buried somewhere for her to answer.

"The man you name in this file is a respected instructor, a man known for his commitment to this institution."

"Yes, ma'am."

"A man whose reputation and livelihood could be damaged irreparably should these allegations come to light. Should a public hearing be chosen."

Allison took a second to respond as she noticed the accusatory edge in the woman's voice. She also noted that it was the second time the word *public* had been thrown at her like a warning. "Ma'am, I understand the reputation of Craig Gerty, but—"

"That's First Mate Gerty. Show some respect." It was the man on the far left, bald, thick glasses, puffy cheeks made red by too many boozy late nights. He looked like a stickler for the rules, and he was one.

"Yes, I'm sorry, what I want to say—"

The bald man held up his hand. "Why did you wait three days to report the alleged incident, Ms. McNeil?"

"I—I was . . ." She took a deep breath to calm her nerves. "I know now that I should have reported the incident right away. I was just trying—"

"Trying to what?"

"I was just trying to—"

"Trying to what, Ms. McNeil?"

"Give the girl a chance," grumbled the man to the right of center. He was younger than the rest, out of place among the graying and the soon to be retired. His quiet comment made the rest of them nervous, and they looked to one another for reassurance. He appeared conflicted, biting his lip as if he were making a decision. When he finally looked up at her, something inside him gave in. He placed his hands on the table in front of him. "Were you told you could have a lawyer here?" he asked.

The others didn't like this at all.

"This is an informal hearing," said the man in charge.

"Seems pretty formal to me," the younger man said. He looked at Allison, his eyes pleading with her to hear his questions as advice. "Do you want to have a lawyer here? You're entitled to one."

"Why did you wait three days to report the incident?" the bald man asked again.

"I was scared. I didn't know what I should do." She had her rhythm, her voice was strong and confident. With a look, she made it clear to the younger man that she wasn't waiting for a lawyer. He slumped into his chair. "Everyone told me not to say anything about it. That this sort of thing happens all the time and that if I wanted a future in the Navy at all, I would just shut up and deal with it." She stared down the woman officer on the panel and wondered whether she would acknowledge her own ugly words thrown back in her face. The woman returned her stare, betraying nothing.

Then the younger man spoke again. "What changed?"

"I refused to believe that rape was—"

"Come now," said the bald man who liked things just so. The word *rape* was not to his liking one bit.

But Allison didn't slow down. Her nervousness had slowly given way to indignation and was well on the way to anger. "I refused to believe that rape was acceptable in an institution that talks so much about honor and moral character. I realized it was my duty to come forward."

"Duty?" the man in charge said with a sneer. "What do you know about duty? Craig Gerty is a decorated veteran. He's served his country in combat. Combat. That's something you will never do."

The younger man groaned and rolled his eyes. Allison felt that she might love him for it. The man in charge whipped his head to his right, and for a second seemed about to ask the younger man what was on his mind. But the man in charge knew what was on his mind, and he wanted no part of it.

"Ms. McNeil," the woman said. "You understand this man's career will be ruined by these charges? Are you certain that you don't want to reconsider the circumstances in which this alleged incident took place?"

"Circumstances? I don't think I know what you mean."

"Well, think about it. You are an attractive girl. There was a party where there was alcohol being consumed. You were wearing," the woman flipped through the files in front of her, "a rather revealing outfit that night."

"I don't think—"

"How many sexual partners have you had since coming to the academy?" the bald man asked.

"Jesus Christ," the young man said.

"She's going to get worse than this in an Article 43. Much worse and you know it," the bald man said. "She should know."

Allison looked to the young man but he wouldn't meet her eye. She got the point. The bald man was right.

"You go to a party full of men," the woman continued. "A girl with a reputation—"

"Reputation? I've been with two people since coming here," she said, hating the defensiveness in her voice.

"Two partners in only two months," the bald man murmured, shaking his head in disapproval.

The woman smiled, enjoying it. "You show up by yourself to this party, dressed provocatively. What kind of message did you think that would send?"

"Ma'am, are you suggesting that the message I was sending was that I wanted to be raped? To be forced to the ground . . ."

"That's enough," the man in charge said.

". . . have my clothes torn off me . . ."

"I said that's enough."

". . . while his friends watched and cheered him on . . ."

"Enough!"

". . . no, ma'am, I do not think I was sending the message that I wanted to be raped, no matter what you think the circumstances were."

Silence. The meeting was not going as planned, and no one seemed quite sure what to do about it. The man in charge did the only thing that came to his head.

"That will be all. Dismissed."

She hesitated, not certain if she heard him correctly, but then got to her feet. She may only have been two months into her time at the US Naval Academy, but Allison McNeil had absorbed enough of the military culture to snap to when her superior officer gave her a direct order. It was a trait that would not last long with her.

She saluted the board, turned on a heel, and walked to the door. Behind her, the board members were already mumbling to one another, not even waiting until she was out of the room before talking about her performance. Without thinking it through, she stopped, turned back, and retraced her steps. The four men and one woman were slow to realize that she was once again standing in front of them and not out the door like she was supposed to be.

"You know," Allison started, announcing her presence. Her voice caught as she talked, and her hands trembled no matter how hard she tried to steady them. "The thing I've learned from counseling over the last few weeks is that the real injuries from rape are not the bruises and scratches Craig Gerty gave me all over my body." Her hands moved slowly around her neck, over her breast, and came to rest near her genital area as if giving a catalog of her wounds. "The real scar is emotional. It's the lack of power you feel. It's the violation. It's the sense that your self-worth and dignity are gone that can make you not report. Not stand up for what's right." She turned to the woman. "I was raped. What's your excuse?"

"Ms. McNeil," the man in charge said. "You are warned that—"

"Thank you sir, but I've already been warned." She continued to stare at the woman. "And it seems the warning was right."

She turned and walked out of the room, her legs shaking so badly that she feared she might collapse before she could make it out of the room. She almost reached the door when she felt the hand on her shoulder. A light tap that she ignored, then the pain of a hand digging into her shoulder from behind. She tried to twist away from it, but it grabbed at her again. She spun around, ready to confront the person, thinking perhaps it's the woman who ran after her.

But then she turned. And it took everything in her to keep from screaming.

Craig Gerty stood in front of her, his pockmarked face creased into an insane grin. His eyes devoured her, red and bulging. Foul breath reeking of vomit and hard liquor blasted into her face. She looked over his shoulder for help, but the panel was gone. So was the room. She was outside and she suddenly knew exactly where. She had been there hundreds of times before in this nightmare.

She blinked and she was on her back, jagged rocks digging into her skin. A sycamore tree curving above her into the night sky. The smell of grass and dirt filled her nostrils. Someone's dog was barking to her left, making her wonder if its owner had seen the men attacking her and was on his way to help.

But there was no help; there was only the fear and the pain.

Then Gerty was on top of her, his saliva dripping on her face as he grunted from his effort. One of his thick, clumsy hands pushed between her locked legs, clawing into her until fingers were inside her, filling her with pain. Then the hand was gone, back up to her mouth to keep her quiet. There were catcalls all around her. Flashlights pointed at her face. Gerty's buddies. Three, maybe four of them. None willing to take a turn but eager enough to show this particular bitch what they thought of women who wore the uniform, the uniform meant for a man alone.

His knees jammed between her legs and forced them open. She thrashed around but she couldn't move; she couldn't even breathe because of the weight on her, because of the hand over her mouth. He was about to penetrate her when his hand fell off her mouth for a second, and she pulled in a lungful of air. It wouldn't do any good; it wouldn't stop what had happened so many years ago, but still Allison . . .

CHAPTER 26

. . . screamed.

She jerked up hard enough to make the seat belt engage. Allison felt the car swerve and then right itself.

"Jesus Christ!" Scott yelled. "What the hell?"

Allison got her bearings quickly. She was in the car. On her way to Virginia. She could feel her heart thudding away in her chest like it was trying to dig its way through her rib cage. It was just the dream. Just the dream.

"Are you all right?"

Allison smiled at the genuine concern in his voice. "Yeah, I'm fine. Sorry about that. Crazy dream is all."

"Must have been some dream. I was trying to wake you up, but you were out of it."

There were a few beats where it seemed Scott expected her to share the dream with him. *Not a chance, buddy.*

"Anyway, that woke me up a little. Better than a cup of coffee."

"What time is it?"

"Nearly eleven. We're only about a half hour away."

"What time's my meeting tomorrow?"

"Oh, you're meeting tonight. As soon as you get in."

"Do you know who's in the meeting?"

"Richard Thornton, for sure. And someone else, I think."

Allison saw Scott try to read her for a reaction on hearing Richard was going to be at the meeting. She didn't give him the satisfaction, although she had to admit she felt a little twinge of excitement knowing that she would see him within a half hour. What had it been, more than two months now?

"Who's the someone else?"

Scott shrugged.

"You're worse at lying than you are at tailing someone. And that's saying a lot."

He shrugged again and said nothing.

Allison gave up the guesswork. She would find out who was going to be at the meeting soon enough. Right about the same time, in fact, that she would find out how much trouble she was in.

CHAPTER 27

Arnie walked along the South Beach, the art-deco buildings barely registering as he thought about his next steps. His phone vibrated in his pocket. He fished it out and answered it.

"You were supposed to call me over an hour ago."

"Good morning to you too," Giancarlo's voice came back at him. It was gravelly and a little hoarse.

"Did you just get up?" Arnie snapped.

"Nix. Haven't been to bed yet. Don't be so jumpy."

Arnie looked out at the ocean stretching ahead of him and forced himself to take several slow breaths. He paid Giancarlo a lot of money to make sure his money and his ass were both protected, but he was a small fish in the lawyer's portfolio. Powerful men, men much wealthier than he, relied on Giancarlo to take care of them, but Arnie still found it hard to be spoken down to by anyone.

"What did you find out?"

"Nothing. Not a thing."

"Giancarlo, you told me that—"

"Before you say anything, is your phone encrypted?"

"Of course it is."

Giancarlo's roster of clients included people routinely under surveillance by the FBI. Because of his involvement on the most detailed level with his client's affairs, it was in his own self-interest to both educate and provide them with the means to circumvent the government's best eavesdropping technologies. Arnie had encrypted phones, traceless Internet access, and sophisticated jamming gear at his house. If the Feds wanted to know what was going on inside his house, they were going to need to beat down the front door to find out.

"All right, I told you I'd run the plate and I did. Must be the wrong number, though, because nothing came up. Hold a second." Arnie heard Giancarlo bark orders at someone; then he was back. "Sorry, Arnie, things are tight around here."

"Anything wrong?"

There was a pause, too long for Arnie's comfort. "Nothing that concerns you, don't worry."

"Listen, about the arrangements we talked about the other day. I need them expedited."

"Are you in trouble? Is there something I need to know about?"

It was Arnie's turn to pause. He smiled as he replied, pleased with the chance to give Giancarlo's words back to him. "Nothing that concerns you, don't worry."

"Fair enough. What do you mean 'expedited'? I can't farm this stuff out, you know. I'm the only one who deals with accounts when they get to this stage. If something goes south for one of my guys, it gets out, and that's not good for business. So don't fuck around here."

"I'm not sure. It might be nothing but I might need an out in the next day or two."

"Arnie, you tell me straight what's going on, right? You tell me what you need done and I'll find a way. Sleep is for the weak."

Arnie scraped his shoe over the sidewalk, pushing a small pile of sand back onto the beach. He planned to fly back to Maryland that afternoon, in time to pull up to his driveway in the early evening. He felt a pang of regret about leaving that house. In the last three years, it had been a real home for him and Jason. Again, he wondered if he wasn't just overreacting.

"Two days is fine," he said, realizing that he didn't intend to use the exit at all.

"You got it. By the way, how's Miami treating you?"

Arnie squeezed the phone tight in his hand, panicked. He whipped around, looking for the telltale van with tinted windows, or the undercover agent with the earpiece radio standing nearby. He twisted in every direction, his breath coming in shallow gasps. Finally he whispered into the phone, "How did you know I was in Miami?"

Silence.

Arnie pictured his highly paid, turncoat lawyer sitting by himself in his office, rubbing his temple as he looked for a way to cover up his mistake. Did Giancarlo have someone follow Arnie? Was he working with the FBI?

But Giancarlo wasn't sweating it out like Arnie thought. He overheard him talking to his secretary, demanding to know why a certain file was not yet on his desk. A few seconds later he came back on the phone.

"What's that, Arnie? You said you like it down there?"

"No, I asked you how the hell you knew I was in Miami."

"You told me, you paranoid fuck. Two days ago you called me from the airport, bragged how you were going to Joe's Stone Crab, remember?"

Arnie exhaled, the tension draining out of him.

Giancarlo came back through the phone with his best father-knows-best voice. "Now, are you going to tell me what has you so spooked and let me help you, or are you going to just suffer out there by yourself?"

"Suffer. I'll call you in two days," Arnie said, and terminated the call.

An old saying crossed his mind, a snippet of bumper sticker philosophy that he either saw at a truck stop convenience store or on the back of an overzealous soccer mom's SUV, he couldn't remember which.

"Just because you're paranoid, doesn't mean everyone's not out to get you."

CHAPTER 28

Allison had never been to Richard's new office, not since he made section chief, anyway. Even though he was technically her boss now, there were a couple of layers of management between them to insulate them from each other. When they had been together, they tried their best to keep apart at work. As ex-lovers, the pattern had held.

They interacted, of course, but no matter the assurances that they gave each other that their past didn't impact their professional relationship, the ghosts hovered around them whenever they were in the same room together. The profiler in her was interested to see what the office would tell her about the man who had shared her bed for more than six incredible months before an abrupt and unceremonious ending.

She chose not to sit while she waited. Instead, she walked the room, stretching her legs after the long drive, working out her nerves a little.

True to Richard's nature, a wall was covered with picture frames affixed in precise relation to one another. She tried to lift the edge of one frame and grinned when she saw she was right; each corner of each frame had a small dab of adhesive to keep from having one tilt and ruin the presentation. It was Richard Thornton's Brag Wall (three presidents, four attorney generals), and he wasn't about to let sloppiness get in the way.

Her smile died as the perfectly placed frames brought Allison back to some of their biggest fights. She threw stuff around. He put stuff away. She lived in clutter. He would rather have his skin peeled off his body than leave a newspaper splayed out on a table for an afternoon.

Of course, the fights hadn't really been about their differences; fights in relationships are never really about the subject people are discussing. It was always about power. About who would exert their will and their needs on the other person. Even with her psychological training, even though she recognized what was going on, it hadn't stopped them from having shouting matches over the smallest things. That's how it had been near the end anyway. Because by then the sex was no longer new enough and exciting enough to get them through the fights. When the end finally came, it didn't surprise either of them. What had been surprising was how clean the break had been. One day they were living together, the next no more than casual acquaintances. At first she hadn't had any hard feelings, something she chalked up to just another sign of how little emotion was left in the relationship. It was like they had simply worn each other out.

But that didn't explain why she had been thinking about him so much recently.

Then again, the fact that he was a couple of pay grades above her probably had something to do with it. Competitive and career-minded, being passed over had hurt enough, but to have Richard as her boss had been hard to bear.

The door opened and Scott walked in first, carefully avoiding eye contact with her. The schoolgirl in her wanted to give him a raspberry and taunt him, "Tattle-tale, tattle-tale." The absurd thought calmed her down as she looked past Scott to see Richard stride into the room behind him.

Dressed in a suit and tie even at midnight, Richard looked the part he had wanted to play all his life. Black hair combed back neatly, angular jaw jutting out confidently, as if daring the world to try and land a punch on him. His gray eyes seemed to take in everything at once, like they were black holes down which all information disappeared, information that could be made to reappear in an instant whenever Richard wanted. His tan, pretty-boy features were offset by a grisly, pale scar that ran from his bulging Adam's apple, under the right side of his chin, then up the side of his face where it disappeared into a well-cropped sideburn. Allison knew the man who had left that mark on Richard. She'd shot him dead herself. It was the first and only person she had killed in her eight years with the FBI.

"Special Agent McNeil," Richard said stiffly.

Allison tried to read his face. He was trying for controlled anger, the supervisor hell-bent on a strong reprimand, but she thought his eyes said something different. Maybe concern, even relief that she was all right. "C'mon, Richard, it's a little late at night for the 'Special Agent McNeil' routine, all right? It's been a long night."

"I heard."

"I bet you did," she said, glancing over at Scott.

"Do you want to explain? Or should I just assume this entire deal is FUBAR and throw it up on the scoreboard as just another complete misadventure of Allison McNeil, destroyer of her own career?"

"I was making progress on the case." Allison cringed at how defensive she sounded.

"No, you brought me your theory and your request to make contact. I heard you out. I denied it."

"I put myself on leave. I wasn't acting under the aegis of—"

"I gave you a specific order!" Richard shouted, slamming the table. "Then I find out from Scott—"

"Who you sent to spy on me!" Allison shouted back.

"To protect you."

"Not your job," Allison said coldly. "It never was. Did Mr. Discreet over here tell you how many times he almost blew my cover? He's the most obvious—"

"Scott's not the issue here tonight, Allison!" Richard shouted. "Jesus Christ, you haven't changed at all, have you?"

Scott cleared his throat uncomfortably. "I'm just going to go—"

"You're staying right here," Richard said. "Both of you have turned a simple surveillance into a cluster fuck. Like it or not, you're in this mess together."

"Sir, I'd like to remind you that I had no authority over Agent McNeil. The steps she took were of her own accord and were against my advice. I don't think—"

"I'm not interested in what you think right now. All I want is for someone to explain to me how a simple surveillance on an unimportant suspect in a stock fraud case turned into boating and dinner with the target."

"You're not jealous, are you, Richard?"

"Oh Jesus, you're unbelievable."

"I'm just going to go and—" Scott mumbled.

"Stay!" Allison and Richard shouted together.

Scott slumped against the wall, obviously wishing he were anywhere else in the world.

"Look, you know what this is really about. I was making progress. There's no way we're going to get anywhere by watching him through binoculars. He's starting to trust me. I saved his kid's life, for chrissake. If I can just—"

"You're done with this one. You're being reassigned."

"What?"

"Allison, you drew your gun on a civilian in a bar. You think I'm going to put you back out in the field?"

Allison felt the fight drain out of her. "I didn't draw the gun," she said quietly. "That's an exaggeration."

"Whatever. Your other theories aside, this is a bullshit stock fraud case anyway. We both know that if we get him, it'll be on a paper trail, not from candlelit dinners on his private yacht." Richard leaned toward her and whispered, "Christ, Allison, this was your chance to get back on track, show that you can be a team player. But once again you had to do your own thing. I'm not going to be able to protect you from this, you know."

The desk phone rang, a soft warbling tone that filled the room like an alarm clock meant to cajole rather than shock a person out of sleep. Richard and Allison stared at each other for two rings.

"Your phone's ringing," Scott said.

Richard waited another beat, then reached over his desk and picked up the phone. Allison looked away, her eyes falling on his Brag Wall. Richard was right. She had never played by the rules, while Richard had never met a rule he didn't like. She was relegated to the backwaters of the Bureau, far away from the work she trained for; Richard was on the wall shaking hands with leaders of the free world. Not for the first time in the past year, Allison found herself wondering if it wasn't time for her to leave the FBI. If she had a clue what else she could do with herself, she might very well pull the plug and move on.

She had zoned out on the conversation Richard had on the phone, but when he hung up she noticed that he looked shaken. The thought crossed her mind that maybe the decision to leave the FBI was about to be made for her.

"Everything all right?" Allison asked.

"Yeah, come with me. The three of us have a meeting to attend."

"A meeting?"

"Yes"—Richard grabbed her by the arm—"and for God's sake, whatever you do, don't be yourself."

CHAPTER 29

Allison followed Richard out of the room and down the glossy lime-green linoleum hallway, a leftover from the remodel in the 1970s. Although she knew there were parts of the building that never let up the hurried pace that came with being the nation's premier law enforcement center, there were few people in this part of the building at midnight, mostly administrative folks catching up on heavy workloads, cleaning people emptying the shredders located next to every desk into giant garbage bags, and young agents trying to impress bosses long since returned home to their tract houses in the Northern Virginia suburbs.

They entered the elevator and Richard swiped a plastic access card through a slot and pressed the fifth floor. The three of them stood in silence as the elevator rose smoothly to the executive level.

When the door opened it was obvious they weren't in admin hell any longer. Thick, blue carpet on the floor and dark-stained wood accents gave the hallway the feel of a luxury hotel. "Tax dollars at work," Allison mumbled, trying to release some of the anxiety building inside her.

Richard grunted. She wasn't sure if it was meant as a courtesy laugh or a sign of disapproval. She couldn't believe she actually cared. But she did.

Then Richard leaned in. "You're in it pretty deep, Ali. I'd go easy if I were you."

"I think I preferred Special Agent McNeil."

"This way." Richard directed her to an open door.

It was a conference room, not much different than ones available on the floor they just came up from. There was no one else in the room waiting for them. Both Scott and Richard took seats, leaving Allison standing.

"So, why are we up here?" Allison asked. "What's the deal?"

"You're here at my request," a voice behind her said.

She spun around and felt her stomach churn at the sight. The man was gray-haired, lanky to the point of being almost too thin, but with a tight-skinned face that spurned any accurate guess about his age. She knew the frail appearance was misleading. The man still ran five miles a day and played tennis against men half his age in a weekly league. He was a legend of the field and even more legendary for his work through the labyrinth of Washington politics. Allison had seen him speak many times, but she had never met the director of the FBI personally.

"Director Mason," she sputtered. "I'm sorry, I wasn't told we would be meeting tonight, sir."

Mason smiled paternally. "It's all right. I asked Deputy Thornton to keep it under wraps. This meeting is outside my normal schedule. Don't hold it against him."

Allison swallowed hard and marveled at the amount of subtext playing in those few words.

I'm not here. We're not meeting. I know about you and Agent Thornton over there. In fact, I know more about everything than you ever will; let's not forget that, shall we?

She nodded as if he had spoken those words out loud. "I understand, sir."

Mason stared at her for a few beats of her pounding heart before nodding. "Good, I believe you do. Now sit down, will you? I hear you've had an interesting go of things recently. I would like to hear about it."

"Sir," Richard started, "I've been briefed by—"

Mason held up a hand and cut him off. "Thank you, Agent Thornton, but I would like very much to get this information unfiltered." He offered an open palm toward Allison, as if inviting her to place something into it, something useful and precious if possible. "Agent McNeil. Your review of the situation, if you please."

CHAPTER 30

Allison finished her story with a retelling of the events only hours before, leaving no detail out since Scott had no doubt already told them everything. She had discussed her rape before with superiors during the psych evaluations and was used to giving the information without emotion, as if it were a case involving some random eighteen-year-old white female victim. But the confrontation with Gerty had put her in a vulnerable place, and she had to stop twice to catch up with her emotions.

Mason listened carefully. Although he did not take notes, Allison had no doubt that every detail was being stored away for later use.

"And then Special Agent Hansford interceded and stopped me from pulling my weapon. We left the establishment, and he transported me here."

Mason tapped the tabletop softly, his eyes never leaving Allison's. "What do you believe would have happened if Agent Hansford had not been there?"

Allison tried to meet the director's stare but withered under the intensity. Somehow she knew he would recognize a lie, and a part of her understood that for some reason it was very important that she proved she would tell the truth under pressure, even if it might end her career.

"I have no doubt—" Her voice broke and she had to clear her throat. "I have no doubt that if Special Agent Hansford had not interceded I would have shot Craig Gerty."

Out of the corner of her eye she saw Richard lean back in his chair, as if physically distancing himself from the damaged goods sitting at the table.

Director Mason raised a single eyebrow and regarded Allison closely. "Shot but not killed?"

"No, sir," Allison said a bit too quickly, "I'm an excellent shot. I'm sure I would have killed him."

"Jesus, Allison," Richard finally burst out.

"Richard," Mason said just loudly enough to ensure Richard cut himself off. "Would you and Special Agent Hansford please excuse us? I would like to have a brief private conversation with Special Agent McNeil. Thank you." He turned toward Allison as if Richard had simply ceased to exist once he had been dismissed. "Do you mind if I call you Allison?"

"Of course. That's fine. I hope, however, to still be a special agent when I leave the room."

Allison thought Director Mason grimaced, but she realized it was actually a smile. A bit out of practice, but a smile nonetheless.

Richard shifted his weight uncomfortably in his chair. Allison looked him over. He was pale and she wondered if it was concern for her career or his own. He seemed about to protest the director's request when Scott, up on his feet as soon as the director's words had cleared his lips, tugged at his arm and guided him out of the room.

Allison cleared her throat, glancing around the room for a pitcher of water, but there was none. When she looked back at the director, he had a smile on his lips.

"Your dossier describes you well."

Allison noticed how old-fashioned the word *dossier* sounded, and she wondered if the effect was calculated. She didn't doubt that Clarence Mason knew more about interrogations and psychological profiling than anyone else in the world. Anything she had learned at the Bureau could probably be traced back to Mason's experience and world-class intelligence. She knew better than to think anything he said was coincidental or arbitrary.

She remembered a quote from one of her classes: "You will be given many opportunities to keep your mouth shut. Take advantage of as many of them as possible." She waited the director out.

"Sharp. Outspoken. A bit of a maverick, they say. An outsider."

Allison tried to control her breathing. She knew that she was blinking too much as Mason threw labels at her. She was sure he was picking up every sign of how nervous she was.

"You have discharged your weapon in the line of duty. Killed a man. Consequent admin review found it was a proper use of lethal force. Saved Special Agent Thornton's life, I understand."

"He had saved mine only minutes before."

"I see," Mason said, flapping open the file in front of him with a flourish, although Allison suspected he knew the contents well enough. "It appears that you have a problem with authority figures."

"I wouldn't say—"

"Took a swing at your old boss Garret Morrison. Clocked him pretty good from what I hear. I guess Garret's legendary tenacity wasn't appreciated in his pursuit of you."

Allison fought back the impulse to explain herself, to remind the director that Garret Morrison had made several inappropriate advances despite her clear indication that she was not interested in what he was offering. But she knew it was in the report Mason held in his hand, likely both the official administrative reprimand she received for her action and Morrison's protest about her. Although a legend in the Bureau for his profiling work in the Behavioral Analysis Unit, he had rubbed enough people the wrong way that his demands for her dismissal were ignored—but not his demands that she be reassigned somewhere far away from the work she loved. She was still in the Criminal Investigative Division but working white-collar crimes instead of violent crimes in the Behavioral Analysis Unit, where she wanted to be. Intellectually, she was able to catch on quickly to the work in financial crimes, but all she wanted to do was get back into the homicide cases. Mason had to already know all this, so she decided not to rise to the bait.

"I suppose Garret deserved it. He usually does." He thumbed the polished tabletop with the tips of his thin fingers. "What do you think about your new friend Arnie Milhouse?"

"I gave you the details of what has happened so far. I think the event with his son brought me closer into his confidence. But there has been nothing so far to conclusively implicate him in the securities fraud."

"Ah yes, the securities fraud. And what do you think of the other matter?"

Allison clenched her hands together beneath the table. The old man's eyes bored into her as if they could see every secret buried behind her defenses. "I'm not sure I know what you mean, sir."

Mason raised an eyebrow in an impossible arc and leveled his stare at her. In the silence, Allison was sure the director could hear her heart pounding in her chest.

She caved to the pressure. "Are you referring to the inconsistencies in the double homicide Arnie Milhouse was involved in?"

Mason nodded. "And the wife. Not so long after, I believe."

"Yes, the wife, Sophia Lane Milhouse," Allison said, self-conscious of the fact she was trying to impress the man now. "Died in a house fire less than a month after the homicides. Seems Mrs. Milhouse didn't know it was dangerous to smoke in bed. The life insurance money gave Milhouse his start in investments."

"Anything suspicious about the fire?"

"Both the locals and the insurance company investigated but found nothing. The wife was a known alcoholic and drug abuser. No one seemed too sad to see her go."

"I didn't ask you what the locals decided. I asked you if there was anything suspicious about the fire."

Allison took a deep breath. "The convenience store double homicide."

"Yes."

"Arnie Milhouse killed the robber by stabbing him in the neck with a ballpoint pen. That's very hard to do."

"How do you mean?"

"I mean it requires a certain amount of rage. The pen was not only stuck into the neck muscle but gouged the jugular, penetrated the windpipe—"

"And why rage? Couldn't it have been from fear? He just saw someone shot in the face. Likely he thought he was next."

"Perhaps, but there's the store's surveillance video too."

"Yes, gone missing. Very odd."

"And never explained. The store owner is on record that there was always a tape in there but it was gone when the police arrived. The locals wrote it off as a nonissue. I suppose they assumed the owner forgot the tape."

"So you think our friend Arnie Milhouse went home with a new appetite for killing, and his poor druggie wife was the next course."

Allison hesitated. "I have no proof that—"

"Forget proof for right now. Talk to me about your instinct."

Allison straightened in her chair. Mason's tone carried with it the undercurrent of command. "In the course of investigating the stock fraud case, I've come to suspect that Arnie Milhouse may have murdered his wife."

"Agent McNeil, you have a master's in psychology from UCLA. You were number four in your class at the academy. You worked under

Garret Morrison in the Behavior Analysis Unit for three years doing psych profiles on some very bad people." Mason pointed a crooked finger at her. "You believe he killed more than just his wife, don't you?"

"Yes, I do."

"You believe he is a serial killer."

Allison swallowed painfully, wishing desperately for a glass of water.

"I don't know if—"

"I didn't ask what you knew," Mason suddenly barked, his voice like a hammer. "What do you believe? Your instinct, Allison."

"Yes, of course," she said, trying not to show her shock. She kept her voice level, even softer than it had been before. Damned if she was going to give him the satisfaction of knowing he'd rattled her cage. "I do believe he's a killer. A blend of serial and thrill. He got a taste of it in the convenience store, felt the rush, and decided to take care of his wife next."

Mason stood and walked around the table, thinking. It wasn't until he was behind her, out of her line of vision, that he spoke again. "You've felt the rush of killing someone yourself, haven't you? 'Elation,' I think you called it. Almost did it again tonight. Does that make you a potential serial killer too?"

Allison rocked back in her chair as if Mason's words were a wall of cold water. Her sudden burst of self-confidence was gone, replaced by uncertainty and nervousness. Obviously, the confidentially she had been promised in her sessions with the Bureau's trauma counselors had not applied to the director if he wanted to see what one of his junior agents was thinking. She searched for something to say but came up empty.

Mason hummed softly, walking back in front of her, watching her reaction. "Come, come. You can do better than that."

Allison leaned forward, using her rising anger at being so obviously manipulated to steel her voice. "Victor Mendez, the man I killed, had a knife to my partner's throat. During my psych sessions I admitted to feeling a rush afterward."

"And that disturbed you."

"Of course. I thought I should feel remorse. Sick to my stomach. Something."

"But you felt . . ."

Allison met her boss's penetrating stare. "Elation. That's the word I used in my counseling sessions. Elated. Not only because I saved my partner's life, but also because I had rid the world of an evil asshole. I had the power to do that."

"A dangerous philosophy, Agent McNeil."

"I would not characterize it as philosophy, sir. It was an emotion, one I can easily control." Mason cocked an eyebrow, and she caught his meaning. "Tonight . . . well, tonight was a lack of control. It was entirely unprofessional and I make no excuses for it. You asked what my instincts were about Arnie Milhouse and I gave you my judgment. Your insinuations that my actions in the Victor Mendez case were anything but professional are both insulting and unwarranted. If we have nothing more to discuss . . ." Allison stood up from the table.

Mason smiled. "Good. Better. Now sit down; I have something to show you."

Allison shook her head slightly, playing catch-up to Mason's pace. She lowered herself back into her chair, aware that everything to this point had been designed to test her. Mason reached down to his side and picked up an attaché case. He removed three eight-by-ten photographs and pushed them across the table to her.

"Suzanne Greenville. Twenty-six-year-old DC call girl. High-class apparently, strictly upper echelon clientele."

Allison inspected the photos, mentally cataloging the parts of the image the FBI's profilers would have picked up on to categorize the killer. Feet and hands hacked off but left near the body. Mouth gaping open, stuffed with a black substance. "The substance in her mouth? Is it feces?"

Mason nodded. "What does it tell you?"

"Both modi operandi have been seen before. In the 1950s, Clifford Forrestal always removed the hands and feet of his victims. The feces in the mouth is just like Beau Rickensaw. New Jersey in the 1970s."

"What does that tell you?"

"I'm sure Garret's team of profilers has—"

"I'm asking you."

Allison took a deep breath and studied the pictures. "He's intelligent. He knows what we look for at a crime scene and he's giving it to us. But it's too much, too self-conscious. There aren't any other killings with these same key factors, are there?"

"Not yet."

"There won't be. There will be more, but with different markers. Likely right out of our own textbooks. Maybe someone who was a profiler at one time." She looked up at Mason. "But it's not, is it? You think Milhouse is connected to this."

Mason pointed to the photos. "Suzanne Greenville was a woman with an exit strategy. Not only did she share the bed of some our nation's rising stars in politics and business, but she kept a diary and an extensive photo record of these fine moments."

"That's a political bomb waiting to explode."

"That's what we thought at first. But while the diary lists some more notable clients and makes reference to the photos and video, her murderer removed all hard drives and data storage. We found a single thumb drive he overlooked. There were a few dozen people on it, mostly nobodies, midlevel people. Thank God."

Allison couldn't help but notice the disappointment in Mason's voice. She'd heard the rumors that he was the new J. Edgar Hoover, with a growing file on the who's who in Washington DC. She had no doubt that a stack of illicit photos of America's top legislators with a dead call girl would have been the find of the century for him. Hell, with that in his back pocket, Mason probably would have been director for life.

"So, I'm here because Arnie Milhouse is somehow connected to all this, right?"

Mason nodded. "Arnie Milhouse is on the one thumb drive we did find. He was contacted by an agent five days ago and shown a photo. We didn't suspect much at the time, just trying to run down all the leads, but something interesting happened after the meeting."

"What's that?"

"Arnie Milhouse left the meeting and went to his banker to make arrangements to leave the country, indefinitely it seems. We've tracked over ten million dollars that have been transferred to an offshore account."

"Maybe meeting with the agent spooked him about the securities fraud."

Mason cocked an eyebrow. "Do you really believe that?"

Allison looked back down at the pictures and tried to imagine the man who she had seen hugging his young son commit the heinous crime in the photos. Even though it was her own theory about Arnie that had put her on his trail, it was hard to reconcile the two images. Still, she felt her gut pulling her toward the conclusion Mason was suggesting.

"I don't know. Before, I was talking about a theory. But that was before I spent time with him. It's hard for me to say now."

Mason said nothing but studied Allison as she continued to pore over the photographs.

"So, you want me to continue my surveillance and see if he's the killer."

"It's a long shot. Like you said, he might be running because of the stock fraud case. But my gut tells me there's something here. And your gut tells you the same thing, doesn't it?"

Allison nodded. "It does."

"I've made more arrests following my instincts than all the forensic science in this place put together," Mason said. "You need to go back in light, and quick. Just like you were doing. Play out your hunch and see where it leads. It's a risky game, so I'm asking you to do it but I won't order you to."

"Backup?"

"One man. My choice. If you think this is too dangerous, I will completely—"

"I'll do it."

Mason smiled. "Good. Very good. I was told I could rely on you." Mason stood up and stretched his hand toward her. She shook it firmly, wondering who had told him that.

"Thank you, sir."

"I know what this could mean for you," the director said softly. "Professionally . . . and personally. Do we need to discuss it?"

Allison met his eye and shook her head. *No, that won't be necessary, you old fox bastard. Is there anything you don't know?*

Mason nodded. "Good. Arnie Milhouse chartered a flight out of the country two days from now. Before he leaves, you need to have brought this to a conclusion. Godspeed."

The director turned and left the room, leaving Allison open-mouthed at the sudden deadline imposed on her and with an over-whelming feeling that Richard had been correct in the elevator. She was indeed far over her head.

CHAPTER 31

"This is complete bullshit," Richard mumbled halfway through the drive back to Annapolis.

Allison kept looking out of the passenger window and didn't reply. She was still conflicted over Director Mason assigning Richard as her backup. It was so outside protocol and Mason was so intent on keeping the mission under wraps that Richard had taken himself off official duty during the assignment.

Then again, the whole business was far enough out of regular channels to make even a hater of the bureaucracy like Allison a bit nervous. She stared at the wall of trees whisking by, lit gently by the first morning light from the sun directly ahead of them, and let the details of the night's meeting percolate through her brain.

Caught up in the adrenaline rush of meeting a living hero in Director Mason, she knew on reflection she had failed to ask even the most basic questions. Were there other suspects in the murder of Suzanne Greenville? Didn't Arnie Milhouse's behavior after the agent interview create reasonable suspicion to launch a full-blown surveillance?

Allison figured Mason played her perfectly. At the heart of the matter, he wanted to stop a serial killer, if that's what Arnie was. But he also wanted the rest of the call girl's photos if they existed. There was a chance her killer had them. If they could be found, Mason wanted them to be recovered with minimum publicity and as few people involved as possible.

Allison wondered for the first time whether Mason might have been on the list of clients.

If not, she wouldn't be surprised if some of the men in the diary were not the same men working to have Mason removed from the Bureau. Just like anyone with power in DC, Clarence Mason had his enemies. Perhaps knowing Mason held files on them would be enough to stop their constant calls for his resignation.

It was politics at its ugliest, but Allison wasn't naïve about how things worked in Washington. If it came down to saving a few sleazy politicos from embarrassment to save the career of a true American hero like Mason, she wasn't going to complain.

In any case, that was just the sideshow. Even if Arnie was the killer she thought him to be, there was only the slimmest of chances that he had possession of the photos. Mason had to know this, which just underscored how badly he wanted them.

She wondered whether Mason knew Arnie's stock fraud case was complete bullshit. That she had made the whole thing up as a cover to dig into Arnie's past. After the transfer to financial crimes, she was toxic goods, so her new supervisor was happy to stay out of her way. Even without proof, it was easy enough to fabricate a scenario where Arnie was named a person of interest, employing her broad powers to comb through every aspect of his life. She had been chasing down her belief that Arnie Milhouse was a murderer for longer than either Richard or Mason could have ever guessed. Even as intimate as she and Richard had been, there were things she wouldn't share. If he knew the truth, there was no way he'd ever let her get close to Arnie.

But that no longer mattered because Mason was her new patron saint. Ultimately, she didn't care about Suzanne Greenville's photos. They were simply an add-on, important to her only because they were important to Mason. As long as he wanted her on the case, it didn't matter what Richard thought.

Of course, Mason's masterstroke was understanding all this and knowing she would overlook protocol for the chance to continue her work. This was her case; her way to get back into the work she loved—tracking down killers.

She wondered, though, if Mason could have guessed that a large part of her was hoping she was wrong about Arnie.

"Who told Mason my theories about Arnie?" she asked Richard.

"I did."

"But why—"

"His name turned up in the Suzanne Greenville murder because his photos were on the thumb drive. The computer kicked out that he was already under surveillance for the stock fraud case, so I was called in."

"Who was there? Anyone except Mason?"

"Yeah, your pal Garret was there with his people."

Allison sighed. "I bet Garret almost shit when he heard my name."

"Yeah, he wasn't too happy, but Mason shut him up in a hurry. Then he ended the meeting and Mason and I finished together. That's when your little theories came up."

"Doesn't that seem a little odd?" she asked, shrugging off his condescending tone.

"No. Mason and I have met privately on many occasions. There's nothing odd about it."

Allison marveled at Richard's ability to be boastful and defensive at the same time. Always aware of hierarchy and proximity to power, Richard assumed everyone around him was as impressed with his status as he was himself. The word *privately* came out as a challenge, as if daring Allison to feel more connected than he was because of her one meeting with Mason.

"No, I mean, if Mason gave any credence to this at all, why wouldn't he want Garret working on this case?"

"Are you kidding? Garret's a publicity hound. Mason wants this thing wrapped tight."

"And that's why you're here?"

"That's why I'm in charge," Richard said. "You will follow my rules out here or I don't give a damn what Mason says, I'll pull you out so fast it'll . . ."

"Make my head spin?" Allison laughed. "You've been watching too many late-night cop movies."

Richard didn't find her amusing. "I'm serious. If you take too many risks, I will close this down. I don't care what Mason says."

Allison smiled. The idea of Richard going against a direct order from Clarence Mason was ridiculous.

"Don't worry, I won't mess things up for you while the big dogs are watching."

"It's not that," he said quietly. He looked over at her. "I'm not going to let you get hurt. If you're right about Milhouse, then you're walking into a situation that could go very bad, very fast. This whole thing worries me."

Allison turned away from him, fearing the path he was taking them down. Farther down that road was more emotion, more worry, more memories.

"Don't worry, I know how to handle Arnie Milhouse. I'll be fine. You just make sure you're around when I call for backup."

"Oh, I'll be there."

"See, then there's nothing to worry about."

Allison went back to watching the trees along the highway stream by as Richard drove back to Annapolis. A shudder worked its way through her body, from her lower back, up her spine, and through her hairline, making her scalp tingle.

She knew a lie when she heard one, especially when it came out of her own mouth.

CHAPTER 32

Charlie felt a little guilty about spying on Allison for a rich prick like Arnie Milhouse, so he decided to drink a gallon or two of beer to make himself feel better. But his sense of curiosity was stronger than his desire to get stinking drunk, and after a couple of drinks, he decided it wouldn't hurt to try and find out who the man was that Allison had tangled with before her odd departure.

More than an hour of drinking later, he had double-oh-sevened himself into the confidence of Craig Gerty. By the time Charlie worked his way into a conversation with him, Gerty was drunk and disorderly in the first degree.

And what he learned about his friend Allison fascinated him. Charlie stayed with Gerty until the bar closed, taking shots of water to match the obnoxious asshole's shots of tequila. By the time they left Middleton Tavern together, they were both staggering down the street. Gerty from being completely hammered and Charlie from trying to walk with his bum leg while his new best friend repeatedly smashed into him to keep his balance. Charlie hammed it up, telling the story for the third time that night about Allison kicking him in the groin, Gerty bent over and howling with laughter, tears coming down his face from the sheer delight of it. Everything about the man bothered Charlie: his looks, his arrogant attitude, the way he disrespected Allison every chance he got. Still, he played along just to keep the pearls of information coming.

To begin with, her name was McNeil, not Davenport. Charlie supposed she could have been married, but if so, she had lied about that too. This wasn't her first time to Annapolis; she had spent a half year at the academy before quitting. Charlie wondered what other lies she had told and why they had been necessary. He supposed he would have spent more time dwelling on it if not for the last thing Gerty had said to him.

"Listhen 'ere," he'd slurred at Charlie. "You wanna fuck tha' bitch Allison, don'tcha?"

"Shit yeah," Charlie slurred back, pretending to be as drunk as his new best buddy.

"I got me some a' that, back in the day. Ere's the deal. You gotta jus' take it from her, cuz she ain't gonna jus' give it away. You gotta throw her uppity ass on the groun', put your han' over her mouth, an' jus' take it, know what I mean?"

Charlie wasn't sure he did know what he meant at first. Even when he realized what Gerty was saying, he couldn't wrap his brain around it. "Are you saying you raped her? Is that why she left the academy?"

Gerty had reared back his hand as if to high-five Charlie, a sneering smile on his face. "You know it. 'Cademy's goin' to the bitches, but Craig Gerty's on the job. Put it there, man."

Charlie put it there, all right. The punch Charlie threw landed with a satisfying wet smack as Gerty's nose erupted in a gush of blood. Charlie spun his crutch around and took a baseball swing at the back of Gerty's right knee. The man dropped to the ground, alternately holding his knee and wiping away the blood draining down his face.

Charlie had felt such rage at the thought of Gerty forcing himself on Allison that he didn't give a damn about whether it was McNeil or

Davenport, or whether everything she had said to him had been a lie. At that moment, gripping the crutch in his hand, with Gerty sniveling on the ground in front of him, all Charlie could think about was how justified he would be to keep beating on Gerty, beating and beating until the sick fuck couldn't pose a threat to a woman ever again.

Fortunately or unfortunately, he still couldn't decide, the rational side of his brain had slowed down the momentum of action and forced his feet a step back from the groaning and bleeding man.

"If Allison so much as sees you again, I'm going to come find you and shove this crutch up your ass. I will beat you senseless, do you understand?" Charlie shouted, feeling very much like he was in one of the action movies he spent most of his spare time watching.

It felt good at the time, but now, hours later, sitting on the bench next to Ego Alley, looking out over the water and waiting for a call back from Arnie, he doubted Gerty would even remember how he came by the broken nose and bum knee when he woke up the next morning. He wondered if he should have done more.

Compounding his building guilt that he might have taken it too easy on Gerty, he had too much time to think whether he was doing the right thing in giving the new information to Arnie. After he'd ditched Gerty, Charlie had almost called Arnie's cell number right away, but he had stopped himself. For the last hour, Charlie had wondered if he shouldn't just keep his night of detective work to himself.

The phone vibrated in his pocket and he dug it out. It read "blocked call," but there was only one person who would be calling him this early in the morning.

He held the phone in front of him, watching the faceplate glow in the early morning light.

The right thing for Allison was to let the phone keep ringing.

"And what's the right thing for Charlie?" he asked the ducks bobbing in the water next to him. "Which way does old Charlie have a better chance to get the girl?"

That was the heart of it. He knew it was. Somewhere inside he held out hope that he still had a chance with Allison. Certainly, given this new information, a crusty old dude like Milhouse would turn tail and drop Allison, leaving him an opening. Not a large opening since she wasn't interested in him at all, but a hell of a lot bigger opening than if Allison was still dating the weird millionaire. Stranger things had happened in the world than a girl changing her mind about something. *Maybe*, Charlie thought, *with Arnie out of the picture, he could help Allison change hers.*

Charlie suppressed his surging guilt, answered the call, and told a very interested Arnie Milhouse everything he knew about Allison McNeil. No sooner had he hung up the phone than he sensed he'd just made a huge mistake.

CHAPTER 33

That afternoon, Allison sat in her room at the Calvert House, thinking through the courses of action available to her. Richard had checked into another room to grab a shower and a power nap. Arnie was not due back in town until that night, so Allison knew she had some time left to figure out what she was going to do. She was still reeling from the deadline put on her by Mason. How could she be expected to bring things to a head in two days? It seemed impossible, especially with Arnie gone for one of those days.

Her phone vibrated on the nightstand next to her. She felt a surge of hope that it was Richard. She followed the unbidden thought by a grunt of disapproval. Richard was all wrong for her, 100 percent. Still, being around him again had rekindled some of the old fire that had driven their relationship; add one part antagonism, three parts pain in the ass, and you had Richard. For the life of her, she couldn't understand her attraction to him. But it was there. Whenever she found herself shaking her head in disbelief that she had ever been with the arrogant bastard, a small corner of her mind couldn't believe she had given him up. Perpetual bad choices in men—that, Allison decided, was her lot in life whether she liked it or not. She answered the phone.

"Hey, Allison. It's Arnie Milhouse."

"Arnie. Where are you?" she asked, already mentally preparing herself in case he was downstairs at the inn.

"Still at the airport. My flight leaves in an hour."

"Was it hard to get through security?"

"No, it wasn't too bad," Arnie said.

"Really? I got a real going-over the last time I flew. Where are you?" Allison bit her lower lip, hoping she sounded natural enough.

There was a pause on the line; then Arnie came through, choppy now. "I'm losing you. Bad reception in airports, you know. Let me try . . . there, that's better. Can you hear me now?"

"Yeah, where are you?"

"I'll be back early tonight, but I have work to do . . . tomorrow ni . . . together?"

"Arnie, you're breaking up again."

"Shit, goddamn phones."

"I heard that loud and clear," Allison said, and laughed.

"Sorry. Before I lose you again. Dinner. My house. Tomorrow at eight?"

"Done."

"Do you know where it's at?"

"Somewhere by St. Michaels, I think, is what you told me, right?" Allison said. Actually, she knew exactly where it was located. She'd taken surveillance photos from all around the property during the past two weeks. She asked him to hold on and pretended to search for a pen to write down directions. Arnie recited the directions for her twice.

"Right then, eight o'clock tomorrow," Arnie said. "They're calling my flight; gotta run."

Allison held a finger to her other ear and listened hard to the background noise coming from the phone. Faintly, she heard a tiny voice over the PA say, ". . . final boarding call for flight 2514 Miami to Reagan National Airport."

Allison smiled and jotted down the city and flight number on the stationery in front of her.

"OK. Have a good flight, Arnie. See you tomorrow."

She closed the phone, picked up the hotel phone, and dialed Richard's number. He picked up after one ring, but she could still hear the sleep in his voice.

"Hey, Sleeping Beauty."

"Who's sleeping?" he said, clearing his voice.

"Give me a break, Super Cop," Allison said. "Listen, Arnie just called."

Richard cleared his throat. "What did he say? Where was he?"

"Miami. Flight 2514."

"Did he tell you that?"

"No. I heard the flight called over the PA system."

"Good work," Richard said, still managing to sound patronizing even in his groggy state. "What else did he say?"

"I have a dinner date tomorrow night."

"Where?"

"At his house."

Richard was silent for a few moments. Allison smoothed out the wrinkles on the bed. She wondered which Richard was doing the thinking: the agent-in-charge trying to decide on tactics or the man whose ex-girlfriend had just been asked to dinner by a millionaire who was also a potential serial killer.

"I don't like it," Richard said. "If he's leaving in two days, why would he pursue you like this? Doesn't feel right."

"Does it matter?" Allison said. "If he is running, we just have to be glad he's not shutting me out. This will get me inside the house and give me a chance to check things out. Maybe the only chance we're going to get."

"What time are you supposed to be over there?"

"Seven tomorrow night."

"All right. I'll make some calls. If you're going to do this, I need to do some work to make sure we have the support in the area."

"I thought Mason said—"

"I've run this kind of thing for Mason before. I know how to handle it. I'll call you later."

Allison held the phone out in front of her as it blared a dial tone. "Good-bye to you too," she mumbled.

As she put the phone back on the cradle, a chill crawled up her spine. She wasn't sure whether it was from the knowledge that in a little more than twenty-four hours she would be having dinner with the man she suspected of being a serial killer, or whether it was from the last thing Richard had said.

I've run this kind of thing for Mason before. I know how to handle it.

She wondered what kind of "thing" she was involved in. And, more importantly, she was starting to suspect that she was the one being handled.

She glanced at her watch. Ten minutes until she was supposed to meet Charlie down at City Dock Café. He had called that morning saying it was urgent they meet, but he hadn't been willing to say why. With Arnie gone, she figured it would do her good to be around Charlie for a little bit to take her mind off things. He was always good for a laugh or two. And that was exactly what she needed to calm her nerves.

CHAPTER 34

"You what?"

Charlie flinched as if Allison had thrown something at him. "Keep your voice down. People are staring."

"I don't care if people are staring," she said, although she did lower her voice. "I can't believe this."

"I know; I'm sorry. I know it was wrong. Right when I got off the phone, I knew it. That's why I'm telling you now," he added, hoping for some salvation in this fact. He figured Allison would be angry with him for spying on her, but she was more than angry. For some reason she looked scared too.

"Outside. C'mon, we need to talk."

Charlie shook his head. "Let's just stay here." He figured that however mad she got, being inside would at least keep her from yelling at him. But the look on her face told him that he didn't have a vote in the matter.

"Outside. Now."

Once they were away from the milling crowds of tourists snapping pictures of the power yachts and sailboats moored along Ego Alley, Allison sat him down on a bench.

"Listen, Charlie, this is real important. I'm not mad at you—"

"Yes, you are."

"OK. So I'm a little mad at you. But that's not important right now. I need you to concentrate, all right?"

Charlie nodded.

"Good. Now, I need you to tell me everything you told Arnie, all right? I mean every detail, got it?"

"Sure," Charlie stammered, a little freaked out by her intensity. "I got it. I mean, it's not like I told him that much. He asked me to keep an eye on you while he was out of town. Gave me three hundred dollars."

"OK, that's fine, but what did you tell him?"

This confession wasn't going at all the way he had planned. He figured she would be a little mad at him but also embarrassed for lying to him too. It didn't seem like she had given that part of the equation a second thought, and it kind of pissed him off. He decided to make things a little easier on himself.

"All I told him was that I saw you at McGarvey's, that some guy was hassling you, and next thing I knew you left the bar and were getting into some other guy's car."

"What else?"

"Nothing, I—"

"Charlie, this is very important, all right? Did you describe the person I left with?"

"No," Charlie answered too quickly. He wished he could roll back the clock, big time, and make this whole confession go away. The guilt had been bad, but now he felt like crap and still felt guilty for lying to her again. But given the way she had reacted so far, there was no way he was going to tell her what else he had found out. Although he wished there was some way he could tell her about him pounding on Craig Gerty. He wondered if that might make her forgive him a little.

"Are you sure?"

"I swear on my mother's grave that was all I told him. What do you want from me?" Charlie pointed a finger at her. "Besides, you're not Ms. Innocent in all this. How about you tell me what your deal is? You tell everyone you've never been to Annapolis before but turns out you spent some time at the academy. What's up with that?"

"Shit. Goddammit," Allison mumbled. "How'd you find that out?"

"Gerty told me."

Allison sucked in a sharp breath and got to her feet. He looked down to her clenched fists, wondering whether he was about to suffer another beating. Allison seemed to notice and relaxed her hands, looking more in control. "Was anyone else around?"

Charlie shook his head. "No, just me."

Allison crouched down until her eyes were level with Charlie's. "Did you tell Arnie?"

"No, I didn't," Charlie said, breezing through the lie without flinching. Lying to women was one thing he had mastered throughout the years, and he was sure she couldn't detect it. "I swear."

Allison reached out and turned his face toward her. "This is really important."

"I swear," Charlie cried. "Cross my heart, all that stuff."

Allison held his face in place and studied his eyes. After a beat, she let go. "OK, Charlie. I believe you."

"So, you gonna tell me what's going on, or what?"

Allison stood with her back to him for a few seconds, then turned around. "All right, but you have to promise to keep it quiet."

"Sure thing."

"I'm an investigative reporter for the *Washington Post*. Arnie Milhouse has been implicated in a complex investment fraud case with ties to organized crime."

"Holy shit. You mean like the mafia. Like *The Sopranos*?"

"You got it. I'm not positive Arnie is guilty, but that's why I'm here. That's why all the secrecy. I'm sorry I lied to you, but I was trying to protect you."

Charlie gulped down his sudden desire to tell her everything. He knew it was the right thing to do, but she was finally calming down. He couldn't bear the thought of how she would react if he told her that Arnie knew her real name, or the fact that she not only attended the Naval Academy but the reason for her leaving.

He was a complete shit for not telling her and he knew it.

But even as they got up and went for a walk, even as Allison made him agree to leave town for a couple of days until her investigation was complete, even then he did absolutely nothing about it. He didn't come clean and tell her the truth. He was not even honest with her that he had no intention of leaving. And he especially made a point not to tell her that he had a meeting scheduled with Arnie that night, which he had every intention of keeping. If he was going to carry the guilt of playing Judas, he was at least going to take the money the son of a bitch owed him.

Allison left Charlie and headed back to the Calvert House. She considered not telling Richard what had happened, but she knew that was unfair. Regardless of their personal history, Richard was her partner on this case. Withholding information like this, information that potentially changed the risk calculus so dramatically, was not only unprofessional but unethical.

She still believed her cover was intact, but there was a doubt now. Although his denials seemed genuine enough, Charlie may have told Arnie more than he let on and that would change everything.

If Arnie was the killer she suspected and he knew who she really was, his invitation to dinner had all the makings of a trap.

CHAPTER 35

Arnie sat on a park bench on the State House grounds across the street from the Calvert House. He wore a baseball cap and sunglasses and pretended to read a newspaper while taking particular interest in the comings and goings of Allison McNeil.

In his pocket was a small digital recorder on which the sounds from Miami International Airport were stored, recorded yesterday before his flight home and recently used to make Allison believe he was still out of town.

Arnie waited a few minutes to make sure Allison did not reappear from the Calvert House, then stood, stretched his legs, and walked around to the back of the capitol building where his car was parked. He would get a sense soon enough of how much Allison and the FBI knew or suspected. With a three-hour window of Arnie supposedly on a plane from Miami, they could execute a search of his house and lock it down under surveillance. If they really had something on him, the FBI would swarm his property within the hour. But if Allison was just playing a hunch, which he suspected she was, then that was a different story all together. If no one showed up at his house, then he had a dinner date to prepare for.

He knew it was reckless. The FBI could track his flight to make sure he was on board. But he didn't think they would. He'd already told them where to find him the next night and so tracking him from the airport was overkill. Unless they had hard evidence against him. In that case they'd be all over his house either way, and he'd be able to adjust his plans accordingly. No, he thought he was in a pretty good position. Still, the undoubtedly smart thing to do was walk away from the whole mess as soon as possible. Call Giancarlo and get the hell out of the country.

But he didn't want to escape. If there was a way to play the game out, he had to do it. All he could think about was the rush he'd feel if he were to pull off a kill right under the FBI's nose. And worse, how it would feel to slink away like some beaten dog, succumbing to fear and weakness.

Still, there was a difference between taking a risk and being a fool. The cameras on his property would tell him everything he needed to know during the next few hours. Until then, he decided to drive up toward Baltimore for some supplies. He had a lot to do in order to get ready for the big date, already just over twenty-four hours away. And he wanted to be sure he was ready to give Allison McNeil the welcome she deserved.

CHAPTER 36

Late that night, they were still undecided about their course of action. As Allison predicted, Richard was adamantly opposed to the idea of her meeting Arnie at his home and was ready to call the whole thing off as soon as she related her conversation with Charlie.

As always, his dictatorial style rankled her and made her argue the other side more vehemently than she felt. By the time they agreed to sleep on it and make a decision the next day, Allison had convinced herself that Charlie had told the truth and that her cover was intact.

Allison lay on her bed, staring up at the plastered ceiling. It didn't make her feel much better. Her real doubts were less about her cover and more about the nagging feeling Arnie was being set up for a fall he didn't deserve. It wasn't the first time she had wrestled with this self-doubt. She knew the risks of being too close to a case and acknowledged that she had long ago lost any semblance of objectivity. The logical part of her worried she'd pushed too hard to make the facts fit her theory. That the patterns of Arnie's behavior, which fed her intuition, were weaker than she wanted to admit. Not a single piece of evidence to take into a court of law. Only her gut telling her that her long search was near an end.

She thought through the case against him and didn't like what she found. It was paper-thin, nothing more than circumstantial evidence piled on top of coincidences and fused with an overactive imagination that tended to see pathologies everywhere it turned. On top of it all had been a level of emotion that typically didn't factor into her thinking.

Sure, Arnie had used the call girl who was later murdered, not exactly a noble act on his part, but he was a single man, and it was a minor transgression compared to the other crimes with which he was suspected. And then there was his liquidating his assets and preparing to leave the country. Not against any law but suspicious given the circumstances.

She just didn't know what to think. If he was guilty, cover blown or not, going to his house was a dangerous proposition. When a serial killer has made arrangements to leave the country and invites a woman over for dinner, Allison reasoned that it was usually not a good thing. Still, if he was the killer she suspected, this was the chance she'd been working toward her entire career. Not only that, but if he got away and someone else died because she was too scared to do her job, she would be responsible for the death too.

But what if she had it all wrong? If Arnie was innocent, she was bringing an awful experience into his life, but more importantly, into the life of his son. The quick bond she had formed with them filled her with guilt that she had taken things too far.

Given all that, she knew what she had to do. And she knew exactly how to get Richard to agree to it.

The knock came at her door early the next morning. She opened the door after checking the peephole and a pissed-off Richard slid inside.

"Guess who I just had a call from?" he asked.

Allison shrugged.

"Clarence Mason just called to tell me I should let you follow your instincts on this case," he said, his voice level in a controlled rage. "That

I shouldn't hold you back. I thought we were going to talk about this together. Decide together."

"Richard, you made it clear yesterday that you were not going to allow me to do this. I know you, and once you draw the line in the sand like that it takes a hurricane to erase it."

"Well, you called in a hurricane, all right. You've got your way. Now we're both in danger here. I hope you're satisfied."

"You don't have to stay. Mason even offered to send someone else out if—"

"Shit, Allison, tell me you didn't—"

"—if you aren't comfortable working with me on this."

Richard took a quick step toward her. "Let's get something straight. I'm still the SAC here. I call the shots. You're working for me, you got it?"

"You can call yourself special agent in charge or Jesus Christ on a pogo stick for all I care, just as long as you're there if things go south tonight. I need to be able to count on you, Richard."

They locked eyes, neither backing down. Slowly, a smile spread across Richard's face. "Jesus Christ on a pogo stick?"

Allison returned the smile and felt the tension melt away. "I don't know; it just kind of came out. Conjures an image, doesn't it?"

"Yeah, one that says you're a freak." Richard plopped himself down in the overstuffed chair by the window as if the conversation had exhausted him. "I'm still pissed you went behind my back to Mason."

"I should have tried again with you first. I'm sorry."

"An apology? Wow, that might actually be a first."

She grabbed a wadded up T-shirt from the chest of drawers and threw it at him. "Don't worry. It wasn't sincere."

"Yeah, well, I'll take what I can get."

Allison sat next to him and took a deep breath, knowing he deserved an explanation. "I just know this is the right thing to do.

If we called it off and it turned out we were right about him, and he killed someone else, I'd always know I could have done something about it."

"No regrets, right?"

She caught a small change in Richard's tone of voice. A softness she hadn't expected. "No regrets," she agreed, wondering if they were still talking about Arnie Milhouse. "No regrets" had been their mantra when their relationship broke up and they had gone their separate ways.

"Well, you were right. I never would have changed my mind." He paused and then added quietly, "I just don't want you to get hurt."

Allison turned away at the words. They had come out full of tenderness and . . . something else . . . maybe expectation? It suddenly felt like the old days. The fights. Shouting. Apologies. The tender words. Then the makeup sex. And that had always been great.

She realized they had gone through most of the cycle, and she wondered if she heard a question underlying his last words.

It would be so easy. A simple nod of the head. Just the right look and she knew they would be on the bed in seconds, tearing off each other's clothes. She remembered the feeling of his hard body against her own.

She was ready with her answer. But when she turned back to look at him, expecting his questioning face, he was gone.

He had gotten up and crossed the room to the door while she had looked away. She realized that he'd taken her body language as a denial. And now, with him leaving, she wanted to scream, "Yes!" She wanted to chase him down and drag him to the bed, but she couldn't do it.

"I'll grab us some lunch. We'll eat here and plan out tonight. You want sandwiches or pizza?" he asked.

"You're the special agent in charge. You decide."

"You kill me, you know that?"

Allison smiled. "That's what I'm here for."

Richard left the room and Allison exhaled slowly, feeling both relieved and conflicted about his departure.

No time to think about that, she decided. Tonight was her command performance as freelance photographer Allison Davenport, and she had to be perfect.

CHAPTER 37

Across the Bay, on his Eastern Shore estate, Arnie Milhouse walked his son out to the waiting car. The driver grabbed the boy's two suitcases and placed them in the trunk.

"I still don't understand why I can't just wait for you," Jason said.

"I told you, Jason. A few things popped up, and I already made these flight arrangements. I can't cancel them so we might as well put them to use."

"But I don't—"

"Enough. I'll be down there in a day, two at the max. This will be good for you anyway. It's good for you to have responsibility. You're not a little kid anymore."

Jason shrugged and looked down at his feet. "I guess."

Arnie kneeled next to him. He took one of Jason's hands and put a sealed envelope in it. "Now, I want you to listen carefully. If I'm not down there in two days and you don't hear from me, I want you to open this envelope. Inside are some phone numbers of people you can call, all right? Don't call anyone else except the people in this envelope. Not your friends, not the house, not anyone. Understand?"

"Why wouldn't you show up? Is something wrong?"

Arnie tousled the boy's hair. "No, your dad's just a worrier; you know that. Just dotting the *is* and crossing the *ts*. You have this?"

Jason nodded. Arnie pulled him into a hug and then watched him climb into the car. He poked his head through the door. "Stay away from the women down there, OK?"

"Dad," Jason protested, flushing red.

"Be careful. I love you."

Jason nodded and gave him a halfhearted wave. Arnie shut the door knowing that was all he was going to get. He watched the car until it drove the entire length of the driveway and turned onto the main road to start the journey to Baltimore-Washington International. A charter plane would take his son down to the Florida Keys, where a small, nondescript aircraft would take him to a private island arranged by Giancarlo. From there, he and Jason would assume their new identities and decide together where to spend the next part of their lives.

Instead of going back into the house, Arnie walked to a small shed on the side of the garage. He took a solitary key from his pocket, inserted it into the padlock, and pulled the heavy chain through the door handles.

Once the chain was removed, the door creaked open a bit on its own and Arnie felt a wave of heat pour out of the small space. He suddenly feared that he'd miscalculated, and the small holes in the shed had not provided enough ventilation.

He swung the door open completely and light poured into the shed. He breathed a sigh of relief as the form on the floor wiggled around spastically. Still alive. Perfect.

Arnie flipped open a small knife and cut the rope wrapped about his prisoner's legs. The bindings on the arms and the blindfold he left in place. With a prod of his knife, he convinced his unfortunate guest to walk to the main house under his own power.

If this was his last night as Arnie Milhouse, he wanted it to be perfect. He went through a mental checklist of what he had to do before eight o'clock. The list of preparations was extensive, and he couldn't afford a single mistake. This chance for a clean break was an unexpected gift, and he meant to take complete advantage of it.

Of course, there was nothing wrong with having a little fun in the process.

Arnie poked the stumbling person in front of him and elicited a short scream as the knife left a small bleeding puncture wound on the left shoulder blade. Arnie grinned.

This was definitely his brand of fun.

CHAPTER 38

Just past seven thirty, the summer sun still filled the sky with a bright twilight, but it didn't stop everything from seeming ominously dark as Allison made the final bend in the driveway. Light filtered through the towering elms and cast flickering shadows as she drove her rented car slowly over the gravel road.

The house loomed in front of her, a traditional brick monstrosity with a symmetrical balance of windows and dormers. Enormous trees on either side of the home provided enough context to make even the third-story gables seem a fitting proportion for the property. The driveway veered to the right and looped around to create a circle in front of the house. Allison stopped the car on the opposite side of the circle and sat there with the engine idling.

She rubbed her hands back and forth across the steering wheel and chewed on the inside of her lower lip. In a slow burn of fear, she wondered if Richard hadn't been right after all. Maybe she was pushing the edge too far on this one. But they didn't have enough to arrest Arnie. If they brought him in for questioning and searched the house, they might find some piece of evidence connecting him to the murders. But if her profile of Arnie was correct, there was no way he was that sloppy.

No, they wouldn't find anything that easily. She had to catch him in the act. The best way to catch a predator was to dangle meat in front of its nose and wait until its true nature was revealed. Only in this case, the prey would fight back. And if she couldn't handle it, the wire she wore would signal to Richard to ride in and help her. Still, even with backup in place, the whole idea was ridiculously risky.

It wasn't only the risk that caused Richard to object, but the clothes she chose that night hadn't thrilled him either. She wore a sleek black dress with straps, the hem short enough that Richard had taken a hard look at her when she came down the stairs at the Calvert House. She'd done her hair so that it fell to her shoulders in soft curls instead of in the usual ponytail she wore. Makeup gently highlighted her eyes and cheekbones in a way that accentuated her natural beauty and tele-graphed that she was making an effort to look her best. She was playing to type in the seduction ritual ahead of her, and Richard didn't like it one bit. A fact she secretly enjoyed.

She felt confident that she looked the part but did miss the com-forting feeling of the ankle holster she usually wore. She'd considered a pantsuit so she could wear the gun but didn't think showing up looking like a career FBI agent was a great idea. A shoulder holster wouldn't work either—too hot and humid for a coat. Instead she had a small purse stocked with makeup, tissues, loose change, and a Glock 44 with a chambered round. She reached into her purse and slid her fingers around the cool metal and felt a little better.

CHAPTER 39

Arnie saw the car stop at the head of the circular driveway. He peered out from behind the plantation shutters in his private office on the main floor and wondered what his guest was doing.

For a second, he worried she was losing her nerve and would turn around and head back to whatever backup was waiting for her on Hawkins Road, the main road outside his property.

He glanced over at the bank of security cameras aligned along the wall behind his desk. One showed the metal gate slowly closing at the main entrance; the others viewed different parts of the property and each direction down Hawkins Road. It was an encrypted wireless system that used cameras smaller than a pinecone. He was certain even a trained FBI countersurveillance squad would miss his setup.

Two cameras particularly interested him. These were at the two small open lots less than a quarter mile south on the main road, the logical staging ground if the Feds were planning a full-scale storming on the property; that is, if they didn't simply close down Hawkins and stage themselves right outside his entrance.

But the lots were empty, and there wasn't a single other car on Hawkins Road. It looked as if Allison had come on her own, still unaware that he might know who she really was.

Arnie grinned. It looked as if he would be able to take his time tonight.

The car started to move forward, and he backed away from the shutters. He walked quickly through the house, checking everything for the last time.

He wanted everything to be just perfect.

He took a deep breath, opened the door, and stepped outside.

"Did you have any trouble finding the place?" Arnie asked, standing on the front steps as Allison walked up.

"No, the directions were fine. I've taken pictures in the area before so I am pretty familiar with it." She craned her neck back. "You have a beautiful house."

"A little too big, if you ask me. But it was a distress sale and I couldn't pass up the deal."

"Divorce?"

"You guessed it. This couple had just finished building the house when the guy found out that his wife and the builder had already christened most of the rooms."

"That's got to hurt."

"Yeah, well, that's the breaks, huh? You look amazing, by the way."

Allison looked self-conscious. "It was this or muddy jeans."

"I would have taken either, but I'm glad you chose this. Come on in. Dinner's almost ready."

She walked into the house, and Arnie noticed the barest shiver passing through her as she did. That slight quiver across her skin, that tangible sign of the fear inside her, gave him rush of excitement. He turned and followed her inside.

CHAPTER 40

Two miles from the house, Richard sat at the communications console in an unmarked van. Two technicians with headphones monitored the audio feed from the small microphone sewn into the side of Allison's dress, toggling the bank of controls to sharpen the sound.

Richard held his own headphones to his ears as he followed the conversation. Right after Arnie's invitation to come inside, a piercing screech blasted through the feed and all three men ripped their headphones off at once.

"What the hell was that?" Richard demanded.

The technicians set to work on their equipment. "I don't know," one of the men said.

"Get her back online. Now! Or you'll be tracing wire intercepts in the Wichita field office this time tomorrow."

CHAPTER 41

Allison jumped as Arnie slammed the door behind her. She turned, half expecting him to come charging at her. But he stood by the door and looked embarrassed.

"Sorry about that," he said. "The wind took it. Did I scare you?"

"No, just surprised me."

"Come on in; let me get you a drink."

She followed Arnie deeper into the house. The open floor plan led to a sprawling two-story great room with a gourmet kitchen off to one side. A wall of glass showcased a spectacular panoramic view of the Chesapeake Bay from the thirty-foot cliff where the house was perched. A thin line of fog obscured the far shore, giving the impression of being on the edge of the ocean. The last remnants of the summer sun poked through the cloud cover and painted the water in bold strokes of light. A single container ship made its way up the main channel toward Baltimore, but the rest of the water was empty. Allison remembered there was a severe storm warning out, a warning recreational boaters took seriously if they knew what was good for them.

"God, that's a gorgeous view," Allison said.

Arnie walked up behind her, two wine glasses in one hand and a bottle in the other. "It's a great vantage point. I believe in being able to see what's coming before it arrives."

"We should see a good storm come in tonight."

"Yes, I saw the warnings just in time."

Arnie's tone was flat, somehow just a bit off. It reminded Allison of the moment on the catamaran after she had saved Jason when, just for a moment, she'd thought she had seen a darkness inside Arnie Milhouse peek out from behind the good-guy persona. She was glad Richard had talked her into bringing the gun.

She nodded to the wine bottle. "Are you going to pour that or is the plan to just stare at it?"

"Of course. It's a pinot noir from a small boutique vineyard in California. It has an excellent bouquet with a strong finish."

"You're a wine connoisseur too?"

Arnie broke out into a wide grin. "Actually, that's just what it says on the back of the bottle. I just liked the anchor on the label. Let's see if it's any good."

And, just like that, dark Arnie was gone and charming Arnie was back. Allison watched him fumble through uncorking the wine and found herself hoping that her instincts were wrong and that he wasn't the monster she suspected him to be.

While he poured the wine, she took further stock of her surroundings. The furniture was an eclectic mix of traditional and modern pieces that somehow worked perfectly together. The artwork was bold but tasteful. But these observations were secondary to where Allison's trained eye fell. She quickly memorized the floor plan, cataloged the exits, and picked out potential weapons she could use in case of a struggle.

"Here you go," Arnie said, holding a wine glass toward her. Allison took it as he held up his own glass for a toast. "Here's to chance encounters."

"To chance." Allison touched her glass to Arnie's and took a sip. Even though she was tense and focused on the business at hand, she had to admit it was a damn good wine. She made a show of checking out the furnishings and artwork in the room. "Impressive. Did you do all this yourself?"

"Are you kidding? Left on my own, this place would probably look like a downscale Motel 6. I paid an interior designer a hefty sum to spend my money."

"She was worth it."

"No one is worth what she charged," Arnie said with a smile. "But Jason likes it, so I didn't mind."

"Speaking of Jason, where is he?"

"Over at a friend's house. I thought it'd be nice to have the place to ourselves for the night. No distractions."

There was an awkward silence as the implication of her spending the night hung in the air. Allison decided not to relieve the tension with a joke but instead smiled and turned toward the windows, taking a drink of her wine. She let the pinot rest in her mouth for a second, savoring the taste, then swallowed it down.

She soaked in the beauty of the view. The container ship made its way steadily up the Bay, its wake extending back a half mile. A dark band of clouds gathered on the western horizon, ready to come gusting down from the Allegheny Mountains and rip across the Chesapeake. Already lightning strikes forked from the sky and struck land in the distance.

"Looks like it's going to be quite a storm," Allison said.

"Nothing we can't handle. The trick is to be ready for anything."

Allison looked back at the container ship. It looked blurry. She squinted, trying to clear her vision. Arnie noticed.

"Are you all right?" he asked.

"Yeah, it's just . . ." Allison took a step forward to balance herself as a wave of vertigo gripped her. Arnie grabbed her arm.

"Easy there," Arnie said, guiding her toward the couch. She let him lead the way, shaking her head as if that would set the tilting world right side up. Muffled alarm bells sounded in the back of her mind, but she couldn't quite sort out what they meant. She stumbled and spilled her glass of wine on the carpet.

The wine. There was something wrong with the wine.

But the thought flitted away before fully forming. She heard her own voice but it sounded far away. "I . . . I'm sorry . . . all over your nice carpet . . ." She fell again and Arnie caught her.

"Careful, I don't want you to hurt yourself," Arnie said. He leaned in and whispered into her ear. "Because tonight, that's my job."

The alarm bells rang through the cloudiness in her mind and screamed at her—

He drugged you.

Do something or you're dead.

She reached for her ankle. If she could just get to her gun, she'd survive. She thought she was moving with blinding speed, but part of her drugged mind knew she was actually in slow motion, barely able to coordinate her movements.

Finally, she reached her ankle. There wasn't anything there. Her gun was in her purse. She blinked hard and looked for it, but found Arnie's face leering at her instead. He held up the gun from her purse and waved his finger from side to side.

Get out of here, Allison. Run, goddammit.

Summoning everything she had, she lunged forward, took one step, and lost her balance. Her legs buckled and she hit the floor.

Sprawled there, unable to move, she shouted into the microphone sewn into the right side of her dress. At least, she tried to shout. But even though her lips moved, she realized she couldn't be sure she was making any sound at all.

Whether aloud or only in her mind, she repeated the two words over and over.

Richard . . . help . . .
Richard . . . help . . .
Richard . . .

CHAPTER 42

. . . pounded on the outside of the communications van. They'd lost the signal ten minutes ago, and the techs still couldn't give him a straight answer for why the FBI's best equipment had just stopped working.

They floated ideas, from a simple malfunction to a blocking device to the field agent disabling the device on purpose. Bottom line was that they didn't have a fucking clue.

Richard knew he should call it. Send in the local PD he had assembled in support. God, he regretted the phone call he had just made to Mason, but the director had demanded to be briefed in real-time on this case. Mason had shared his opinion that Richard give Allison time. It was against every protocol the FBI had in place for field operations, and as SAC it was his call to make.

But he hadn't climbed this far up the food chain by being a fool.

Mason's opinion was as good as a direct order. And a special agent foolish enough to think otherwise would find himself out of the ladder-climbing business and in the shit assignments business in a hurry.

Five minutes.

He would give her five minutes to make contact or he would go in, whether Mason wanted him to or not.

The pit in his stomach told him he was making a bad call for all the wrong reasons. He climbed back into the communications van to see if his idiot techs had any good news for him.

CHAPTER 43

A stab of pain tore through Allison's body. It started in her chest and shot out her arms and down her legs. She jerked her head up, gasping for air. Every muscle in her body flexed at once. Her back arched and rope dug into her skin. The realization came to her hard and quick.

Jesus Christ, I'm being electrocuted.

No sooner had the thought materialized than the current passing through her body disappeared, and she slumped forward in the chair, panting for breath. Her heart pounded so hard that she thought she might be going into cardiac arrest.

She strained against the ropes tying her to the chair, desperate to orient herself to her surroundings. Concrete walls. A musty smell in the air. She was in a basement. A table directly in front of her had a small television set on it. It didn't make any sense. One minute she had been talking to Arnie, looking at the view, when . . .

She froze. It wasn't that she saw him. Rather, she felt him standing immediately behind her.

"How long have I been out?" she asked.

"Not that long," Arnie replied. "I had to wake you up once I found this."

His hand reached from behind her head and held up a tiny electronic device between his thumb and forefinger.

"I almost missed it. You guys are good."

"Then you know they're already on their way," Allison said, her heart still pounding in her chest. "We can roll this back. Let me go and you can just walk away."

Arnie smiled as he walked around her chair. The facade he usually wore around her was gone; his face and eyes bore the signs of mania she'd seen in the images of so many killers she had studied.

"You can walk out of here, Arnie. Think of Jason."

Arnie reached out and slowly slid the strap off her shoulder. Allison felt her skin prickle where his hand brushed against her skin.

"They're going to be here soon," she whispered, hardly able to breathe.

Arnie slid his hand down her neck and placed it on her chest. He stared blankly into her face as he held his position for several long seconds. Finally, he removed his hand.

"Your heart is reacting to the adrenaline shot I gave you to counteract the drug. I wasn't sure how much to give you to bring you out of it. I hope I didn't overdo it."

"Arnie, I'm a special agent with the FBI. I have backup all around the property. They listened to us the entire time. No way you're getting out of here."

Arnie rolled the tiny microphone between his fingers and then tossed it on the floor. "The thing is, I have toys of my own just in case. A signal scrambler, for example. They haven't heard a thing since you've been here."

Allison struggled against the ropes holding her. She knew it was futile, but she had to try and buy more time. Arnie crossed to the wall and flipped a light switch. Electricity poured into her body from the wire contacts attached to each of her hands. It was a small jolt, but Allison got the message: if you don't listen, you will be punished.

"Standard operating procedure," Allison said when she got her breath back. "The minute they lost contact with me, they started to move in."

Arnie picked up a remote control and turned on the television. The screen showed an image of the road outside Arnie's property. Empty. Arnie pressed button after button, showing different parts of the property. There was no one coming.

Allison choked down a surge of panic. *Why weren't they coming?* She tried to remain calm in front of Arnie, not wanting to give the bastard the satisfaction of seeing how scared she was.

"Yes, I was surprised too," Arnie said. "Then I saw this."

He clicked the button one more time and it showed a long view of the main entrance road. Arnie pointed to a little blotch on the screen far down the road. He toggled another button on the remote, and the camera zoomed in on that part of the image. "Wait for it," Arnie said. "Wait for it."

Slowly, the white communications van with two police cruisers parked behind it came into view. "Not very much backup," Arnie said. "Seems not everyone is taking this very seriously. Should I feel insulted?"

"They'll still come eventually. If you stay, you're going to die. Is that what you want?"

"I'm glad you asked that question," Arnie replied. "Because you know what I really want?"

He waited for Allison to ask him, but she was done with the games. She just stared at him.

"I'll tell you," Arnie continued. "I want you to use this phone to call the special agent in that van and tell him exactly what's written on this card."

He held it up to Allison for her to see. She read through it quickly and broke out into a harsh laugh. "You know I won't do that."

"Oh, I think you will."

Arnie pressed another button on the remote and the screen changed to a bedroom scene. In the center of the screen was Charlie, arms and legs tied to an old-fashioned wooden chair. His face was a bloody and swollen pulp, so battered that Allison almost didn't recognize him at first. His body shook and, even without sound, she could tell he was sobbing. There was a car battery on a table next to him, and two cables snaked their way across the floor and disappeared under his shirt. Thick bands of tape wrapped around his chest to hold them in place.

Jesus. A pain gripped her chest, her breathing reduced to short, ragged gasps. She yanked and jerked against her bindings. A futile effort, full of rage and anger. When she stopped, she was breathing even harder. "Let him go," she barely managed to say. "He has nothing to do with any of this."

Arnie pulled a transmitter from his pocket and pushed a button. Allison watched the TV screen in horror as Charlie's body twitched and jerked. His mouth was open, screaming, but she didn't hear a sound. Which meant either Charlie was in a different location or the basement was soundproof. Arnie kept the button pressed and Charlie continued to flail around.

"Stop! You're killing him!" Allison cried.

"Are you ready to make the phone call?" Arnie asked calmly.

Charlie was only here because of her. Deep inside, she knew both of them were as good as dead, but she had to try. She nodded to Arnie, and he let go of the button. Charlie sagged forward in his chair, moving just enough that Allison could see he was still alive.

Arnie held the phone in front of Allison, ready to dial for her.

"Deviate from the script I wrote by one word, and I'll cut off both of his arms while you watch. Understand?" Allison nodded. "Good. Fifteen seconds into the call, poor Charlie gets the juice." He held up the transmitter for emphasis. "And he keeps getting it until you get off the phone."

"You're a sadistic asshole."

Arnie grinned. "You have no idea."

CHAPTER 44

Richard was just about done waiting. His self-imposed twenty-minute mark had passed five minutes ago and still nothing. Every second that ticked by ratcheted up the guilt he felt for not moving in right away. The techs were out of options, even though they were still going through the motions of adjusting their equipment.

"To hell with this," he muttered to no one in particular. "We're going in."

He pushed open the back of the van and waved to the police officers milling around their cars. As he did, his phone rang. It was a Maryland number he didn't recognize. He almost slid it back into his pocket, but the caller ID showed it came from the immediate area.

"Hello?" he said into the phone.

"Richard, it's me."

"Jesus, Allison, what the hell—"

"No time," Allison's voice came across rushed and breathless. "My phone doesn't work out here. I'm guessing my mic doesn't either."

"Yeah, we lost you when you went inside."

"I think it's some kind of electronic jammer. I used this landline to make contact."

"Come out, now! Make any excuse; just get the hell out."

"I've got it under control. I'll contact you again. He's coming. Got to go."

Click.

Richard almost threw his phone into the empty field next to the van.

"Goddammit, Allison!"

He looked up and saw the police officers watching him carefully. He smiled and waved at them, all the while steaming at Allison's maverick behavior. Some things never changed. He just hoped it wasn't going to get her killed someday.

CHAPTER 45

Allison watched Arnie put the phone in his pocket along with the transmitter. The entire call had taken less than fifteen seconds. Charlie remained hunched over in the TV image, unaware how close he had just come to another electric shock. Allison racked her brain on how she was going to get out of the mess she was in. There hadn't been any time to somehow alert Richard that things were not well. Usually, there were code words to use when speaking under duress, but Arnie must have known that.

An hour. She had to survive the next hour before she'd have another chance. She watched Arnie open a case on a side table and realized staying alive was going to be no easy task. Inside the case, lined up perfectly in a molded spot for each piece, was a set of silver-plated surgical instruments. He passed his hands over the tools slowly, his fingers lingering on each piece. Arnie's expression showed he was a million miles away, a slight smile on his lips, as he reverently looked over his hacksaw, his scalpel, his suturing hooks.

Based on that expression, Allison doubted she would make it the next hour. She had to think of something and she had to do it quickly.

She looked around the room, desperate for anything that might give her an out. The possible solution came from the unlikeliest of sources. It was a long shot, but it was all that she had. An expression from her father reared up in her mind. *The chances are between slim and none, and slim just left the building.*

But she pushed the thought aside. With no other options, she grasped onto the small glimmer of hope she had spotted and used it to focus her attention. If it were going to work, it would need all of her effort plus some good old-fashioned luck thrown into the mix. One thing she knew for certain. If it didn't work, both she and Charlie were as good as dead. And that thought just pissed her off.

CHAPTER 46

Arnie loved this part. The foreplay right before the main attraction. The anticipation. The infinite universe of possibilities. Once he started, once he chose which FBI profile to mimic, then the choices narrowed. After he cut into flesh and chiseled through bone, the choices narrowed even more. Then there was the delicate dance between his fun and the moment where his subject lost consciousness. The game didn't end there, but without the reaction of a live subject, it became a butcher's job. But he had grown to like that part too.

He justified the gruesome killings as part of his strategy to throw off the FBI, but part of him knew he was chasing the high from his first kill twelve years ago. Part of him knew that no matter what he did, he was chasing the wind. Elusive and forever out of reach.

But every kill still gave him a taste of that first exhilaration, not nearly with the same intensity, but enough to make him feel alive. And that was the trick of it. He needed this thrill, this sense of power, so that he didn't slide back into the thing he once was. Weak, confused, unwilling to stand up for himself or for his son.

He'd tried to give it up. For Jason. The odds of evading capture were against him, after all. Serial killers got caught. And when they did, everyone in their lives was branded with the stigma. So once, several years ago, he'd packed his tools away and resolved to find other outlets for his dark yearnings. It was the only way to protect his son.

But after only a few months, the itch started. Quietly at first. A whispered suggestion in the back of his mind when he crossed paths with a good candidate for his knife. An attraction to reading true crime books of the world's most notorious killers. Worst of all, self-doubt and anxiety reentered his mind like water pouring into a boat with a ruptured hull.

He was a terrible father.

He'd only been lucky in the stock market.

He was ugly, and women only approached him for his money.

He was a fraud.

These insecurities were weights around his neck, bearing him down deeper and deeper until he realized he was regressing back to the terrible person he'd been before the convenience store. Before he set the bed sheets on fire around his passed-out wife. He understood then that he couldn't stop. Not unless he wanted things to go back to the way they were before.

So, he'd killed a waitress in a motel near Orlando. After he fed her piece by piece to gators and basked in the glow of a fresh kill, Arnie decided all of the commercials were right. Orlando actually was the happiest place on Earth. He bounced right back. No more insecurity. No more voices. Only the sense of total power.

After that, he never let anything get in his way. And that included the goddamn FBI.

CHAPTER 47

Charlie slumped forward, the zip ties that bound his wrists to the wooden spindles of the chair digging into his skin. He blinked hard, trying to clear his eyes of the tears and blood obscuring his vision. Every part of his body hurt. There were small knife cuts across his arms and legs that bled long rivulets of blood down his limbs. Each breath he took sent shockwaves of pain through his body from cracked and broken ribs. His head ached so badly that he shook it thinking there might be some kind of diabolical tool attached to him, squeezing his skull until it popped. But he didn't feel any extra weight, and the shaking only made it hurt worse. The pain was from inside his head, and it felt like his head was going to explode

He whimpered as his eyes followed the two wires appearing from under his shirt, leading down from his body, across the plastic sheeting on the floor beneath him, and terminating into a car battery nearby. The most recent electric shock left him limp, left his nerves raw and tingling. He didn't know if he could stand another round.

The only thing worse than the pain and the anticipation of the next electric shock was the lack of sensation on his face. That felt completely numb. Just deadweight hanging onto his skull like a thick callus peeled back. There were no mirrors in the room so he couldn't see himself. Not that he really wanted to. His thinking was clear enough to remember the beating Arnie gave him. And he remembered the way the asshole smiled while he did it.

Charlie felt a wave of guilt for the way he begged and whimpered for Arnie to stop. Toward the end, he didn't even feel human, just an animal trying to crawl away from the monster killing him one small cut at a time.

But the final blow never came. There was a reason for that, but Charlie couldn't remember what it was.

God, he was thirsty. He tried to swallow, but his dry throat constricted so forcibly that he felt choked. He gasped for air, then coughed hard, sending a splatter of blood across the plastic sheeting. The memory of a TV show came to him. A serial killer who laid out plastic before he finished off his victims. But in that show, the killer only murdered bad people. Charlie was no saint, but he didn't deserve this.

Neither does Allison.

The thought hit him with the power of another electric shock. His head jerked up, a rush of adrenaline clearing his head. He remembered Arnie goading him, the bastard listing the things he planned to do to Allison once she got there. He recalled the flat edge of a knife blade dragged across his chest as Arnie whispered how he would finish Charlie off once he was done with Allison. He promised it would be a quick ending. A mercy gesture meant as a thank-you. After all, he said, without Charlie, he would never have known what a threat Allison was to him.

And there it was. The truth that hurt more than anything Arnie could do to him. Charlie wasn't just going to die, but he was going to die a sniveling coward who was responsible for getting an innocent woman tortured and killed. He pictured Allison locked in the basement dungeon. He imagined her screams as the bastard cut into her flesh.

And it was all on him.

He looked up, his vision clearer now, the distance from his last shock giving him time to recover. He noticed the small webcam for the first time on the table facing him. Somehow he knew that Arnie was on the other end of the camera. That he was using him as a tool to control Allison just like he promised he would.

Rage built up inside him. There was a power behind it unlike anything he'd felt before. It was animalistic and primal. And he let it flow through him.

He bucked and arched his back. Struggled against the zip ties, his wrists turning slick with blood. His grunts filled the air. The zip ties cut deeper into his skin, but he was beyond caring. He twisted and jerked in the chair like a wild animal caught in a steel trap.

One of the chair legs buckled and Charlie collapsed to the floor, landing on his side. He cried out in frustration and kicked his legs.

Only this time one of them came free, the chair leg still attached by the zip tie to his ankle, but free of the rest of the chair.

An involuntary chuckle mixed with a sob as he allowed himself the first hope that he might be able to get free. He looked sharply at the webcam, wondering if Arnie already knew he was breaking out. But he couldn't, otherwise the car battery would be doing its worst to him.

He used his free leg to reach out to the battery cables and kicked at them frantically, paranoid that the voltage would hammer into him at any second.

But it didn't. The wires were taped tight to his chest, but by wrapping his leg around the cables he was able to get enough leverage to yank them off of his body.

He gasped for breath from the exertion, but the adrenaline being pumped through his system gave him strength he wouldn't have believed he had only minutes before. He stood up, balancing on one foot, then threw himself at the nearest wall, smashing the chair with his body.

The world flared hot white from the pain, and he dropped to the floor. But Charlie growled like an animal, rolled over, and got back up to do it again. The pain didn't matter, not anymore. All that mattered was survival.

He reared back and smashed into the wall again, this time the spindle attached to his right hand broke free.

He paused for a second, holding his bloody hand out in front of him for balance.

Charlie's swollen, misshapen face twisted into a grin.

He intended to do more than just survive.

CHAPTER 48

"If you're going to kill me, at least tell me why you're doing it," Allison said.

Arnie removed the instruments one by one from the case and laid them on the table. "I think you already know the answer to that, don't you? Let's not be boring." He held up a nasty-looking metal suture hook. "The more interesting question is what brought you to my doorstep? Why did you come looking for me?"

"Your name was flagged on a white-collar crime case. Stock manipulation," Allison said. "Then again in the Suzanne Greenville case. A prostitute killed in the District."

"I know all that, but I want to know why you chased me down so hard. Why you were so sure I was guilty."

"Just trying to be thorough," Allison replied, trying to sound smug. She did everything she could not to look at the TV screen that showed Charlie's room. He was nearly free of the chair now. He only needed another minute or two to be free and then at least he could get the hell out of there. But no matter how hard she tried not to look, whenever Arnie turned away for even a second, her eyes involuntarily went to it. She needed to stall Arnie longer.

Arnie laughed. "You need to be a more convincing liar to play this game, Special Agent McNeil. I've had time to piece things together. The way you happened to be at McGarvey's. The way you slow-played me when I first hit on you. How you even said no to the boat ride the first day. I admit, you played me like a pro."

Arnie started to turn around. Allison's stomach clenched. Her one chance about to be blown.

"The problem was," Allison blurted out, "I was attracted to you."

Thankfully, this stopped Arnie in place. Allison tried not to show any emotion, but relief washed through her. By his reaction, Arnie hadn't looked at the TV screen.

But it was short-lived as Arnie smiled and shook his head.

"That's a little heavy-handed, don't you think?" he asked. "I expected better from you."

Allison pressed on. "It wasn't supposed to happen that way, but it did. There were ghosts for me in Annapolis, ghosts that made me feel weak. I'm tired of feeling that way. And I think you can relate to that. I think you figured a way out from that feeling."

Arnie hesitated. It took every bit of willpower for Allison to keep from looking at the TV right behind him.

With her peripheral vision, she could see that Charlie was no longer on the screen.

Arnie only had to turn around to see that his prisoner was gone. Allison had to keep his attention on her. She decided to throw all her cards on the table.

"That's why you killed those two at the convenience store in Baltimore, right? To take control?"

Arnie took a quick step forward and sliced through the air with the metal hook. Allison flinched as he pressed it hard against her cheek, its point making a depression on her skin. "Why do you think I killed both of them?" he snarled. "Who else thinks it?"

Allison ignored the ugly hook right below her eye. His reaction was just what she had hoped for. She stared him down and savored it. Because for that moment, she was in control.

"Just me," she said. "My theory. But I'm right, aren't I?"

Arnie didn't flinch as he sunk the tip of the metal hook into Allison's cheek. She whimpered from the pain and felt a trickle of blood dripping down her face.

"I want to know everything," Arnie said calmly. "Who else in the FBI thinks I killed both of them?"

"I told you, just me. It was a case study at the academy."

"Bullshit!" Arnie shouted, losing his cool. He quickly brought himself back under control. "This can be quick or this can be more painful than you could ever imagine." Allison cried out as the tip of the hook pierced through the inside of her cheek and sank into her gums above her back teeth. "Tell me."

She chanced the shortest glance she could manage at the TV screen and confirmed that Charlie was long gone.

She wondered whether he would run or call the police. If he found a phone, word would get to Richard right away and she might have a chance. If he ran, there was no telling which direction he would go and whether Richard's team would spot him. Either way, Charlie would be safe. Now she had to figure out how she was going to survive.

"Don't believe . . . if . . . don't want to," Allison said, her words coming slow and garbled from both the pain and the hook in her mouth. Arnie retracted the instrument so she could speak. "If I don't come out of here alive, they're going to know you're a killer anyway, so what do you care?"

"Because it's my secret!" he shouted. "It's my private moment! Not yours! Mine!" Arnie took a deep breath and fought to get back under control. "Perhaps you're right. Maybe we should just move on." He started to turn, only a short motion away from seeing that Charlie had escaped.

"Wait!" Allison cried. Arnie looked at her, the first time she thought he looked suspicious of her. "I just . . . I want to know. I basically threw my career away on this. Maybe my life too." Her voice changed to a whisper. "Why? Why the kid behind the counter?"

Arnie smiled. "The first one. The criminal. That was just rage. The second one was a decision. I had to know I could do it again. I had to know I could have that feeling of pure power whenever I needed it. It changed me. It changed everything."

Allison fixed him with her eyes. "That's why I came here, even suspecting who you really were. I want what you have. I want that power. The FBI doesn't give a care about me. It's still a bullshit men's club."

"And when they know about Craig Gerty, it makes it even worse, doesn't it?" Arnie said with a smirk at Allison's surprise. "Oh yes, I know all about that. Your friend Charlie," he swung around and pointed to the TV screen . . . and froze.

The screen was empty.

That same second, Charlie burst into the basement. His face twisted into an animal snarl, spittle hanging from his chin, his shirt covered with blood.

He ran at Arnie, a butcher's knife in one hand and a metal fireplace poker in the other. Weapons picked up from the house above.

Arnie dodged the knife thrust but took a smash from the poker to the side of the head.

He gripped Charlie's wrist and bent it backward until Charlie screamed from the pain. The knife tumbled to the floor.

Allison watched helplessly as the men fought back and forth across the room.

Charlie broke loose and swung the poker mercilessly, bashing Arnie's forearms and shoulders.

Then he swung low and slammed Arnie behind one of his knees, dropping him to the floor. With a flurry of blows, Charlie pounded Arnie into submission. Striking his torso, his legs. Anything exposed.

Arnie curled up, doing his best to protect his head from the brutal onslaught.

Finally, Charlie stopped, holding the poker like a baseball bat, ready to strike again if Arnie moved.

He didn't.

Charlie lowered the poker and slowly turned to Allison.

"Are you OK?" he mumbled through swollen lips.

CHAPTER 49

Allison nodded, fighting back tears. "Christ, Charlie . . . Look at you . . . I'm sorry . . . so sorry I dragged you into this."

Charlie waved her off. "Let's just get the hell out of here." Charlie tugged on the ropes around Allison's arms, untying the knots. Once loosened, she wriggled out of the rest.

"I can undo my legs. Did you call for help?"

Charlie shook his head. "I came straight down here. The bastard had me here for a while, so I knew where to look."

Allison pulled on the knot around her ankles. "There's a cordless phone in his pocket. Grab it and click redial. There's backup just down the road."

"Backup. I like the sound of that." Charlie grabbed his poker and carefully approached Arnie's still body. He stuck the sharp end of the poker between Arnie's shoulder blades and poked him roughly. No movement. "I think maybe he's dead," Charlie whispered. "I've never killed anyone before."

"Charlie, listen to me. Just block all that out, OK? Grab the phone and make the call."

Charlie nodded. He reached into Arnie's pocket and slowly pulled out the phone. He held the phone in one hand and tried to hit the redial button, but his hands shook too hard.

"I can't," he said. "My hands won't stop."

Allison fought the last tangle of rope around her legs. "Take a breath. You can do it. Just try."

Charlie stabbed at the phone with his finger. He stared at the screen for a second then broke out into a wide grin. "I got it. The call's—"

Charlie's scream was so unexpected that it almost made Allison roll out of the chair for cover. He dropped the poker and clawed behind his head, reaching for his back.

"Charlie!" Allison yelled.

He sagged to his knees, revealing Arnie, bloody and snarling, standing behind him. Charlie twisted as he fell to the concrete floor, the butcher knife sticking out between his shoulder blades.

Arnie's and Allison's eyes met. For a beat, they froze and stared at each other. Allison felt a rush of hatred fill her, a cold and brutal emotion that made her heart pound fast in her chest and every muscle in her body flex in preparation for action.

Arnie's expression was the same one she'd seen flicker across his face on the boat after saving Jason's life. Only this time the good-guy persona didn't reappear. Only the pure anger and hatred remained.

A voice broke the silence. It was soft, barely intelligible.

"Hello? Who is this?"

Richard. His voice coming from the phone that had skittered across the basement floor when Charlie had fallen.

The call had gone through.

Arnie sprinted toward the phone.

Allison tore at the final knots holding her legs as she screamed, "Richard! Help! In the basement. Richard!"

Arnie stomped on the phone and smashed it into the floor.

Allison pulled the last of the rope away and sprang from the chair, searching for a weapon. She grabbed the poker and held it in front of her.

"You're not getting out of here, you bastard. They'll be here in a minute."

Arnie looked too calm. She didn't like that one bit.

"You're half-right," he said, picking up a steel pipe leaning against the wall. It was the length of a baseball bat and wrapped on the bottom with rubber grips. "They're coming, but I won't be here." Arnie crossed to the door. Next to it was the breaker box. "We'll have to pick up where we left off at a later date. But don't worry, I won't forget about you." He opened the panel and put his hand on the main breaker. "And don't try to follow me. I'd hate to see you get hurt in such a crude way. Bye for now."

Arnie smashed the breaker box with the steel pipe. Sparks burst from the wall and the lights turned off. She heard the basement door slam, but the sparks had been short-lived and the room was pitch black. She froze in place, thinking it might be a ruse. She imagined Arnie stepping carefully through the dark room, step-by-step, the pipe raised over his head, until he was right in front of her. But as she listened, she heard the unmistakable sound of steps on stairs. He was on the run.

Allison crawled on the floor until she was next to Charlie. She felt for a pulse. It was there, but weak.

She propped him up so he wouldn't roll back over on the knife. She looked in the direction of the door, then back at Charlie.

"I'm sorry, Charlie," she whispered. "They'll be here in a minute to help you."

She walked carefully through the room, her hands outstretched until she found the door. She flung it open and ran up the basement stairs to the main floor.

CHAPTER 50

It was night now, and none of the lights were on in the house. Wind howled outside and rain pounded on the windows. Allison couldn't see anything. She put her hand on the light switch and flipped it on. Nothing. Arnie had killed the power to the entire property. But she realized the dark could be an advantage either of them could use.

She grasped the metal poker, willing her hands to stop shaking, and walked along the wall.

Get control of yourself.

Allison didn't know if she was still feeling the effects of the drugs mixed with the adrenaline shot, but her heart thumped in her chest so hard that she thought the sound might give her away.

Lightning lit up the sky, casting sharp shadows through the two-story living room.

The door leading to the patio was open, swinging open and shut from the storm raging outside.

He's going to the boat. That's his way out.

Thunder rattled the windows as she sprinted across the room, using light from more flashes of lightning to make her way.

She flung open the door—and ran right into Arnie.

His hands gripped her shoulders.

Fingers digging into her skin.

She shouted and brought a knee up into his groin.

It wasn't a direct hit, but enough to make him slump forward and loosen his grip on her.

She reared back with the metal poker over her head.

"Goddammit, Allison, stop!" the man shouted in her face over the thunder. "Allison!"

Lightning flashed and she saw that it wasn't Arnie; it was Richard. She lowered the poker and hugged him, allowing herself a few seconds to feel safe. But the reunion was short-lived. "There's a hostage in the basement. He's hurt badly."

"Where's Arnie?" Richard said.

"I think he went to his boat. But I can't be sure. He might still be in the house."

Richard raised a radio to his lips. "Go, go, go."

Behind them, the front door burst open and police entered the house, guns drawn.

"Friendly in the basement. Needs immediate medical," Richard shouted.

Allison pulled away from Richard but he still held her arm, as if reluctant to let her too far from his reach. "I'll check the boat; you clear the house."

"No way," Richard said. "We're sticking together. Let's go."

Together, they ran across the stone patio and down onto the gravel trail that led to the cliff edge. Leaves and loose twigs flew through the air as the trees around them were blown mercilessly by the storm.

They reached the wooden stairs that zigzagged back and forth across the cliff face before ending at the pier thirty feet below. Arnie's catamaran was docked there, and a light glowed inside the main cabin.

Richard checked his gun. "Come on! Let's get this son of a bitch!" he yelled over the howling wind.

She grabbed his arm. "Wait, something's not right."

"He's going to get away. No chance he can fly in this mess. It's just us."

Allison heard Arnie's voice in her head.

Don't try to follow me.

Allison looked at the wooden stairs leading down the cliff face. Right under them was a bulkhead of jagged rocks.

I'd hate to see you get hurt in such a crude way.

"C'mon. Let's go," Richard yelled.

"Richard, trust me," Allison pleaded. "I have a bad feeling about this."

"No time for that," he shouted back. "We have a job to do." He turned and sprinted down the stairs.

"Richard, wait!" Allison shouted.

It was too late. Richard took the first three steps at once and jumped onto the first landing. The entire thing gave way in a sickening crunch of splintering wood. Richard spun, arms flailing wildly for a split second . . . and then he was gone.

"No!" Allison screamed.

Carefully, she climbed down the steps that remained bolted into the side of the cliff until she could look down. Richard lay sprawled on the rocks, his back bent at an impossible angle. He wasn't moving.

"Oh God! No. No," Allison cried. She saw movement on the catamaran and shrank back into the shadows. Arnie walked to the edge of the hull and looked at the collapsed staircase. A flashlight came on and it danced back and forth across the cliff, lighting up the wreckage. Allison pushed back behind a bulge in the rock. It didn't cover her completely, but she hoped it would be enough given the distance and the rain.

The flashlight beam passed within inches of her and stopped. She sucked in a breath and pushed back harder against the rock face. If she had any chance at all, she needed the element of surprise.

The light hesitated for a few seconds and then moved on. She exhaled slowly but caught her breath and stifled a cry when the flashlight beam swung over to Richard's unmoving body. It lingered there for nearly a minute before turning off.

She leaned back against the rock, fighting to control her emotions. Her chest felt like it was being crushed by a vice. She was underwater, unable to catch her breath. Her trained mind recognized the signs of a panic attack, but the animal part of her brain, the part wired with the fight-or-flight instinct, didn't care about the diagnosis. It only knew that Richard was likely dead, and Arnie was going to get away with it. Unless she did something.

Instead of fighting her instincts, she decided to give herself over to them. If her choices were fight or flight, she reached deep into herself and picked between them. It was a decision forged from a decade of anger and pain. She would fight. And with the decision, as if preparing for action, the pain in her chest released its hold on her, and she was able to catch her breath finally. She steadied herself, feeling an unnatural calm come over her, and got to work on how she was going to get down to Arnie before he escaped.

Allison examined what was left of the staircase. It still looked sturdy below the section that Arnie had booby-trapped. She saw Arnie moving deliberately around the catamaran, preparing to sail in the middle of gale-force winds. Her only hope was that he would be so focused on getting ready that he wouldn't reexamine the stairs.

Allison eased her way down to where the wooden pylons had broken away. She tested her weight on each step, cautious that Richard may have only found the first of many traps.

I'd hate to see you get hurt in such a crude way.

For once tonight, Allison agreed with the serial killer she was chasing.

The gap in the stairs was a good eight feet wide. There was still a twenty-foot drop if she fell. With the real reason she was chasing Arnie

Milhouse front and center in her mind, she didn't think twice about the risk.

Giving it everything she had, she jumped through the air.

As soon as she launched herself, she knew she was going to come up short.

She arched her body and reached out as far as she could, bracing for the impact.

With a whack that knocked the air out of her, she hit the stairs with her chest.

She slid backward, clawing for a handhold on the wet, slippery boards.

At the last second, she wrapped a hand around a half-broken support post and stopped her fall.

Her entire body dangled in open air, buffeted by the winds and rain.

She pulled herself up onto the stairs with a grunt and took a second to catch her breath. She rolled her head to the side to see if Arnie had noticed her. Even with only the small amount of light coming from the main cabin, she could tell he hadn't seen her.

She breathed a sigh of relief . . . until she realized that Arnie had just cast off one of the main lines.

He was about to leave.

She pulled herself up and sprinted down the stairs. There was no time to worry about any more traps. If she had a chance at all, she had to go, and go fast.

Three steps at a time. Then four. She flew down the steps, half running, half falling.

She reached the bottom and hit the pier running.

The catamaran was already underway.

She sprinted the length of the pier, digging her heels hard.

The catamaran slid along the edge of the pier, a second away from being out of reach.

Allison planted her foot and jumped through the air—

—and landed on the back hull, grabbing a handful of rigging to keep her on board.

She got her balance and crouched down low to the deck. Arnie was busy piloting the catamaran from the wheel in the middle of the boat, and the sound of the rough water had disguised her hard landing.

Allison held on tightly as he steered the cat into the center of the Chesapeake and straight into one of the most violent storms of the year. She had no idea what she planned to do next, but she knew whatever it was, she had to do it quickly while she still had the element of surprise on her side.

CHAPTER 51

The Bay matched the thunderstorm in its rage. Whitecaps rolled up and over the twin hulls of the catamaran, and massive swells bashed violently against it. Arnie steered diagonally through the waves, the catamaran's twin Mercury motors whirring loudly when their rotors pulled completely out of the water. The sails remained tied down. The howling wind would give them breakneck speed, but it would also either slash the sails or flip the boat over.

Even with just the motors, the catamaran plowed through the Bay. The wide design gave it more stability than a regular boat. The thousands of gallons of water that poured over the side with each wave simply drained through the netting stretched between the hulls, both aft and stern.

Arnie white-knuckled the wheel. Not from the stress of sailing into the storm—that was a cakewalk. He'd sought out days like this to challenge himself on the water. No, he didn't like how messy things had become in the last few hours. Control was the essential ingredient to evading capture, and both here and in Miami he'd made bad choices. Choices that left a trail and put him in danger.

The real problem was that he knew he was exposing himself to these risks on purpose. The adrenaline rush of the kill wasn't enough anymore. It wasn't enough to hold a life in his hands, squeezing it until there was nothing left but pulp and bone.

The close calls with law enforcement had taken it all to the next level. He hadn't felt more alive and powerful in years. And that's what made it dangerous. He was playing with fire. Even tonight, if the FBI had come with a SWAT team, or if the storm hadn't been bad enough to keep a helicopter from tracking him, or if Allison had picked up that something was wrong and used a gun, or . . . or if a hundred other things had gone differently, he'd be on his way to prison or lying face-down in a pool of his own blood.

And where would that leave Jason?

An orphan. Probably a ward of the state once they found him.

That wasn't acceptable. Arnie decided right then that he would make a clean break and go back to the way things used to be. With his new alias set up in Florida, he and Jason would live under the radar. Giancarlo assured him that he'd done this exact thing for people dozens of times. That he and Jason would be safe.

He would kill, of course. That always had to be there. But he vowed to stop taking these ridiculous risks. Life was too short to spend it in prison. And a boy needed his father.

Even in the middle of the raging storm, Arnie felt himself relax. The FBI was behind him. He wondered how aggressively Allison would seek him out. She'd proven more resourceful than he'd expected. More tenacious. But if it hadn't been for Charlie escaping, she'd already be dead.

No, Arnie didn't think she had the stomach to chase him for long. She'd had a taste of what he could do. How he could exert his power over her. There was no way she wanted more of that. He doubted he would ever have to worry about Allison McNeil again.

Allison stared Arnie down from the back of the boat. She wrapped the rope from some of the rigging around her arm to keep the waves from sweeping her off the deck and into the roiling churn of water. She considered for a second that she could hide out until Arnie reached whatever destination he had planned and then attack him there. But she knew it was wishful thinking.

The second Arnie turned around to check the rear of the catamaran, he would spot her. There was no place to hide. And if he had a gun on board, which seemed likely, she'd be an easy target.

Well, maybe not easy, as the bucking deck and the rain would make shooting her a challenge, but he would have as many shots as he had ammunition. If that happened, her only option would be to jump overboard. One look at the black, angry water around her and she knew that was near-certain death.

Like it or not, she had to make her move now.

She lay flat on the deck and pulled herself along using whatever she could get her hands on. This kept her profile low so that the waves washed over her and minimized the chance Arnie would spot her if he looked over his shoulder.

Closer and closer.

A massive swell caught the boat at an odd angle, plowing the entire hull under water. Allison gasped for air at the wrong time and choked down a mouthful of water. She felt her entire body lift off the deck as the swell nearly ripped her from the boat. Only the rope in her right hand kept her from being tossed across to the other side of the catamaran and probably off the boat entirely.

When the hull popped back to the surface, Allison hacked water out of her lungs, gasping for air. Her legs dangled over the netting stretched between the hulls. She quickly pulled them back in and eyed Arnie.

He continued facing forward, as calm as if he were motoring on the Bay in eighty-degree weather with glassy surface conditions.

She looked around to see what she could use as a weapon. Everything had been secured for the bad weather, so there weren't any poles or gaffs lying around.

Her hand found a coil of extra rope tied off on a strut. She quickly unwound it, estimating it was about twenty feet long. She tied one end into a crude hangman's noose. It wasn't great, but it was all she had.

Fighting the waves, she crawled toward Arnie, the rope clutched to her side.

Only a few feet away, she tied the end of the rope to a rail and climbed to her feet. Holding the noose in front of her, she rocked with the motion of the boat to keep her balance. She'd only get one shot at this. And, at that moment, she was totally exposed. If Arnie turned around, he'd be looking right at her.

She leaped forward, slid the rope around his neck, and yanked back as hard as she could.

Arnie spun in place, arms flailing.

Allison fell but held on to the rope, cinching it hard around Arnie's throat.

Arnie grabbed at the rope.

Lightning flashed and Allison saw his face twisted in a grotesque mask of pain and surprise. His eyes bulged out of their sockets. His mouth gaped open for air.

Then he did the unexpected; he ran straight at her.

Allison braced herself for the impact.

Snarling, he bore down on her.

At the last second, she turned, grabbed the side of his body, and used his momentum to heave him past her and over the side of the boat.

The catamaran hit a wave right as he flew through the air. The rope, tied to the railing, snapped tight.

His body jerked, neck twisting nearly backward, then slammed into the water.

The railing held and the rope pulled taut as Arnie's body was dragged behind the boat.

Allison went to grab the rope, ready to pull him in. She hesitated, looked back into the darkness of the storm, and thought better of it. Instead, she flipped on the high-powered floodlight next to the wheel and swiveled it until it pointed behind the boat.

Arnie's body dragged lifelessly through the water.

It wasn't worth the effort to haul him in.

Allison let out a sob, an emotional release that it was finally over. The chase that had started more than a decade ago was done. The promise she'd made had been kept.

It wasn't how she'd imagined it would turn out. There would be no trial. No final confrontation. No satisfaction when he found out who she really was and why she had spent her adult life preparing to bring him down.

Still, without all those things, she was happy the son of a bitch was dead.

Now she just needed to make sure she didn't join him in a watery grave.

She staggered over to the main hatch that led to the large living area down below. There had to be a radio down there. Maybe even an emergency beacon. She timed opening the door with the waves, aware that it would only take seconds to flood the hulls. With a yank on the hatch, she ducked inside into the dry safety of the cabin.

Only after she slammed the hatch behind her did she realize how loud the storm was outside. Even inside, sealed off from the worst of it, the wind howled and thunder rattled the windows.

She flipped the switches on the wall and the cabin lit up. It looked like the living room in a high-end furniture catalog, completely out of place compared to the dark world outside.

It made sense to her that the radio would be near the door for easy access, but she didn't see one. She tore open the cabinets and rifled through closets. Nothing.

Allison crossed the room, searching the cabinets in the hallway leading to the stateroom in the catamaran's bow. Bingo. The boat's emergency kit. In a clear plastic tub, she found a flare gun, a strobe light, and, most importantly, an emergency transponder. No sign of a radio anywhere, but she hoped the transponder would do the trick.

She ripped open the directions that were taped to it and poured over them. She was halfway through when she heard a sound that made her stomach turn.

It wasn't the grating sound of the hull on rocks.

It wasn't the gush of water pouring into the hull.

It was the sound of the storm filling the cabin as the hatch opened, followed seconds later by the hatch reclosing and the relative quiet returning to the cabin.

Quiet, that is, except for the sound of wet footsteps across the floor.

The closet doors blocked her view of the main room, but she knew who it was.

Arnie.

CHAPTER 52

Allison cursed herself for not pulling his body in and making sure he was dead. How could she have been so stupid?

She grabbed the flare gun and crouched to the ground, trying to get it loaded. The steps paused.

"Allison," Arnie whispered hoarsely. "Come out, come out, wherever you are."

The flare shell tumbled out of her fingers and hit the floor. The boat tilted precariously to the side, and the flare rolled down the hall toward Arnie.

"I can see you," Arnie called out. "C'mon. Let's play."

Allison slid past the closet door and took a firing stance, the flare gun gripped in both hands. She froze for a second on seeing Arnie. Blood poured from a ragged gash across his throat, covering his clothes. His eyes were wild. Bruised, swollen lips were pulled back in a snarl showing blood-stained teeth. He looked more like an animal than a man. "On your knees, Arnie! Right now."

Arnie smiled. "There you are. I've been looking for you."

He stumbled a little as the boat rolled. He seemed out of it. Maybe in shock. But Allison knew better than to underestimate him. She wasn't taking any chances.

"I said get on the goddamn floor, Arnie!" she yelled. "Or so help me, I'll shoot you right here and now."

Arnie lowered his head, cowed. "Don't want any problems, OK? No muss, no fuss."

Arnie held a hand to his throat as blood trickled out. He was pale, his lips blue from the cold water. "I'm so fucking smart, I'm stupid. Right? Isn't that right? My wife always said . . . she always said I was. No muss, no fuss."

He wasn't making sense now. Allison didn't think he could stay on his feet much longer.

"Sit down, Arnie. Right over there."

Arnie ignored her. "Why?" Arnie mumbled, fighting to keep consciousness. "Why did you . . . did you . . ."

Allison chanced a glance at the flare shell, rolling back and forth on the floor with each swell. Even in Arnie's weakened state, she knew she'd feel a lot better with the gun loaded. She moved toward it slowly as she spoke.

"Why did I risk everything to catch you?" Allison asked. "It could be that I'm ambitious and wanted to prove myself. But that's not it." She trapped the shell with her foot. "It could be that I needed to do this to prove to myself that I could take control and not be a victim." She bent down and picked up the shell. "But that's not it either."

"Then what?" Arnie slurred. "What was it?"

Allison slid the flare shell into the gun's chamber. "My sophomore year in college, I got a phone call from my dad. He was crying. Dad never cried." She snapped the gun in place. "It took me a minute to understand what he was saying. Then I finally got it. My kid brother was dead. Only a high school senior, and he was dead."

Arnie's eyes went wide as he pieced it together. Allison savored the moment. This was the script she'd written and rewritten in her head for all those years. This was the scene she'd played out in her mind during the long hours of studying her criminal justice courses. During the years of training in the FBI. During the hundreds of off-duty hours put into cold cases and tracking down dead-end leads. This was it.

This was the way it was supposed to go.

"Oh my God," Arnie whispered. "Edgar. The kid in the convenience store."

"Don't say his name," Allison spat. "You don't deserve to say his name."

"No, no. He taught me how . . . he taught me t-t-to fly. I jumped . . . from the canyon wall. H-h-h-e made me who I am."

"How dare you say that? He was just a kid."

"I'm sorry . . ." Arnie mumbled.

"I pledged to find his killer . . ."

"I'm sorry . . ." Arnie's eyes sagged.

". . . and avenge his death." Allison said, her voice stone cold.

Arnie's head hung low. "I'm sorry to disappoint you . . ." he mumbled, barely audible. "But that's not how it's going to work out."

With surprising speed, Arnie lunged across the room. All the disorientation and weakness had been an act. And it worked. Allison was caught off guard. Arnie smashed into her, and the flare gun went flying.

Allison fell and Arnie landed on top of her. The blood from his neck wound poured onto her face and mouth. She spit and hacked it up, wrenching her body left and right to get him off. But he was too strong.

Strong hands wrapped around her neck.

She looked up and it wasn't Arnie anymore. It was Craig Gerty. Red-faced and straining. She closed her eyes to block out the image. When she opened them it was Arnie again, his face contorted in anger. The edges of her vision blackened.

Then something in her clicked.

I'm not giving in, you mother fucker. Not this time.

Allison used the slipperiness of Arnie's own blood and slid her hands into his grip. In one motion, she leveraged the pressure points on his wrists and collapsed his hold on her neck.

But Arnie wasn't going easily. He head butted her, and she almost blacked out from the blow. Arnie used her disorientation to lean back and slam a fist across her jaw.

He leaned back again, but this time she was ready for him. She rolled to the side, and his punch smashed into the floor.

She rolled the opposite direction, pinning his arm to the floor and bending it backward at the elbow. She flung a wild elbow and it connected with Arnie's temple.

He sagged to the floor, but only for a second. With a grunt, he got back on his knees, too exhausted to stand. He pulled back to punch her again, but Allison was too fast. She lunged forward and delivered a vicious punch to his throat.

Arnie rose up, grabbing his wound. She took the opening and pulled up her right leg, then landed a kick across his jaw.

Arnie flew back and landed hard on the floor.

Allison scrambled for the flare gun, grabbed it, then shoulder-rolled up into a crouched firing position.

Arnie ran at her. Hands outstretched. Mouth open in a primal scream, foaming with spit and blood.

Allison didn't hesitate. She eased back on the trigger just like the tens of thousands of times she'd practiced on the range, pretending Edgar's killer was on the receiving end of each shot.

Instead of a small caliber bullet making a small tear in a paper target, the flare projectile exploded from the gun and found its target.

Right into Arnie's mouth.

It shattered a few teeth on the way in, but it fit.

The flare ignited inside Arnie. White phosphorus blew through the thin skin of his cheeks. Ripped out the soft tissue of his sinuses. Melted his eyeballs and shot out from his sockets.

Impossibly, he fell to his knees and remained upright, his head shaking as the flare burned hotter inside his skull.

Allison couldn't take the sight anymore. She kicked Arnie's side and he toppled over, his head now engulfed in light.

The boat hit a swell hard, and Allison had to grip the wall to stay on her feet. It was a reminder that even with Arnie dead, she wasn't safe yet. Gasping for air, she grabbed the emergency beacon and made her way to the hatch.

The wild gust of the storm was a welcome relief as she climbed back on deck. She took long, deep breaths, trying to settle her stomach.

She punched a button and activated the emergency beacon. It came to life in her hands, lighting up and pulsing comfortingly. She grabbed the steering wheel and turned the catamaran into the wind. Given the conditions, she wasn't sure how long it would take them to come for her, or even if anyone would. But if the Coast Guard showed up, they wouldn't find her huddled in a corner waiting to be rescued. That Allison was gone forever.

Instead, she gripped the wheel and set her course toward lights in the distance that she hoped would be a shoreline. As the catamaran cut through the waves, she allowed tears for both Richard and Charlie to flow freely down her cheeks. She cried for the life her brother never had a chance to experience. And she kept part of her grief for herself and for the gaping hole in her that had so long been filled by her need for vengeance. A hole that now still felt empty.

She allowed the sadness in because she knew now that she was strong enough to handle it. The walls she'd erected around herself were no longer necessary. She knew a truth that Arnie Milhouse never grasped. Allison understood that true power didn't come from dominating others; it came from peace within herself. From being comfortable in her own skin and confident in who she was.

With a smile, Allison rode confidently into the storm. Unsure of her destination but more ready than ever for the journey.

EPILOGUE

The debriefing after the raid on Arnie's house took a couple of days. Director Mason did his part to exert control over the turf war that erupted over jurisdiction of the case, not to mention the inevitable media frenzy right afterward. He only asked her once about whether the call girl photos had ever come up. When she told them they had not, he seemed inclined to leave things at that.

Arnie's son, Jason, was found in Florida three days later from an anonymous tip. The working theory within the Bureau was that whoever was supposed to take care of the kid in the case of Arnie's death had gotten cold feet when the case drew national media attention.

Garret Morrison flew down to Florida personally to take custody of Jason from the local authorities. Allison wasn't surprised to hear that Garret was wedging his way into the case. A fourteen-year-old raised by a serial killer was too good of a study subject for the head of the Behavioral Analysis Unit to pass up. Allison knew she wouldn't be involved in the conversations with Jason regardless of Garret's involvement. The twenty-four-hour news cycle was filled with the story of an unnamed female FBI agent who had fought and killed mass-murderer Arnie Mil-house in self-defense. Jason was a smart kid. He knew it was her.

Still, she felt an obligation toward the boy. When the FBI Cessna taxied into the private hangar at Reagan National Airport, Allison was in a side room watching as the team handling his case waited for him. Counselors, psychiatrists, doctors. The Bureau needed answers to find all of Arnie's past victims, and, whether he knew it or not, Jason likely had clues that would help them.

Garret appeared at the door first, his square jaw set, surveying the hangar as if he were on a security detail. He turned and motioned behind him. Jason appeared framed by the Cessna's metal door. Garret reached out and placed a hand on Jason's shoulder to guide him forward. Jason shrugged it off and glared at him. Allison wasn't sure what she expected. Maybe someone looking lost, eyes red from crying, a little boy scared what the future held for him. Instead he looked over the assembled group with nothing but pure hatred in his eyes.

Jason seemed to turn right toward her and catch her staring at him. She pulled back farther in the shadows, even though she knew it was impossible for him to see her from his position. Still, the look in his eyes unnerved her. She'd seen that look before. And, as they guided Jason away, something told her she might see it again someday.

She could have used Jason holding her hand two days later during Richard's memorial service. It was small consolation that the initial medical report showed that a broken back from the fall had killed him instantly. At least he hadn't suffered. But the same couldn't be said for the living. A collection of friends, family, and colleagues that numbered in the hundreds cried and laughed together as they celebrated his life and mourned his death.

Director Mason gave a eulogy of Richard's professional life that would have made any agent proud. Allison ached from the loss and from the possibility of what might have been between them if he had survived.

Allison made a quick appearance at Jay's Saloon, Richard's favorite dive bar, where his Bureau friends congregated after the service to share stories and get drunk even though it was barely past noon. But she couldn't take the sympathetic looks, the awkward words of consolation, the whispered conversations that followed behind her as she walked across the room. It was all too much to bear. So she mumbled a quick good-bye to Richard's closest friends and snuck out a side door.

The drive was welcome downtime to clear her head. She rode with the windows down, brisk air filling the car. She headed toward Annapolis and within an hour, she was at the Naval Academy Main Gate with a marine scrutinizing her credentials. She was early to her appointment, but he waved her through.

She expected to feel a sense of dread as she entered the campus, but there was none. The midshipmen looked like kids to her now. Fresh-faced, pimply college students. Worried about their grades. Worried about a date they had that night. There was no menace. No ice pit in her stomach.

She walked to Dahlgren Hall, the massive administrative building in the center of campus. The last time she had been there was for her panel interview regarding her rape allegations. Walking across the wide concrete courtyard where the brigade held its twice-daily formation, she remembered how small she had felt all those years ago.

She didn't feel small today.

A young lieutenant met her at the building entrance. He explained that, although she was early, the commandant had cleared his schedule and was waiting for her. Allison followed the officer into the building, never more confident in her life that she was doing the right thing.

◆ ◆ ◆

An hour later, Allison emerged from her meeting, satisfied that the commandant had heard her out, dissatisfied that he intended to do not a damn thing with the information. Despite the assurances that an investigation into Craig Gerty's performance would be conducted, she knew a patronizing smoke blow when she saw one. She shook hands with the commandant and said she would follow up in a month to see if there was any progress. Allison could tell the commandant didn't like the implication that she didn't believe there would be any, but he bit his tongue and asked the young lieutenant to show her out.

When they reached the door, evening formation had already begun. All four thousand midshipmen fell into their platoons, ready to be counted and inspected prior to evening meal. The ceremony had yet to begin, so the lieutenant walked them through the middle of the courtyard. Halfway across, Allison spotted Craig Gerty walking straight toward her.

She shook her head. The old boys club was still at work at the academy. Someone had already tipped him off that she was there and why. The lieutenant escorting her said a hurried good-bye, turned, and walked back toward Dahlgren Hall.

Allison faced Gerty, squared her shoulders, and waited for him.

Gerty came to a stop in front of her. "Just what the fuck do you think you're doing?"

"Right now I'm talking to a piece of shit," she said.

"What do you think is gonna happen?" Gerty said, leaning in. "Just 'cause you're FBI now, you think they're gonna believe you?"

"Worth a shot."

"No, it's not. Know why?" Gerty asked. "It's 'cause they don't wanna know. When are you gonna get that through your thick head? You got raped. So what? It happens. Suck it up and be a soldier."

"Is that what you teach the young women here at the academy, Gerty?"

"Just the lucky ones," he said with a sneer. "Shit, you weren't even that good. I like it when they fight more. After I forced your legs open and got inside you, you just kind of gave up. Remember?"

Allison met him eye to eye. "Trust me, I remember. Turns out, I don't give up anymore." She pulled back the lapel of her jacket and revealed a small microphone.

"What the fuck is that?"

"That's your confession, asshole. Enjoy your time in the brig."

Allison pushed her way past Gerty. Behind her, she heard him growl, "Come back here, you bitch."

She felt him grab her roughly on the shoulder.

It was exactly what she'd hoped would happen.

She reached back and grabbed his wrist. In a fluid move, she spun his arm around and bent his wrist back painfully.

He took a wild swing at her with his other hand, but she dodged it and swept his leg. As he dropped to the ground, she kept the pressure on his wrist and elbow.

Gerty's arm broke with a sickening *crack*.

His scream filled the courtyard, and four thousand midshipmen turned to watch.

Allison yanked harder on the broken arm, grinding the bones together. Gerty screamed again, tears coming down his cheeks. Allison put one foot on his neck and leaned in so only he could hear her.

"Who's the bitch now, Gerty? Look around. They all know it's you. Don't you ever forget it, or I'll come back . . . and next time I swear to God I'll kill you."

She threw Gerty's arm down and it flopped uselessly on the ground. He used his other hand to cradle it to his chest.

Allison looked all around her, at the entire Mother Brigade staring back at her. From somewhere in the back came a soft sound, barely discernible at first.

A single person clapping.

Then another joined in. And another.

Allison picked them out of the crowd now.

It was the women. They knew what Gerty was. And, somehow, they seemed to understand why the public beat-down they just witnessed had happened.

Soon, there were dozens clapping. Then hundreds.

Finally, the entire brigade cheered. Men and women. Allison looked back at the main entrance to Dahlgren and saw the lieutenant and the commandant standing in the doorway. They didn't look happy.

Allison waved and smiled.

Now she was satisfied.

An hour later she was at Anne Arundel Medical Center in Annapolis. Even though she wasn't family, a quick flash of her FBI badge gave her admittance to the room she wanted.

The patient was asleep and, according to the nurses, resting well. One of them told her he must be getting better, because he'd made not one, not two, but three passes at her that day.

Allison smiled. Yep, Charlie was definitely on the mend.

Allison knew the real healing he would need wasn't going to come from physical therapy. The psychological effects of being held prisoner, tortured, and coming so close to death would take years of work. He had responded to the pressure of the situation by being a hero. Without him, she would have died that night. She owed Charlie her life, and she hoped that would help his healing process. If nothing else, she had a sneaking suspicion he was going to milk that for more than a few free beers.

She made herself as comfortable as possible in the hospital chair and closed her eyes.

"Hey, good lookin'," Charlie said.

Allison smiled, got up, and crossed the room to the edge of the bed.

"Hey, yourself. How are you feeling?" she asked.

"I've been worse. Once I had this crazy woman karate chop me on the beach and then get me in a car wreck."

"Sounds like you should stay away from her."

Charlie laughed but quickly grimaced and pressed the button that released his pain meds.

"Can I get you anything?" Allison asked.

"A pint of Guinness would be nice."

"I'll work on it."

A comfortable silence filled the room while Allison held Charlie's hand. His expression relaxed as his meds did their work.

He rolled his head toward her. "How about you? Are you all right?"

Allison thought about it, taking the question seriously. "Yeah," she replied. "Actually, I am."

For the first time in more years than she could remember, she felt the comfort of those words as she realized they were the truth. "I'm all right," she said confidently, letting the words fill her.

Charlie nodded, his eyelids growing heavy, his voice slurring slightly. "Good. Good. You deserve to be all right."

Allison let go of his hand long enough to pull up a chair next to the bed. Then she took his hand again. "Go ahead and sleep. I'll be right here when you wake up."

Charlie was already out. Allison patted his hand and smiled, thankful he had survived. She leaned against his bed and whispered a prayer for him. She prayed for Richard and felt the pang of loss all over again. She asked that Jason receive protection and comfort. She even said a small prayer for Arnie Milhouse, asking that his tormented soul find peace.

She left Craig Gerty off the list.

Fuck that guy.

AUTHOR'S NOTE

Dear Reader,

Thank you three times.

First, thank you for supporting a fellow human being's passion. I think it makes you a good person and makes up for that one thing you did in high school. (You know what I'm talking about.)

Second, thank you for being part of the community of readers. Each time you write a review, recommend a book to friend, or share a new novel through social media, you help keep the fire for books alive. Those of us who scribble stories late into the night are completely in your debt.

Last, thank you for your time. As a father of five and an avid reader (labels that can seem mutually exclusive at times), I recognize every book you open represents a hard choice among thousands of options. I'm awed and humbled that you chose to spend your valuable time within these pages. I hope that I proved to be worthy of your trust.

With appreciation,

Jeff Gunhus

PS: If you would like to support this book, the best way is to share it with a friend and then share it with the world with a review. Even a sentence or two would be great. Thank you in advance for your help; it means more than you could imagine.

ACKNOWLEDGMENTS

I love to write. I can't help it and I can't do without it. When meeting a friend's sister at a restaurant recently, I saw her eyes narrow as she put together who I was. She shook her head in sympathy and said, "Oh, you're the compulsive writer-guy." Yep, guilty as charged.

I've been this this way since I first lost myself in good books, when I discovered that writers like Tolkien, C. S. Lewis, and Frank Herbert had carved out vast worlds that I could visit simply by cracking open a book. It was long before I tried my own hand at the business of creating lives out of ink and paper. It was exciting and liberating and I loved it. I knew that when I grew up, I would be a paid writer. Only that didn't happen . . . until it did.

Instead, I started and grew a business, married a perfect woman, and became a father . . . five times over. But along the way, I kept writing when I could. Late at night. Before work. During lunch. Novel after novel. Then screenplays. Then novels again. Never selling a thing.

Winston Churchill said, "Success is going from failure to failure without the loss of enthusiasm." It's a handy quote, but hard to pull off. There were definitely times of self-doubt, of wanting to pack it in on this writing thing and take up golf. But my wife, Nicole, refused that as an option. Whether it was her Midwestern work ethic or her slightly misguided trust in my writing ability, her enthusiasm and her confidence in me never waned. Every person should have a cheerleader clapping for you even when you fumble the ball. Nicole is mine and I couldn't be more thankful.

A thank-you to my kids, Jackson, William, Daniel, Caroline, and Owen. It never ceases to amaze me how so much noise can come from such little bodies. But I know someday soon I'll sulk around an empty house, willing to pay any amount to have it filled again with your young voices. Every message about morality and ethics in my books are really just me talking to the five of you. I hope you look at those as a piece of your dad . . . as opposed to just the cuss words and torture scenes.

Special thanks to my business partners Jay Reid, Matt Stewart, Spencer Pepe, and Tracy Meneses for supporting this other side of my life. Especially Jay, who is always one of the first five people to read anything I write and who pulls no punches in his feedback. Thanks to Blake Crouch for taking my call to discuss his experience with Thomas & Mercer and for offering sage advice to a newbie writer. Thanks to Stephen King for his book *On Writing* that I read twice a year and quote endlessly in Q&As with new writers.

Special thanks to Mandy Schoen who did the very first developmental edit on this book and kicked it into shape. Emily Mitchell, an amazing local photographer, who supplied the photo on the original cover. Thanks to my talented brother, Eric, who did the original cover and who has been so supportive and instrumental in all of my books. Thanks to Mom and Dad, who always told to me to stop whining and get to work. Pretty damn good advice.

I originally self-published this book, loving the freedom that came with owning my own rights. Then Kjersti Egerdahl from Thomas & Mercer called and suggested I work with her and her team to bring the book to a wider audience. I was leery, but her positive attitude and enthusiasm were impossible to resist. The experience with T&M has been everything she promised. Fun, professional, and inclusive.

She brought in David Drummond, who created the inspired cover you see today, the perfect image for a book where nothing is what it seems. Bryon Quertermous who got a front row seat to see how hardheaded I am and yet still managed to improve the book through his developmental edit. Donald Weise worked his deft touch on the copyedit, not only as a guru of grammar, but catching tone and story issues at the last hour that made all the difference. Lauren Bailey swooped in at the final hour and used her fine-tooth comb to catch the last few details that needed attention. As an indie author, I'm used to doing things on my own. This time around I'm excited to have Tiffany Pokorny (author relations) and Jacque Ben-Zekry (marketing) on my side. It only took one meeting to know I was in good, capable hands that would treat this book with care and love.

My last acknowledgment is to my readers. I've been humbled and overwhelmed by the positive response to my books. Writing fiction is a very personal endeavor that strips you bare, leaving you naked and exposed to the world. Your reviews, encouraging e-mails, and support on social media have meant more to me than you know. Your acceptance of my work, even when it's a bit out there, has encouraged me to push the envelope and dig deeper to give you something unexpected. I hope *Killer Within* meets with your approval and that we ride this train together for years to come. If you're ever in Annapolis, stop by City Dock Café, look in the back corner, and if you see someone with earbuds rocking out while he pounds away at his laptop, it's probably me. Come say hello. This compulsive writer-guy would love to buy you a cup of coffee and thank you in person.

With gratitude,

Jeff Gunhus

ABOUT THE AUTHOR

Photo © 2014 Connie Groah

Jeff Gunhus is the author of the Amazon bestselling novels *Night Chill*, *Night Terror*, and the middle-grade/YA series The Templar Chronicles. The first book of this series, *Jack Templar Monster Hunter*, was written in an effort to get his reluctant reader eleven-year-old son excited about reading, a journey shared in his book, *Reaching Your Reluctant Reader*, and featured on Amazon's main home page. In his spare time, Jeff runs a national company with more than three thousand employees, chases his five kids all over Maryland, and constantly wonders why his wife puts up with him. After his experience with his own kids, he is passionate about helping parents reach young, reluctant readers and is active in child literacy issues. In rare moments of quiet, he can be found in the back of the City Dock Café in Annapolis working on his next novel. He loves to hear from his readers and can be contacted on social media or at www.JeffGunhus.com.

www.facebook.com/jeffgunhusauthor

www.twitter.com/jeffgunhus